Praise for Neil Cross:

'Neil Cross is an astonis[...] ble at a stroke to fill you with [...]
Time Out

'Cross excels at uneasy landscapes, be they urban, [...] psychological . . . everyday settings are so subtly infected with menace it takes a while to locate just what is making the narrative so frightening'
Metro

'Cross holds it together with tough prose, skill and nerve'
Guardian

'Cross's writing is relentlessly absorbing'
Big Issue

'Distinctive, original . . . powerfully atmospheric and hypnotically rendered. You may not be able to say precisely where you've been, but you'll know you've taken a hell of a ride'
Literary Review on *Holloway Falls*

'A masterpiece . . . seductively readable . . . dangerous'
Daily Telegraph on *Natural History*

'A terrifically scary and all too believable tale . . . brilliantly written in taut, humorous prose, while being exceptionally well observed and paced'
Daily Mirror on *Burial*

'Stunning . . . It has been a long time since I've read a novel so compelling, chilling and satisfying'
Peter James on *Burial*

Neil Cross is the author of several novels and the top-ten best-selling memoir *Heartland*, and is one of the most sought-after TV writers around. He has been lead scripwriter for the two most recent seasons of the acclaimed BBC spy drama series, *Spooks*, and continues to write widely for the screen. He lives with his wife and two children.

Also by Neil Cross:

Mr In-Between
Christendom
Holloway Falls
Always the Sun
Heartland
Natural History
Burial

Always the
Sun

Neil Cross

POCKET
BOOKS

LONDON • SYDNEY • NEW YORK • TORONTO

First published in Great Britain by Scribner, 2004
First published in paperback in Great Britain by Scribner, 2005
This edition published by Pocket Books, 2009
An imprint of Simon & Schuster UK Ltd
A CBS COMPANY

1 3 5 7 9 10 8 6 4 2

Simon & Schuster UK Ltd
1st floor
222 Gray's Inn Road
London WC1X 8HB

www.simonandschuster.co.uk

Simon & Schuster Australia
Sydney

A CIP catalogue record for this book is available
from the British Library

ISBN: 978-1-84739-462-0

This book is a work of fiction. Names, characters, places and incidents
are either a product of the author's imagination or are used fictitiously.
Any resemblance to actual people living or dead,
events or locales is entirely coincidental.

Printed by CPI Cox & Wyman, Reading, Berkshire, RG1 8EX

For Nadya, Ethan and Finn – to whom
this book is a kind of promise

I couldn't show you
But I hope to one day
Pretty promises to teach the tender child
To welcome madness every Monday

'Perfumed Garden', *The Chameleons*

'I'm gonna be like you, Dad'

'Cat's in the Cradle', *Harry Chapin*

1

Sam steered the dirty-white hire van to the nearside kerb and killed the engine.

It was the last week of June, two days before Jamie's thirteenth birthday. For a while, they sat motionless and silent, listening to the slow tick of the engine. Then they exchanged a guarded, excited glance and raced each other to get out first.

The driver's door was dented and obstinate; Sam forced it with his shoulder, but he was too late. Jamie was already waiting on the kerb. Sam ambled over to join him. He laid a hand on Jamie's shoulder and together they looked at their new house.

The house stared back at them, blank and imperturbable. Scudding summer clouds were reflected in its windows, and a mismatched father and son. Sam was sunburnt and brawny. A messy head of corn-blond hair. Broad face on beefy shoulders. Pale-blue eyes and a knobby cudgel of a nose, broken long before and never properly re-set. Jamie was skinny and feline, the subtle echo of his mother. Skin like amber. Long, unkempt chestnut hair that hung over his collar and obscured his eyes. Both wore blue jeans faded to white, washed-out T-shirts and scuffed Adidas.

The house on Balaarat Street was a detached, double-fronted Victorian building that presided in tired majesty over the corner of Magpie and Cobden Avenues. Sam had known it since he was a boy. Through the street-wandering years of childhood and early adolescence, he must have passed its chipped green gate and inviolable hedges many hundreds of times. He'd never caught sight of whoever lived there. Although it had not developed the unhappy reputation of most long-empty houses, and despite the lack of broken and boarded windows, he'd always assumed it to be uninhabited.

It was Jamie who'd chosen to live here. They'd come house-hunting three months before. Sam remembered a cold, squally April day. The estate agent's confected enthusiasm was depleted by the morning's visits to several other properties, each of them found in some way wanting. With a disconsolate air, he parked his Golf GTI on Balaarat Street.

In the back of the car, Jamie looked up at the house.

Using his copy of the *Sun* for an umbrella, the estate agent hurried to the front door. Huddled into their jackets, Sam and Jamie followed.

Junk mail was piled behind the front door. The hallway was bare and uncarpeted and their footfalls and voices echoed pleasingly. The sitting room was high-ceilinged and cavernous. The kitchen was shadowy, with translucent blinds hung, rotting, at the windows. The appliances were antiquated, in chocolate browns and mustard yellows, furry with grease and dust, broken at the hinges.

Jamie used the heel of his hand to wipe a porthole in the wet kitchen window, through which he briefly inspected the garden. Then he turned and stamped upstairs.

Sam waited in the kitchen with the estate agent, who placed his rain-dappled newspaper face-down on the grimy work-surface to read the sports pages. Sam listened to the empty-house sounds of doors opening and slamming shut. He waited a few minutes before following Jamie upstairs. The floors were bare, laid here and there with brittle old newspapers. Spent bulbs, burnt nicotine yellow, hung from frayed cords.

He found Jamie in the master bedroom. He was standing at the bay window, looking down on the quiet street below. Sam crossed his arms and leant against the cold, glossy wall, the colour of custard.

He said, 'Shall we check out the garden?'

'Seen it.'

Sam laid a hand on his shoulder.

'Come on, sunshine. Have a proper look.'

They turned and clumped heavily down the naked stairs, along the hallway and through to the kitchen, where the estate agent was by now making a call from a mobile phone so tiny that Sam wondered briefly if he was speaking to his empty palm, like a street-corner nutcase. By training, Sam was a psychiatric nurse. Sometimes he saw the symptoms of disorder wherever he looked.

The garden was broad and high-walled; a tangled, rain-sodden, knee-deep wilderness. At the far end stood a collapsed shed. In one corner leant an ancient, perilous-looking apple tree, its root-base embedded deep in ancient mulch.

'What do you think?' said Sam.

Jamie stooped and picked up a small nugget of damp, brittle masonry that lay on the weedy patio. He inspected it, crumbled it between his thumb and forefinger, then skipped it across the wild lawn like a pebble on a reedy pond.

He shrugged his shoulders.

'Dunno. It's *big*.'

'Which means?'

'It's all right.'

'Good all right? Or bad all right?'

'Depends.'

'On what?'

He wiped his fingers on his jeans.

'Do *you* like it?'

Sam crossed his beefy arms and nodded his head twice.

'Yeah,' he said. 'It's good.'

'Am I allowed to choose my room?'

'I don't see why not.'

'What if I want the big one?'

Sam scratched the back of his neck.

'If that's the room you want.'

'And you're going to get it done up? Decorated and that?'

'Of course.'

'Decorated how?'

'I don't know. Decorated. You know – done up. We'll get someone in.'

'Can I do my room how I want to?'

'Well, that depends on how you want to do it.'

'Could I have PS2?'

'What, generally – or for the room?'

'Both.'

'We can talk about that.'

Jamie chewed at his downy upper lip and crossed his arms, upon which there seemed to hang no muscle. He brushed the hair from his eyes and scrutinized the garden. There was a rash of small pimples across his forehead. He scuffed his Adidas across the damp surface of the loam where it met the weather-damaged patio.

'All right then. If I can have the big room.'

In that moment Sam missed his wife more acutely than he would have believed possible. It felt like homesickness. He disguised it by pinching at the knotty bridge of his nose and resting his palm on the crown of his son's head. He closed his eyes and tried to remember her scent, the warm softness of her belly, the musky incense of her throat and underarms.

Sometimes he was able to forget what she had become. Instead he recalled the woman who married him, the woman inside whom his son had budded, a secret efflorescence, a polyp unfolding from nothing, reaching for the sun.

Their London flat had already found a buyer, a property developer who was happy to ignore its poor decorative order, paying cash at fifteen thousand pounds less than market value. Even that figure was a great deal more than Sam and Justine had paid for the property, sixteen years earlier, and Sam was able to return to his home town and buy a house outright, using the equity alone. He left Justine's life insurance payout untouched.

To go house-hunting, he and Jamie had driven from London in a hired car. They camped at Mel's for a week. Into the spare room, Mel had jammed an elderly, steel-sprung camp-bed and a tatty futon. Upon these Sam and Jamie had laid out their sleeping bags. It was a squeeze, but that only added to the sense of adventure. It was like camping, without the unhappy imperative of being outside.

Since he was a tiny child, Jamie had been scared of cows. In return, cows seemed abnormally attracted to him. They would cross any field to procure his company. They would slowly gather round, nuzzling at him as if he were an object of singular curiosity.

At Mel's, Jamie and Sam woke early. There followed extravagant arm-stretching, grunts of discomfort and smacking of sleep-gummy mouths. In T-shirt and boxer shorts, Sam plodded downstairs to make a cup of tea, which they drank in companionable, masculine silence. When the mugs were empty, Sam told Jamie to take a shower.

When Jamie emerged from the bathroom two minutes later, barely wet, Sam was waiting for him on the landing.

'Now try again,' he said.

Jamie rolled his eyes and turned back to the shower.

This time, he was gone so long that Sam began to worry. He stomped from the bedroom and pounded on the door, shouting that he needed to piss.

There was a pause: the rustle of a shower curtain being pulled back. Bare feet slapping on wet tiles. Clutching a towel to his waist, Jamie answered the door. His hair was in wet, shampooed spikes. There was no fat on him. His avian bones and musculature were tight-packed in olive skin. His taut, paler belly bulged slightly above the towel. Sam was overcome by tenderness. He wondered if Jamie had been using the sound of the shower to disguise his sobbing. Sam still did that, sometimes.

Jamie loped back to the still-running shower. Sam stood before the lavatory and forced out a meagre trickle. He glanced at Jamie from the corner of his eye. He was massaging his soapy hair. Foamy white rivulets ran between his scrawny shoulder-blades.

Sam went downstairs again, this time to make them breakfast.

By now, Mel was up. She had bed hair and was smoking a cigarette at the kitchen table. She wore a silky, ivory-white dressing-gown and oversized, fluffy bedroom slippers.

Sam rummaged in the kitchen cupboards. Eventually he found the frying pan. Its base was blackened and its handle, melted in places like volcanic glass, had come loose. He spent a few moments tightening the greasy screw with the round tip of a bread knife.

Mel yawned into the back of her hand. She was tall and slim and caustic and languid, with a Roman nose that, earlier in life, had caused her much misery. She drew on the cigarette in a manner that suggested another age and a different class.

'Do you know where you'll be looking?'

Sam went to the fridge. He inspected the sell-by date on a box of eggs.

'I only bought them Tuesday,' said Mel.

Sam put down the eggs and hunted round until he located a pint of milk and a humble chunk of butter bandaged in silvered, papery rags.

'Dunno really,' he said. 'The Merrydown Estate's still nice.'

'It's lovely round there,' said Mel. 'They've got a brand new whatsit. High Street. Nice shops.'

Merrydown was the name of the private estate that bordered the council estate where Mel lived. She'd moved in twenty years ago, shortly before she and Unka Frank were married. The house had been too big for her since he left.

'We'd be close to you,' said Sam.

Mel scratched at her bed hair and yawned like a lion. It was still early and she had never been good at mornings. All around, the house was the same mess it had been since the day she moved in, an excited eighteen year old.

'Will you send Jamie to Churchill? Or go private?'

Sam cracked four eggs into a plastic measuring jug. He added pepper, salt and a drop of milk and beat the mixture with a fork. His back to his sister, he shrugged.

He said: 'I don't see what's wrong with Churchill.'

'It's a bit rough.'

He turned to face her and laughed, a touch incredulous.

'We went there,' he said. 'We did all right.'

She sipped at her milky coffee.

'It's different now.'

'Mel,' said Sam. He laughed. He didn't want to be patronizing. 'Jamie and I are living in *Hackney*. Compared to that, Churchill Comprehensive will be like Disneyland.' He saw her expression and softened. 'Look,' he said, 'he's grown up in London. It's a rough place. This doesn't even feel like a city to him. He thinks it's the *countryside*.'

'And he's told you this, has he?'

He poured the beaten-egg mixture into the delicately sizzling frying pan.

'Yeah,' he said. 'Well, not in so many words.'

'In how many words, exactly?'

'I don't know. He thinks it'll be like a permanent holiday. And he's looking forward to having you near. He thinks it'll be like TV. Dropping in on his aunt on the way home from school. Do you want eggs?'

'Please.'

'How do you want them?'

She looked at him along her nose.

'Do them a bit firm. I hate it when you do eggs like snot.'

The toaster popped. He hurried to butter three rounds of toast before stirring at the bubbling eggs with a plastic spatula.

Jamie came downstairs, barefoot in clean orange T-shirt and dirty blue jeans. He smelt of shower gel. He'd combed his wet hair from his face. He kissed Mel on the cheek.

She said, 'Your dad's doing bogey eggs for breakfast.'

'Gross,' said Jamie. 'Can I have Crunchy Nut Cornflakes?'

'No,' said Sam. He tipped the frying pan in order that Mel and Jamie could see inside, and prodded the mixture with a fork.

'See?' he said. 'Nice and firm.'

'Is there any bacon?'

'Not that I'd actually eat.'

'God,' said Mel. 'Is that still *in* there?'

She went to the fridge and looked inside.

When breakfast was done, Sam left the washing-up soaking in hot water. He knew it would be there when they got back. He and Jamie met the estate agent at 9.30 a.m. They saw four houses in the Merrydown Estate before arriving at Balaarat Street.

Jamie had never had a garden, nor access to any park that Sam and Justine considered safe in the absence of direct adult supervision. Although he professed no interest in the wilderness at the back of Balaarat Street, at the rope-swing that hung from a high bough of the inclined apple tree, and although it was raining, Sam could see the light in his eyes – a late, welcome glimpse of his diminishing childhood.

Jamie buried his hands in the pockets of his Levi's and sauntered inside, just as the estate agent was slipping the tiny phone back in his trouser pocket.

In a few hours the deal was done. Later, Sam whistled over the washing-up.

It took nearly four months. There were contracts to be exchanged and renovations to be completed. Sam employed Mel to liaise with the contractors and to act as point of contact with the site manager. He knew well how fearsome she could be, and it was a successful stratagem: disregarding a few details, the work was completed only five weeks behind schedule.

But the wait was dead time, like waiting in a foreign airport for a delayed flight home.

They were ready to move long before there was anywhere to go. Months before, Sam began to pack their essential belongings into boxes and crates. Everything else he got rid of: clothes, video cassettes, broken and tarnished items of Justine's jewellery, odd earrings, half-empty perfume bottles that didn't smell of her any more; postcards, letters, her wedding dress and shoes.

His mother-in-law had started this process while Justine was still alive. Diane was ash-blonde, clipped, efficient. She suggested they gather those clothes her daughter would euphemistically 'not be needing', and take them to a charity shop. Sam agreed. He insisted only that the charity shop should not be in Hackney. He didn't want to come across strangers dressed in his wife's clothes. He and Diane stuffed the clothing into garden sacks, which Sam loaded into the back of Diane's estate car. She drove the stuff home to Bath.

The same day, Sam packed their wedding and holiday photographs into a number of boxes and sealed them with tape. In blue marker pen, he wrote: *S&J wed, etc*, *B-bados 92*, *Turkey 89*, *Devon 90*, *mil. eve 00*.

He stared down at the boxes. Their marriage, codified.

The degenerative brain disorder that killed Justine was called 'fatal familial insomnia'. It was a vanishingly rare condition caused by the action of prions, the enigmatic rogue proteins that also caused scrapie in sheep and bovine spongiform encephalopathy in cattle. Justine withdrew from them bit by bit, minute by minute until, near the end, it was impossible not to wish what remained of her more speedily gone.

The first sign had been difficulty in sleeping. But Justine was an art teacher in the local College of Further Education, which was underfunded and understaffed. She was stressed. They didn't think much of it.

Within a few weeks, the ability to sleep – but not the longing for it – had deserted her. Her GP assured her that all chronic insomniacs slept far more than they imagined, and she prescribed pills. The pills didn't work. Later, different doctors ran tests. Working shifts in a controlled environment, they observed the passage of forty-eight entirely sleepless hours. By now, Justine was debilitated and bewildered. She so very badly wanted to sleep.

Before the condition was diagnosed, Justine's sanity left her. She was awake until being awake drove her insane.

Even when she became deranged, being awake gnawed at her bones, confining her eventually to a wheelchair. She could no longer distinguish between dream-states and waking reality. She passed randomly from one to the other. There came a time when she no longer knew her mother, her husband or her only son. During those final months she was shrunken and grotesque and sometimes violently maniacal, curled like a cricket and shrieking at chimeras and imaginary colours.

In the early days, Sam tried to take care of her. He took leave of absence to become her full-time nurse. Even when he unmistakably became unable to cope, he refused offers of Local Authority assistance. Instead, he relied on Diane. At first, she merely visited them often. But as the disease progressed, Diane moved in with them. She and Sam took it in turns to sleep. Diane slept on her own linen in the marital bed, while Sam was consigned to a sleeping bag on the floor of Jamie's room.

In the evenings, when their waking moments intersected, Sam and Diane prepared a meal and sat together, watching television while Justine gibbered and dribbled and shrieked in her wheelchair. Weekday mornings, they prepared Jamie for school and tried hard to pretend this was normal life. On Friday afternoons, Diane took sole responsibility for Justine. Sam spent those few hours in a curious blank. He sat in empty cinemas and watched films whose plot he was unable to follow.

Privately, each of them dreamt of an ultimate flicker of clarity. Justine would fall silent. An expression of saintly peace would settle her wracked features. She would whisper: *Sam*, or *Mum*, or *Jamie: I love you*.

But no such moment came, and the disease that devoured Justine eventually vanquished Sam and Diane too. One day, Jamie came home from school to find his mother gone. Diane and Sam had worked hard to prepare a speech for him. Sam would tell him that Mummy was in hospital, where properly trained nurses would look after her, keeping her safe and comfortable. And although she was very, very ill, she was still his mum and she loved him very much. He could visit her any time he wanted.

Jamie took one long, acute look at his exhausted, baggy-eyed father and grandmother. Then he dumped his schoolbag in the middle of the floor and went to make himself a crisp sandwich.

Diane stayed another week. She and Sam went through Justine's effects with an efficiency that resembled malice.

The evening that Diane returned to Bath, Jamie cooked the supper. He'd learnt in Food Science how to do lasagne. It took a long time and the result was nearly inedible, but Sam ate three portions, nevertheless, and a green-leaf salad whose dressing Jamie made himself, adding vinegar to olive oil and flourishing the bottle like a cocktail shaker.

Jamie never saw his mother again. Soon after entering the hospice, Justine contracted the viral pneumonia from which she did not recover.

Sam didn't have to break the news. On his way home from school, Jamie saw Diane's Volvo parked outside the flat and guessed. From politeness, he hugged Diane and assured her that yes, he would be a brave boy.

Jamie didn't go to the funeral. That was the worst argument he and Sam ever had, except only Sam was arguing. Jamie's detachment bordered on the autistic. He looked at his ranting, weeping father with gentle but utter lack of comprehension, as if Sam might be rehearsing a play in Latin. He sat there and absorbed without recoil everything Sam pitched at him, including threats of violence. When Sam's ire was exhausted, Jamie returned his attention to the GameBoy.

Sam recalled the infuriating, circular trilling of the game's melody. He thought the meaningless sound might drive him insane. Jamie's lack of response was dreamlike and claustrophobic.

Sam walked out of the flat, slamming the door behind him.

It was late winter, and he didn't stop to pick up his jacket. The air was cold and filthy, a particulate miasma. He wanted to punch someone, but the hordes of Hackney flowed by, without anyone meeting his eye. He went into a brightly-lit corner shop and bought a pack of Marlboro Lights. He bitterly enjoyed the

urdity that, after everything, it should take an argument
h a child to drive him back to cigarettes.

Shivering in his shirtsleeves, he sat on a much-vandalized
nicipal park bench. He watched the traffic and the buses
l the people. He chainsmoked half the pack of Marlboro,
n walked home.

He found Jamie on the sofa, watching *Buffy the Vampire
yer*. The GameBoy was discarded on the cushion alongside
1. Neither he nor Sam mentioned the argument, and Jamie
his way: on the morning of the funeral, he was collected by
ne's neighbours, who'd driven all the way especially, and
en for a day out.

Sam barely knew the neighbours. They'd been guests at the
dding, and over the years they'd exchanged pleasantries at
ious Christmas parties and midsummer barbecues. But
y'd known Justine since she was four years old and Sam
s touched by the quiet modesty of their desire to help.

They had mapped a full day's itinerary. Jamie would not be
owed an instant in which to become bored or reflective. Sam
tched from the window as they drove him away. He could
him, tiny and regally serene, perched on the back seat of the
tra estate.

Sam didn't know how to get through the day without him.
He barely remembered the funeral. At the wake, he was offi-
usly anxious for everybody's comfort. For the first time since
nie's christening, he hugged Diane. She hugged him back,
l that was the moment when he thought he might break,
zing into pieces like a cheap vase. He allowed Justine's sister
ob on his shoulder. He said '*There. there.*' He smiled tightly

at her husband, whom he knew to have had a number of extra-marital affairs, and whom he very much disliked.

By the time Jamie came home, everybody had gone. Sam was alone among the paper plates and uneaten sausage rolls. He was lying on the sofa. The new shoes had worn his black socks translucent at the heel.

Jamie was wearing his Walkman. Sam could hear the rapid, tinny sibilance of sequenced hi-hats. Jamie stomped through to the kitchen and began opening and closing cupboards. He returned with a plate of chocolate HobNobs and a can of Dr Pepper.

He swept Sam's feet from the sofa and sat.

He looked at the TV.

He said, 'Are you watching this?'

Sam wiped his eyes.

'Not really.'

Jamie flicked over to Sky 1. They watched *The Simpsons*. Terrified and exhilarated, Homer sailed over Springfield canyon on Bart's skateboard. He almost made it to the other side. But he fell at the last, as Homer always did.

'Can I watch *Die Hard 2*?'

Sam sat up. Jamie was shaking his shoulder. He had fallen asleep. He wiped his lips. Ran a hand through his tangled hair.

'Of course you can. Go on.'

At the end, they both cheered.

A week after the funeral, Sam woke to find Jamie asleep on the floor at the foot of his bed.

He knew he should return him to his own room. Instead, he lifted Jamie and laid him in the bed, on Justine's side. The presence of his sleeping, delicate son filled him with a tenderness that blunted the jagged edge of his grief. Sometimes Jamie whimpered in his sleep and thrashed his limbs. Twice he wet the bed: Sam was woken by a warm jet of urine on his lower back and thighs. Jamie, still sleeping, turned his back and curled foetally at the cool, dry edge of the mattress. Sam chuckled, quietly and fondly, and never mentioned it.

The further Justine's death receded, the harder it grew to mention it. In those strange days, Sam and Jamie wandered like spectres within decreasing boundaries. London lost all meaning. The edges of their territory drew together like a drawstring purse, until it was defined by a few Hackney streets and convenience stores. The flat was no longer the place where they'd once been happy. It was simply a place where terrible things had happened, long ago and to other people. It had a dusty, museum feel. It became dirty as well as disordered. They stopped washing up. They ate off paper plates. The curtains were seldom opened. There were mice, and a urinous cockroach stink in the kitchen. At night, wrapped tight in a greying white duvet, Sam imagined the skittering of tiny claws. He dreamt of a tangled rat-king hidden among the decaying mementoes of their dear, dead days.

Early in March, Diane arrived to visit them. Pointedly, she opened all the windows, letting in the winter cold. Sam remembered that he'd not washed the sheets for many weeks, not even after Jamie had pissed on them. He supposed they smelt like a zoo, two helpless mooncalves locked away with the windows and curtains forever drawn on the world. Sometimes Sam forgot how old Jamie was. Sometimes he seemed as flawless and innocent as a toddler; at others, as clumsy, angular and raw-boned as an adolescent.

He told Diane that he'd resigned his job.

Her mouth pursed, lipstick-bled at the edges.

She said, 'It's too late to fall to pieces now, Sam. You got through the hard part. Now look at you. Has Jamie been going to school?'

'Of course.'

'Have you been doing the laundry?'

'Yes.'

'How often?'

'Diane, I don't know. But I've been doing it.'

She wrinkled her nose. Once, it might have been endearing, even sexy.

'Sam,' she said, 'I'm sorry to say it. But you smell, darling.'

Surreptitiously, he sniffed at his armpits. He smelt sour and yellow, vaguely feline. He ran his hands through his hair.

He said, 'Oh Christ, Diane. Please.'

'Don't *please* me,' she said. 'You're not a student. You have responsibilities to that child.'

'Di, he's fine.'

'Living in *this*?'

He looked around him.

'Who makes his breakfast?' she said.

'He's nearly a *teenager*, for Christ's sake. He needs some independence.'

'He's a child, and he needs supervision. Do you make his breakfast?'

'He made his own this morning.'

'What did he have?'

'I don't know. Cereal. Eggs or something.'

'And do you have fresh milk and eggs? A loaf of *bread*?'

He closed his eyes, massaged his forehead.

'Yeah,' he said vaguely. 'We went – I did the shopping. A few days ago.'

She crossed her arms.

'Gather your things.'

'I beg your pardon?'

'Throw some clothes in a suitcase. And some of Jamie's. You're coming back to spend some time with me.'

'I can't. He's got *school*.'

'It's practically half-term. A few days off won't hurt him.' She looked eloquently around herself. 'Quite the contrary.'

By the time Jamie came home, his shirt untucked and one lace trailing, Diane had cleaned the kitchen and the bathroom and made inroads into the sitting room. According to her instruction, Sam had shifted as many of the boxes and crates as possible into Jamie's room.

'Hello, Grandma,' said Jamie.

'Hello, darling.' In rubber gloves and pinafore, she gave him a quick hug.

'All right, Dad?'

'All right, mate.'

Jamie dumped his weight on to the sofa and dug the GameBoy from his bag.

Sam looked at him. His blazer was too small. The shirt was yellowish, missing a couple of buttons. His trousers were nearly through at the knees and one of his trainers was split along the insole. His hair needed cutting.

Sam lit a cigarette.

'We're going to spend a few days at Grandma's,' he said.

Jamie looked up. 'Cool,' he said, without inflection, and returned to his game.

Diane's house, white and well-appointed, backed on to farmland.

Sam woke to the sound of sheep and cattle. He was in a clean room, in crisp bedding. It had been Justine's childhood bedroom, the room they stayed in when they came to visit. They'd had sex there, on the single bed, many times before Jamie was born. He endured a desolate erection at the memory.

It was a guest bedroom now. He lay for a while, enjoying the spring sunshine through the curtains. His skin was still faintly scented with last night's shower. Just inside the bedroom door was a plastic laundry basket, full of freshly washed and pressed clothing. Diane had probably been up since before dawn.

He pulled on a fragrant, white dressing-gown and padded downstairs. In the big, bright kitchen, Jamie sat in football shorts and T-shirt, reading the comic section of the previous week's *Sunday Times*. Diane was in the garden, hanging out more washing. Sam looked without embarrassment at his underwear swinging on the line.

He put the kettle on, made himself a cup of tea and Diane an instant coffee, the way she liked it: half-water, half-milk, cooked in the microwave.

She came in and wished him a brisk, busy good morning. The microwave pinged before he could answer; he took out the hot mug and handed it to her. She thanked him graciously and offered him a biscuit. He said no thank you.

'Diane,' he said, 'I've had an idea. Tell me what you think.'

She set the coffee down and crossed her arms.

'Go ahead.'

'I'm thinking of leaving London.'

He waited for a response.

'What do you think?' he said.

'I think it's an excellent idea. Where will you go?'

'Home.'

She knew he didn't mean Bath, and he was surprised to see that, on some level, this hurt her. She masked it well. She took a small, scalding sip from the coffee.

'It'll do you both the world of good,' she said.

After buying the house on Balaarat Street, Sam and Jamie returned to Hackney. Sam carried a single, borrowed suitcase full of clean clothing. Neither of them was pleased to be back in London. They found it difficult to believe they'd become accustomed to negotiating teetering piles of dusty boxes in the half-lit hallway. The disorganization in the living room had become intolerable, boxes piled on crates piled on more boxes. As the leaving day approached, there was no tug of nostalgia. Moving would be like leaving prison; like drawing a breath of clean, country air.

A few days before they left for their new house in a new town, Sam phoned out for Chinese food. They watched a video and ate Chicken Chow Mein. Shadowy henges of cardboard loomed behind them and in the edges of their vision; seemed to lean into their conversation.

Sam offered to throw Jamie a leaving party.

Jamie lowered his head and shovelled Chow Mein into his mouth.

'Nah,' he said.

'Why not? Don't you want to say goodbye to everyone?'

'Done it.'

'What? All of them?'

'Pretty much.'

'When?'

Another shrug. Another mouthful of Chow Mein.

'You know.'

'What? Even Danny?'

'Danny's in California. With his dad. Disneyworld or something.'

Jamie made a face.

'Oh,' said Sam. 'Right. What about that Nicola?'

There was a long silence.

'Don't be *stupid*,' said Jamie.

'Who's being stupid? I thought you were friends.'

'No way. I hate her.'

'You didn't used to hate her.'

'*Dad*. Grow up.'

Sam hid his smile with a forkful of Chow Mein.

They loaded the hire van on a scorched, suffocating London morning. Jamie insisted on shifting a number of boxes that were too heavy for him, accepting no offer of assistance. He tugged and levered them precariously downstairs, one corner at a time, bracing himself against the wall. He dragged them down the communal hallway.

By the time Sam nosed the van into the London traffic, Jamie's eyes were heavy and drooping. He was asleep when they reached the North Circular. At the lights, Sam fiddled with the radio, tuning from Radio 1 to Radio 4.

He'd never driven a high-sided van before. He wasn't comfortable taking it on the motorway, particularly since its bodywork bore the disheartening dents and scars of previous collisions. Instead, he took an indirect route of B-roads and dual carriageways, which extended their journey by a third. They arrived at the house on Balaarat Street late in the afternoon. By now, Jamie was awake and eating a bag of wine gums, three at a time. Sam parked carefully. He didn't want to prang any of his new neighbours' cars. He noticed that a yellow mini-skip was still standing on the corner with Magpie Avenue. He clicked his tongue against his palate, irritably.

After racing each other from the van, they saw that Mel was waiting for them. She sat on the concrete doorstep, smoking a cigarette and reading a *Daily Mirror*, three of whose corners she'd weighed down with a disposable lighter, a pack of Silk Cut and a small pebble. The fourth corner flapped occasionally, like a dying bird. Mel looked up, shielded her eyes with her hand. She smiled and waved.

Sam thought of a photograph, as if this moment were already a memory of lost times.

He rolled his head on tired shoulders, then he jingled the van keys in his palm and walked through the green gate. It was no longer rusty, but it still squeaked. He made a mental note to buy some WD40. The front lawn had yet to be laid; the turned black earth was laced with glistening slug-trails.

Mel stood to greet him. They hugged. Sensitive to the fact that Jamie might not wish to be embraced by his auntie in public, Mel batted the crown of his head twice with the rolled-up newspaper, then whacked him on the bony arse with it.

She linked an arm through Sam's. With the other, she reached out and pushed open the front door.

She said, 'Welcome home.'

The house smelt of sawdust and varnish: new smells. The floorboards had been stripped and sealed, the walls painted. The banister had been replaced and the stairs repaired. Mel walked to the kitchen: the same, echoing footfalls, full of potential: a space waiting to be filled. She put the kettle on to boil, brought along from her own kitchen that morning.

The kitchen was newly fitted – pearwood and porcelain, brushed aluminium and slate. There was a breakfast bar, faced with four high stools. Looking at it, Sam was saddened to think of the remnants of their previous life, still packed in the van: their cheap, tarnished cutlery, the tea stains, the dried yolk set fast between misaligned tines.

'Well,' said Mel. 'What do you think?'

He was surprised to find that Mel's pride for a job well done touched him. He gave her another hug, longer this time. She smelt of grapefruit soap and hair conditioner and washing powder and cigarettes: unchanging and comforting.

She disengaged from the hug.

'Cheer up,' she said, and nodded stealthily in Jamie's direction.

Jamie was opening and closing empty cupboards. With the pointy tip of his tongue, he tasted the trace of sawdust that adhered to the whorl of fingerprint. He opened the fridge and looked inside. It was empty and spotless. He put his head in and said, 'Hello hello hello.'

Mel dropped tea bags into three mugs, topped them up with boiling water. Jamie joined them. He perched side-saddle on one of the bar-stools.

'What do you think?' said Sam.

'Cool. Can I see my room?'

'You can do what you like. It's your house.'

Jamie vaulted off the stool and thundered upstairs.

Mel scooped the tea bags from the mugs; squeezed them with her thumb, dropped them on the granite worktop. Broke the seal on a warm carton of milk.

'You don't think it's over the top?' said Sam.

She handed him the cup of tea.

'There's no sugar,' she said. 'What do you mean?'

'You know,' he said. 'Is it all too much, just for the two of us?'

'Don't be stupid. Anyway, it won't be just the two of you for ever.'

'Yeah,' he said. 'Right.'

Jamie came crashing down the stairs and back into the kitchen. Sam handed him a mug of tea. Jamie took it in two hands and went stomping in the direction of the living room. He paused in the doorway; noticed the door was missing a handle.

He said, 'Do we have to unpack today?'

'Afraid so.'

'But I'm knackered.'

'Me too, sunshine.'

'Is Frank going to help?'

'We'll see,' said Mel. 'He promised to try.'

Frank was Mel's ex-husband.

Sam reached into his trouser pocket. He fished out a crumpled ten-pound note and a number of pound coins, balled them and threw it to Jamie. 'Here,' he said. 'Run down the chippy. The one down the Merrydown shops.'

'That's *miles*.'

'It's five minutes. And it's nicer. I'll have cod and chips – large if they've got it. Mel?'

'Jumbo sausage.'

'Get Mel a saveloy. And get whatever you want. Get a bottle of Coke too.'

'What about Frank?'

'Pasty and chips,' said Mel. 'I expect.'

'Can I keep the change?'

'If there is any.'

'Cheers, Dad.'

He ran off down the corridor.

Sam called after him, 'Do your laces up!'

But Jamie didn't hear. Or if he did, he ignored him.

'And watch the *road*!'

Jamie returned unlaced and undamaged. They ate their chips on the floor of the living room, watching motes of dust describe slow, incandescent spirals in shafts of late-afternoon sunlight. They waited for Unka Frank. But Unka Frank didn't show, and he didn't phone. So, as the sun grew low in the sky, Jamie, Mel and Sam unloaded the hire van. There wasn't much to unpack. Most of their bulkier furniture, including the beds, Sam had sold for a pittance to a 'house-clearance specialist' – a cadaverous creature in whose company he would not have chosen to spend one second more than entirely necessary.

That night, they slept in sleeping bags on the smooth, wood-fragrant floors of their respective bedrooms. Sam was awakened by the early sun bursting through the curtainless window. Excited, he rose almost immediately. He crept through to Jamie's room. It was already a mess.

Sam stood behind a pile of boxes, looking at his sleeping son. In yesterday's T-shirt and pants, Jamie lay on his back. He was starfished across his sleeping bag, his bare heels touching the floor. He'd flung a thin forearm across his eyes, warding off the morning.

2

It took a couple of weeks to get the house in proper order. So much jumble remained that Sam found it difficult to recall exactly what he'd worked so hard to sort out and throw away. In bin bags and boxes he found ancient chequebook stubs, wads of yellowing bank statements, folded and peeling beer mats, dead batteries, coverless paperbacks swollen and stained with ancient coffee spillages and a toddler's crayon swirls; unmarked cassette tapes, empty video-cassette boxes; jackets and trousers he could never wear again, even if he wanted to. There was so much crap. He couldn't imagine what he'd been thinking, bringing it all the way here. Finally, in a fit of self-directed pique, he dumped it all, still boxed and bagged, in the smallest of the spare bedrooms and closed the door on it. He resolved never to set eyes on it again, at least until the day when he would pay somebody to visit the municipal dump on his behalf.

On Friday morning, he took Jamie into town. They had McDonald's for breakfast, then went to choose the boy some bedroom furniture; a single bed and wardrobe, a chest of drawers, a desk for his PlayStation and television. It was all delivered the following week. They hauled the flatpacks and plastic-wrapped mattress upstairs, unzipped them with carpet knives, threw angular blocks of Styrofoam packaging into the far corner. All morning, they worked silently to assemble the furniture.

Just before lunch, a flat-blade screwdriver slipped from the head of a Phillips screw and gouged a chicken-skin wound in Sam's thumb. He ran the cut under the cold tap in the bathroom while Jamie went hunting for the Elastoplast. After lunch, Sam watched with a mug of tea and a plate of Jammie Dodgers as Jamie erected blinds at the bay window. Although they hung slightly and variously askew, they at least stayed attached, and Jamie was proud of the job done.

Soon Jamie's room was ready. There remained a great deal of summer to kill. Jamie spent most of it at Mel's.

Jamie and Mel had begun to grow truly close when Jamie's lack of siblings began to impair Sam and Justine's cheerful attempts at family holidays. Jamie was never able to make new friends quickly, and too much exclusive parental company bored and embarrassed him. So Mel looked after him while Sam and Justine were in Tuscany or North Africa or Rome. And because Mel didn't mortify Jamie the way his parents did, it was she who took him away. Together, they'd been to Cornwall, to Brighton, to Spain, Disneyland Paris, and three times to CenterParcs.

Usually, Mel cooked the kind of food Jamie wasn't allowed at home. But she made him wash the dishes, too, and sometimes do the vacuuming. Mysteriously, Jamie didn't mind taking out the rubbish, or cleaning the upstairs windows, or running to the shops to get milk and cigarettes, as long as it was Mel who asked him to do it.

Mel always phoned if Jamie was staying over and – although Sam knew she'd feed him on frozen potato waffles and Findus crispy pancakes, and that she wouldn't make him bathe if he didn't feel like it, or go to bed until he was staggering with fatigue, or make him clean his teeth, or put on clean underwear – he always said yes. But when he suggested that Jamie should keep some clothes – just a few T-shirts, some socks and underwear, perhaps a toothbrush – at Mel's, his sister and his son took lofty offence and he was forced to apologize, as if for barging in on a private game.

One afternoon, Mel and Jamie walked to the Dolphin Centre to return a rental video (*The Evil Dead II*). Propped against the NSS newsagent's window, Jamie noticed a mountain bike that he recognized as belonging to Stuart Ballard, a ratty little kid he'd known since they were both three or four years old. Sam had always thought that Stuart belonged to another age: he should have been dressed in grey shorts and tank tops, clambering, scabby-kneed, over postwar bombsites or collecting tadpoles in a jam jar with string for a handle. Once, Stuart's parents had been Mel's neighbours. Three years ago, they'd moved to a slightly smaller house on the Merrydown Estate.

Stuart was inside the NSS, buying a PlayStation magazine

and ten Silk Cut for his mum. Mel and Jamie surprised him on the way out. Stuart went back to Mel's with them, pushing his bike. They pulled the curtains on the afternoon and watched *Halloween H20* on fizzy, jumpy VHS. Stuart warned them it was crap, but they enjoyed it anyway. That afternoon, Jamie ate his tea at the Ballards'; grilled lamb chops, chips, peas and HP fruity sauce.

Sometimes, two or three days might pass without Sam catching sight of Jamie, and when he did come home, he'd be worn out and crabby, still wearing the clothes he'd left in. The trousers would be grass-stained, the collars grease-blackened, the socks mossy-damp and odorous. Sam took care to welcome him jauntily, repressing the powerful urge to order him immediately upstairs and into the bath.

Sam wasn't due to start work at Agartha Barrow, the local mental hospital, until October. He had never spent so much time alone. But it wasn't so bad. At first, he kept busy by unpacking the stuff he hadn't crammed into the smallest spare room. When that was done, and when he'd found a place to put everything, the house felt emptier. It swallowed those belongings by which he was content to be surrounded. The rearing expanse of living-room wall miniaturized the television and sofa. The rug, still grubby with their London footfalls, was a postage stamp.

Although Sam lacked any real sense of aesthetics, he'd long ago become adept at second-guessing Justine's taste. It started as a survival mechanism contrived to abbreviate shopping trips; now he found himself furnishing the house on Balaarat Street as if Justine might soon arrive at the door, browned and relaxed and pleased to see him after an extended painting holiday (to where? Morocco? Andalucia?). She would clap her hands to her mouth and exclaim her surprise and delight in his cleverness, his thoughtfulness, his eagerness to make her happy.

Engaged by this fantasy, he allowed consideration of the tiniest domestic details to fill his day. He would rise, shower, shave, then make breakfast and wander to the bus stop. In town he might spend an entire morning examining and comparing curtains or lampshades, rugs or kettles. He bought curtains to please Justine – bleached Egyptian cotton, just long enough to brush the wooden floor. He hummed and hawed and scratched his big, square jaw, examining items of cutlery from all angles, testing them for weight and balance and quality of line.

In the evenings, when the curtains were hung and the cutlery was in the drawer, when the new kettle or new toaster stood in its appointed place in the kitchen, when the new mirrors were hung in the hallway and bedroom and bathroom, when the telephone stood on its new table in the hallway and the CDs were ranked in their new shelves, when the new towels hung folded on the heated rail, the walls receded from him.

Justine was not coming back from holiday and he missed his sister and his son, eating oven chips and fish fingers and tomato ketchup in a small, crammed, chaotic, tobacco-smelling house half a mile down the road. It didn't occur to him to join them. He was as unwelcome as he was loved.

Instead, he watched television and yearned to sleep. Often, he consulted his watch to find it was somehow 2 or 3 a.m. He couldn't read. For weeks, he'd been carrying round the same spine-broken and unread paperback. Several times a day, he attempted to read a page, but even if he was able to muster the necessary concentration, he'd lost his place and the passages he read and re-read lacked context and continuity.

Television didn't relax him. It flickered and glimmered, spectral blue on the walls behind him. As it grew late, he lowered the volume. Yet it seemed to shriek ever more stridently. In direct proportion to diminishing content, the programmes became frenetically edited until, after 1 a.m., it was easy to believe he was watching a random, flashing sequence of unconnected images, most of which depicted young people shouting at one another.

Once or twice, he tried the radio instead. But the sound of a small, intimate voice echoing from the unadorned walls of the big, empty house made him feel lonely and spooked. Sometimes when he was alone, he thought he heard movement upstairs – footsteps on the hallway and bedroom floor. Quickly, he turned on the television.

Eventually, he went upstairs. He had yet to buy a bed for himself and was sleeping on the bedroom floor, cocooned in a sleeping bag. In the morning he woke with a sexless erection, solid and springy as a rubber cosh. According to his need to urinate, it soon deflated. He looked down sadly as his penis relaxed in his hand like a dying bird.

Eventually the day arrived when he decided it was no longer quite rational to keep delaying the purchase of something decent to sleep on. His clothes, although few, hung neatly from a chromium rack at one end of the bedroom. His socks and underwear were stuffed and rolled into the top drawer of a new, glue-smelling chest that had arrived, flatpacked, with Jamie's. It seemed stupid to be sleeping on the floor.

He caught a bus to John Lewis. He wandered round the bed department, his hands clasped Napoleonically at the small of his back. Once or twice, he tested how a certain mattress was sprung. An assistant, a nervous woman in outsize spectacles, asked if he required help. Hastily, Sam selected a bed and demanded to buy it.

It was delivered a few days later by a high-sided, racing-green van. Sam signed for it and, alone, he lugged the flatpacks and plastic-wrapped double mattress upstairs. It wasn't easy. He sat on the daytime twilight of the highest step, sweating and breathing heavily. Then he went to his sunny bedroom and assembled the bed. When it was finished, he stood back and admired his work. The bed was iron-framed, with a new-smelling, unstained mattress whose protective plastic, ripped open, was now unfolding itself loosely in the doorway. He tested it by springing up and down on his arse. Soon he remembered that this was the only bouncing on beds he was likely to get up to for some time and he stopped bouncing and looked disconsolately around himself. He realized that he'd neglected to buy any bedding. He spent another night in the faintly odorous sleeping bag, like a giant pupa on the naked mattress.

In the morning, he returned to John Lewis and, somewhat sheepishly, wandered again around the bedding department. He was worried that he might appear to be some kind of fetishist, but the nervous woman wasn't there and no other member of staff gave the least sign of remembering him. Back home, it took him a great deal of time and effort to stuff and cajole the new duvet into its cotton sheath. That had always been Justine's job and, he had long supposed, more trouble to learn than it could ever be worth.

When the job was done, the bed looked virginal and white. He thought of a photograph in a magazine. It seemed a pity to defile it by sweating and dribbling into its crisp, cotton whiteness. That night, he laid the sleeping bag on the wooden floor alongside the iron bedframe. He bundled up an old jacket to use as a pillow and set the still-unread and much deteriorated paperback talismanically alongside him.

Once he felt settled in, there was nothing to do. During the day, he sometimes allowed himself to wander round to Mel's, even if it risked spoiling their fun.

He'd walk through her front garden gate and round the back of the grey, pebble-dashed house. If the weather was very good, Mel would be in the scurfy, psoriatic back garden whose half-collapsed fence backed on to a cul-de-sac of garages. The garages were a design-feature of the estate, and for years they'd been put to most frequent use by kids: during the day they were playgrounds, somewhere to ride bikes and play football and cricket. During the hours of darkness they were the location of those heady adolescent pursuits that in hindsight seem so innocent. In such terrain, Sam lost his virginity to a girl called Tina Marie, both of them drunk on cider. He remembered the T-shirt gathered and ruched at her neck, the raindrop pattern of lovebites on her breasts and neck, her cigarette breath, her chipped nail varnish, her knickers hooked on one ankle, her doll-blank eyes. He remembered something like dread as the orgasm surged at the root of his penis.

At the far end of Mel's garden there stood the rusty swing she'd bought for Jamie, second-hand, ten or eleven years ago. Despite its decrepitude, she still treated it as a bench. As he approached the house, he knew by its gentle creaking if Mel was in the garden. It was a sound he associated with midsummer torpor.

Mel would be talking in a gossipy murmur to her friend, a woman who for so long had been known as Fat Janet that all the insult had drained from it. (When opprobrium was called for, she was known instead as Janet the Planet.) Fat Janet had baby features packed into the centre of her face and fine, blonde hair pulled into a ponytail that was hazy-tipped with split ends. In theory she had a husband called Jim, a limp, grey cardigan of a man. But Sam couldn't remember meeting him since a party in the mid-1980s, when he'd made a pass at Justine and she had laughed, assuming he was joking.

Sam would join Mel and Janet on the grass, or on a patch of dry soil where grass had once grown. Wordlessly, he would accept the cigarette one of them chucked at him. Sometimes they said nothing at all. But mostly, they discussed ephemera, local and celebrity gossip. Janet had a joyful, malicious sense of humour. Her cackle erupted from the garden like a startled crow.

Sometimes Jamie and Stuart Ballard roamed by. They were hungry or thirsty or both, and summer-scruffy, in need of haircuts, engaged in conversation from which adults were excluded by intent and temperament. When the mood struck him, Sam would stand, brush his arse clean of grass and dried soil, and go inside to make a round of tea, or to watch TV. Jamie and Stuart might be huddled on the sofa, watching *The Simpsons* or *Robot Wars*.

One afternoon, Mel and Sam challenged Stuart and Jamie to an improvised, half-arsed game of badminton. The rackets were crumpled and half-strung, and the shuttlecock was fletched with a few desultory feathers. Despite Sam and Mel's best and genuine efforts, the boys won easily.

Sam welcomed the first muddy trainers in the hallway of the house on Balaarat Street, and the first rank of dirty T-shirts hanging on the banister; the first wet-trampled towels in the bathroom. Such were the first cryptograms of domestic normality. Jamie was beginning to feel at home.

One day, Sam wandered upstairs with a bundle of laundry folded in his arms and came across Jamie and Stuart, cross-legged before the portable TV, playing *Gran Turismo III*. They were surrounded by crisp bags and biscuit wrappers, crushed, empty Coke cans, toppled mugs and glasses. They spoke a language foreign to him, a cant of cryptic insults and surreptitious debasements.

Without letting them know he'd seen them, he sneaked downstairs and turned on the TV.

Cigarette smoke drifted down. He closed the door on it. Before *EastEnders*, he dialled Domino's Pizza. He called Stuart and Jamie down when the pizzas arrived. They mixed and matched slices, piling them on plates that had not yet been used. Without thanking Sam, the boys sat on the floor and commandeered the television. Stuart went home at 9.45 p.m.

Sam crushed the pizza boxes and put them in a bin bag, and loaded the dishwasher. Then he stretched out on the sofa with his hands knitted behind his head.

He said, 'No smoking in the bedroom.'

Jamie grunted. His head bobbed twice on his shoulders; an irritated affirmative.

'It's a mug's game anyway,' said Sam.

'You do it.'

'That's not the point.'

'Shot *down*,' said Jamie. He made a gesture with clenched fists, like a triumphant sprinter.

Sam rolled a sheet of Kleenex into a ball and chucked it. It bounced off Jamie's head.

Jamie rubbed at his crown.

'Oi,' he said. 'Fuck off.'

'Watch your language.'

Jamie chucked the Kleenex back over his shoulder.

'Fuck off,' he said again. 'Please.'

Sam laughed and changed the channel.

3

Unka Frank turned up late in July.

Far away, along the quiet length of Magpie Avenue, they heard the familiar coughing of an antiquated, badly tuned motorcycle. Jamie stopped what he was doing and looked up, his jaw canted like a deer tasting the air at the forest's edge. Then he ran to the window and waited there until Unka Frank came round the corner.

Frank was a thin man with bad teeth and long hair, who liked motorbikes. More than twenty years ago, Mel had introduced him to their parents and announced their intention to marry. Frank was thirty-five and of no fixed abode. Mel was eighteen.

A miscalculated ultimatum from their father – that Mel finish with Frank, or never darken his door again – made Mel technically homeless and, because she chose never to see her mother or father again, an elective orphan.

She was also pregnant. According to the points system by which the Town Council tallied people's lives, she and Frank qualified almost at once for a house on the Robinwood Estate. By the time they lost the baby it was too late: their names were on the tenancy agreement.

The marriage lasted for thirteen years. This, as Mel was still glad to point out, was twelve years longer than many had predicted. Frank had proved to be a good and attentive husband, in his own way, and Mel to be a good and attentive wife, in hers. When they needed money, Frank worked hard for it. When they didn't, he didn't. Mel barely worked at all. They had no children, although for several years they tried, and they loved one other with an unaffected, infectious merriment.

Nobody knew for certain why they separated. One night, they argued about something stupid. Neither could remember exactly what. But whatever it was, Mel told Frank to get out of her sight and he did – for fifteen months. Mel sometimes drunkenly rehearsed her last vision of him, Frank her husband: his spine erect, spluttering haughtily down the road on his elderly Triumph.

When he returned, it was not as a married man.

In a variety of ways, Unka Frank was among the least trustworthy men Sam had ever met. He'd not only served at least one prison sentence before meeting Mel; he'd spent a year inside since they separated.

In partnership with a shambling, ursine biker friend called Yeti Moocow, Frank spent a number of lean months working as a landscape gardener. While he and Yeti were constructing a gazebo in a particular suburb of Manchester, it came to Frank's attention that certain wealthy dog lovers, mostly elderly, smothered their pets with the kind of affection more commonly reserved for very young children.

At much the same moment, it further occurred to him that the police, who were required to target their limited resources, were unlikely to share this depth of attachment. Frank thought the police wouldn't be interested in investigating a few abducted West Highland terriers.

And he was right. Simply by doing some online research and bundling a series of lolloping, silver-brown Weimaranas or bewildered Afghans into the back of a Morris Traveller, followed by a couple of sinister phone calls, Unka Frank and Yeti Moocow made two-hundred thousand pounds in less than eighteen months.

If the research was done well, and Frank ensured it was, the entire affair could be over in less than twenty-four hours. During this time, Frank and Yeti Moocow usually took their charge to the local park where, for a blithe hour, it was permitted to chase soggy, balding tennis balls, or gnaw promotional Frisbees. The hounds were seldom less than grateful; Great Danes and snuffling prize bulldogs paraded for Unka Frank like cantering ponies.

Only once in this brief but remunerative dog-napping career did Frank's research prove to be less than thorough. The master of his final victim had some familial (or possibly Masonic) senior-level connection to the police force. As soon as Yeti Moocow parked the patchouli- and fur-smelling

Morris Traveller beneath a motorway flyover, ready to exchange their panting contraband for a bag of unmarked twenties, their car was penned in by wailing, blue-flashing police cars.

Freed of his captors by a grim, uniformed dog-handler, Bonny Prince William immediately escaped the tearful embrace of his owner, bounding back to Frank's spindly, welcoming arms. Such was Frank's shrewd but fond affinity with animals. He had enjoyed kidnapping them. Each pampered poodle was like Patty Hearst to him.

Although he served twelve months of a two-year sentence, Frank still believed this idea to be possessed of criminal genius.

Frank had nearly completed a doctoral degree in Marine Biology.

It was late one Christmas night when he told Sam about it. Jamie, a baby, was tucked away upstairs. Justine and Mel were asleep in their chairs. Head back and mouth open, Mel snored softly.

Frank poured Sam a whisky and lit himself a cigar. Then he told Sam about a trip he'd taken in the early 1970s: a descent to the deepest part of the ocean. He'd been alone in a spherical submersible, a ball of steel. There was only room inside for one person. Frank told Sam about the slow descent through the swarming, teeming deep blue to the deeper gloom, the depths where sunlight did not penetrate. Even here, the ocean abounded with life.

But Frank descended still further, to the edge of the Abyssal Plane. Here he encountered a darkness so terrible he could not properly speak of it. Several times he glimpsed the transient, flickering bioluminescence of species as yet unknown to science. And still he descended: a single, fragile point of light in eternal, freezing blackness. Finally, the lightless and utter solitude blew a network of psychic fuses behind Frank's eyes. Panic swelled inside him. He yelled and howled and begged and demanded to be returned to the surface. It took a while. He was a long, long way down.

When finally the submersible was landed on the deck, the crew had to lift Frank from it. He was a jabbering ruin in khaki shorts and cheap flip-flops. Two weeks later, he returned the remains of his research grant and flew back to England.

Frank was never able to describe exactly what it was that terrified him to the point of madness. Sam wasn't sure he was able to do so. When the Abyssal Plane was alluded to even tangentially, all the jest and tomfoolery deserted Frank's hatchet face and he fell silent and introspective, staring at the blue Ace of Spades tattooed on his right forearm.

It was Jamie, at two years old, who named him Unka Frank. It wasn't the first nickname he'd acquired; Sam had also heard him called Carnie Frank. But it was the name he liked best. Frank made Jamie few promises, but he kept the promises he made. He rarely sent birthday cards, but he might turn up unannounced on a Sunday afternoon and offer to take Jamie to Brighton, or to a motorcycle rally, or deep sea fishing.

Shortly after Justine died, Frank turned up to spend the weekend with them in Hackney. He took Jamie to the cinema, where they saw *The Mummy Returns*, and he came home clutching a litre bottle of Jack Daniel's. That night Unka Frank and Sam worked their way through the bottle and didn't mention Justine. Frank talked about his new bike, his new girlfriend, some bad acid he'd dropped at the Reading Festival in 1982, various high-paying construction jobs he always seemed to be on the verge of getting, the predatory habits of Great White Sharks. Every few minutes, he topped up Sam's tumbler, and Sam didn't remember the end of the evening. When he woke, still on the sofa, Frank was gone. But before leaving, he'd wrapped Sam in a towel for a blanket, removed his shoes and left out for him a tumbler of water and two aspirins.

He hadn't seen Unka Frank since. Mel said he might be there to help them move in, but he hadn't turned up and had never explained his absence.

Jamie loved him. So did Sam.

They waited at the window and watched the bike chug to the kerb.

'Go and let him in,' said Sam.

Jamie broke for the door and launched himself along the garden path. Astride the bike, Unka Frank waved a gauntleted hand and dismounted, somewhat stiffly. Jamie threw himself into Frank's arms. Frank hugged him back.

Still at the window, Sam smiled.

Frank straightened. He removed his helmet and upended it, then stuffed in the gauntlets. He posted his wrist through the open visor and wore the helmet like a handbag. He had a narrow, craggy face with a great beak of a nose.

Sam thumped twice on the window. Frank looked up and smiled. His gold tooth glinted in the sunlight. He walked through the gate and down the path, bandy-legged as a cowboy with a ponytail at the nape of his neck.

As soon as Frank came in, Sam could smell him – strong smells, but not unpleasant: fresh tobacco, engine oil, fresh sweat, leather. Exhaust fumes.

Frank looked around.

'This it, then?'

'This is it,' said Sam. He was leaning against the doorframe with his arms crossed.

'Do you want to see my room?' said Jamie.

'In a minute, mate. Let me say hello to the old man.'

'I've got PS2.'

Frank assessed this information with a turned-out lower lip.

'Nice one,' he said, and nodded approvingly.

Jamie looked at Sam.

'Frank's got a new bike,' he said.

'So I see.'

'It's a Triumph.'

'It looks like a bit of a triumph,' said Sam.

Frank cackled. Phlegm rattled in his scrawny throat, silver-bristled round the jaw.

'She needs a bit of twiddling,' he said. 'Here and there.'

Frank's bikes were always English and they always needed a bit of twiddling. When a bike didn't need any more twiddling, Frank sold it and bought one that did. To Frank, twiddling was its own reward.

Frank unzipped his jacket and dropped heavily upon the sofa. He set the helmet down next to him. It was black, and still bore the gummy edges where various stickers had been removed. He shrugged out of the jacket and dumped it on the floor. He wore a tight, washed-out Budweiser T-shirt. He sat there in his oily ripped jeans and biker's boots and asked for a beer.

Jamie ran to the fridge. They heard the pop and fizz of a bottle being opened, then Jamie ran back in to give the bottle to Frank. Sam rolled his eyes, then went to the kitchen and got a beer for himself.

He got back to find Jamie cross-legged on the floor, wearing Frank's helmet and gauntlets. Frank had propped his feet, crossed at the ankles, on the boy's head. He was rolling a cigarette while Jamie continued the single, unbroken sentence he'd begun when Frank arrived.

'Last time I was here,' said Unka Frank, while Jamie's prattling continued, unabated, at his ankles, 'it was a building site. They were putting the kitchen in. Cowboys, like.'

He licked the gummed paper and put the cigarette in the corner of his mouth, then lit it with a brief, complex ballet of wrist and thumb and brass Zippo lighter.

Sam sat on the floor, his back to the cool wall.

'They did all right.'

'Oh, they did all right,' Unka Frank agreed. 'Once Mel had said her piece.'

He grinned; crooked teeth and gold. His little eyes were lost in complex tributaries of laughter lines and sun-wrinkles.

He removed his feet from Jamie's head.

'Are you all right in there, sunshine?'

Jamie raised the visor.

'Do you want to play *Gran Turismo*?'

'In a bit. You want to take that crash-hat off. It's a bit hot in here.'

'I'm all right.'

'Jamie,' said Sam, 'take off the helmet.'

'He's all right,' said Frank. 'He can wear it if he likes.'

Jamie cocked his oversized head to one side.

'See?' he said, muffled. 'It's all right.'

'Whatever,' said Sam. He hugged his knees. 'How are you, Frank?' he said. 'We missed you.'

'Yeah,' said Frank. 'Sorry about that.'

'What happened?'

'You know how it is,' said Frank, although Sam didn't know how it was, which was why he was asking. 'Anyway, it doesn't look like I was needed. Where's all your stuff?'

'He sold it,' said Jamie. He put the visor down and began to breathe like Darth Vader.

'You what?'

Sam sipped lager.

'It made sense,' he said. 'There was no point hiking it all the way from London. Half of it was knackered anyway.'

'You had some nice stuff there. Designer and whatnot. There was that . . . cupboard thing. And the doodah.'

Jamie began to walk like Frankenstein's monster, his arms held horizontally before him.

Sam leant to one side, to see past him, and made a dismissive face.

'I didn't want it,' he said.

'Fair enough.'

Unka Frank slapped his skinny shanks. He drained the bottle and loosed a mighty belch. Jamie stopped being Frankenstein and said, 'Oh gross,' with much evident pleasure. Frank offered him a skinny hand, blue-tattooed on the web between thumb and finger.

He said, 'Come on then, sunshine.'

Jamie took his hand and Frank allowed himself to be dragged upstairs.

Sam left his lager, half-drunk, in the fireplace. He went to the hallway, picked up the phone and invited Mel over. He checked his watch and then the weather, then went into the garden and lit the barbecue.

Mel arrived in a Fiat Uno driven by Fat Janet. They'd each brought a bowl of salad and a couple of bottles of Frascati with screw-top lids. Fat Janet had also brought a portable stereo. They joined Sam in the garden, where he was barbecuing sausages, chicken wings and pork chops, flattening the meat with a greasy spatula and watching liquid fat dance and sizzle.

Unka Frank and Jamie came down to join them. Frank had loosened his hair and it hung in two lank, grey-streaked curtains on either side of his fatless, haggard face. He hugged Mel and slapped Fat Janet's arse.

He said, 'All right, Jan?'

Then he knelt down and turned up the volume on the mini-CD player. Sam Cooke.

Sam flipped a chop and sipped lager. Behind him, Unka

Frank waltzed with Mel and Jamie waltzed, haltingly, with Fat Janet.

He wouldn't have believed it was still possible to be that happy – not even for an hour, in the summer, with Mel and Frank and Jamie and Sam Cooke on the stereo. But it was.

4

Early in September came Jamie's first day at Churchill Comprehensive School. As the day approached, Sam grew more nervous on his behalf. He couldn't sleep.

He remembered his own first day at the same school. When he thought of himself, big and clumsy in his new uniform, he felt a kind of pity, a strange desire to reach back through time and comfort himself. But it hadn't been so bad for him. He was one of nearly three hundred First Years, blinking in the bright new light. And of course, he had Mel, his big sister. Mel was in the Third Year, as it then was, and Sam didn't question that, for all they were sworn enemies at home, Mel would look after him at school. Mel had a reputation. Nobody messed with her, be it boy, girl or teacher. Sam believed then, as part of him believed now, that she was almighty and indestructible.

Because the idea made Sam nervous, Mel took Jamie to shop

for his uniform. She came round at 10 a.m., and they didn't get back until late that afternoon. They'd bought everything Jamie needed: a new blazer, slightly too large in the shoulders and arms, to allow for growth, a yellow, blue and red striped tie, five polycotton white shirts, black Caterpillar boots and a full sports kit with reversible rugby sweater.

Mel laid the stuff on the bed for Sam to inspect. It looked crisp and dense with the future. Sam looked at the school tie and felt his testicles retract. He remembered knotting an identical tie at his own throat. And he remembered the first few, terrified weeks of the first year. He remembered walking home at 3.40, dragging his bag on the pavement behind him.

He hung the clothes in Jamie's wardrobe. The sight of them, hanging there, made him feel sick, and he went to make a cup of tea.

On what had become known as Jamie's last night of freedom, Mel came round to cook a special tea. They had steak and chips and peas. It was well known that Mel cooked the best chips in Britain. They ate the meal on their knees, in front of the TV – a DVD of *Attack of the Clones*. Mel was loud and brash. Sam could tell she was nervous. Jamie seemed the most tranquil of the three of them. But he went to bed early, before the film had finished.

Five minutes later, Sam pretended to Mel that he needed the lavatory. He sneaked upstairs, pausing and cupping his ear at Jamie's bedroom door. He heard nothing. He wanted to knock on the door and march in there like a sitcom father, to sit on the edge of the bed and be strong and wise. But he didn't feel strong and wise.

Downstairs, Mel was curled on the sofa, watching *Crimewatch*. She had lit a cigarette, and threw one to Sam. He caught it with a hand-clapping motion and flopped in the armchair.

He whistled at the ceiling.

'Jesus,' he said.

Mel expelled smoke through her nostrils.

'He'll be all right.'

'Oh Christ. I hope so.'

Tears welled in his eyes and he blinked them away.

'He's my little boy.'

Mel rubbed his forearm, as if warming it.

'No, he's not,' she said.

Sam knuckled his eyes.

'I know,' he said. 'I know.'

'He's a young man,' said Mel. 'He's a teenager.'

'I know.'

He went to the kitchen and got himself a whisky.

He woke in time to make them a full English breakfast — sausage, egg, bacon, tomato, hash browns, a fried slice. Jamie came down in his boxer shorts and a T-shirt. It was clear by the obliged way he picked and prodded at the fry-up that he had no appetite.

'Now,' said Sam. 'Go and have a proper shower. None of this dodging the drops business. And wash your hair. With shampoo. And clean your teeth.'

Jamie stamped obligingly upstairs. Sam fussed around, placing pens, pencils, a ruler, a compass and a pocket calculator into Jamie's schoolbag. He paused, tilted his head. Over the sound of the shower, he could hear Jamie vomiting. He tried not to listen. He turned up the radio and sang along.

He'd rehearsed what he wanted to say, but there was no opportunity to say it. When he went upstairs he found that Jamie, his hair still wet and glossy, was knotting the tie at his throat. When that was done, he tucked the fat end inside his shirt, as children had apparently done since neckties were invented. Sam had no idea why, but he'd done the same. Then Jamie shrugged himself into the blazer. A squirrel was mechanically embroidered on the badge, eating an acorn. Same badge, unchanged for God knew how many years.

Sam wanted to reach out and hug his son and kiss him on the forehead. Instead he leant back, the wall cold on his shoulders, and crossed his arms approvingly.

'It looks all right.'

Jamie looked down and made pigeon toes.

'The shoes look stupid.'

'You chose them.'

'They're *shoes* though. I hate shoes.'

'You can't wear trainers every day.'

'Why not?'

'Anyway, they're boots – and they cost a lot of money. They look all right. Christ, you should see what *I* had to wear.'

'That was before fashion was invented.'

Sam smiled, but Jamie wasn't looking and he let it fall.

Jamie's voice rose and quickened.

'They look naff. They're all *new*.'

'I don't know. Scuff them up, then.'

Jamie looked at him.

'Duh,' he said. 'I don't want to look *poor*.'

Sam retreated.

At 8.30, the doorbell rang. Sam opened the door to Stuart, who looked tiny and mammalian in his uniform. He'd had his gingery hair cut so it stuck up on the crown. He had not tucked the fat end of his tie into his shirt.

'All right, Stuart?'

'All right, Mr Greene?'

'You coming in?'

'All right.'

Stuart shambled in, his trousers baggy and gathered at the ankles. He wore new boots identical to Jamie's.

He sat on the sofa and picked up the remote control.

'Can I watch some telly?'

'Of course.'

For a couple of minutes, Sam stood behind him, his arms crossed, and watched.

Then he said, 'It's terrible. The first day back.'

Stuart shrugged. From his bag he removed a chocolate Tracker and began to unwrap it.

'It's all right.'

'I used to hate it. I was always really nervous.'

'We're a year older now though,' said Stuart. 'We're not the youngest any more.'

'No,' said Sam. 'I suppose not.'

'It's them that'll get the hard time. All the new kids.'

Jamie came clomping downstairs and into the front room.

'All right, Stu?'

'All right, Jamie?'

Stuart stuffed the uneaten half of the Tracker into his blazer pocket and wiped his palms on his lapel. He slung his bag over his shoulder.

Jamie said, 'See you later, Dad.'

Sam wanted to say something. He wanted to clap Jamie manfully on the shoulder and wish him half-ironic good luck, as a good coach might. But Jamie gave every appearance of confidence, of hardly being aware.

So Sam fought the urge to stand in the doorway, watching the boys wander down the street, towards the new term. They were deep in some meaningful conversation about a subject Sam would never be able to understand. He closed the door and went to the kitchen and put the kettle on. While it boiled, he sat on the garden step and smoked a couple of cigarettes. He looked at his watch and wondered what Jamie was up to now, if he'd met his future classmates yet. He went back inside and poured boiling water over a tea bag. He left it there to steep.

When, with a grunt of surprise, he remembered it, the tea was already cold.

When Jamie came home, Sam pretended not to be waiting. But his heart cracked in his chest when the front door slammed. He started to potter in the kitchen, as if he hadn't spent the last two hours sitting at the breakfast bar smoking, watching the clock, staring into the middle distance.

Jamie looked hot. His hair was in sweaty disarray and the stripy tie was loosened to his sternum. He kicked off his school shoes in the hallway, then went to the fridge and took out a can of Diet Coke.

Sam said, 'If you're thirsty, drink water.'

Jamie glugged the can half-empty then replied with a long, fruity belch.

'What?'

'Nothing. So?'

'So, what?'

'So how was it?'

'What, school?'

'Duh. Yeah, school. How was it?'

'All right.'

'What did you do?'

'Nothing.'

'Did you make any friends?'

Jamie shrugged and drank off the remainder of the can.

'Nah.'

'It's early days yet,' said Sam. 'You'll be all right.'

Jamie shrugged again.

'I *am* all right.'

He crushed the can, left it on the worktop and stomped upstairs. Sam listened for the sound of the PlayStation engaging.

He called upstairs for Jamie to hang up his blazer and tie, but when he went up, later, they awaited his attention from an indecorous pile on his son's bedroom floor. Jamie was playing *Tekken*. Sam watched from the doorway with the blazer folded over his forearm. Oblivious of his presence, the boy was playing a tiny Oriental woman with an elaborate top-knot. She was comprehensively beating the shit out of a procession of baddies. Sam slipped the blazer on to a wire hanger and hung it from the door handle. Its skirts brushed the floor.

Then he went back downstairs.

5

Agartha Barrow was a bus ride away, on the edge of Hollyhead.

It was a Victorian hospital complex, centred round a garden square. Many of its annexes had fallen into disuse and disrepair. Its main function now was as a Low Secure Psychiatric Intensive Care Unit. Although it stood close to a main road and a busy shopping street, the complex had a faded, disused air, like a place about to be shut down.

But Sam had needed a job, not least because he needed something to do, or risk going mad himself. His former boss had placed a few phone calls on his behalf, and a position was found for him at Agartha, subject to the usual formalities and a number of qualifications. The position was at a lower rating and at a lower wage than he had become accustomed to, and the vacancy didn't start until October. Agartha was, therefore, getting an experienced member of staff, cheap and on its own terms. Sam didn't mind.

On his first morning, he gave an intra-muscular injection of Lorazepam, followed by one of haloperiodol, into the arse of a man with an eye tattooed on each buttock. They watched Sam while he jabbed.

On Tuesday he was punched by a manic-depressive prostitute, the first time he had been successfully assaulted since he qualified, more than a decade before.

By Friday, he was feeling more on top of things and Mel came to meet him for lunch. Tired, he shuffled to reception like a patient. Mel was wearing new jeans and an old leather coat that flared at the waist and fell to her ankles. She'd done her hair and make-up.

Sam wrestled himself into his overcoat and wound the scarf round his neck, then pecked Mel briskly on the cheek. It was cold. She linked her arm through his. He felt the light, all-seeing gaze of Molly the receptionist pass across them like a zephyr. He turned to face her, so quickly that Mel stumbled in her heels.

'Molly,' he said, 'this is Melanie. My sister.'

Molly said she was delighted to meet Mel, although this did not, strictly, appear to be true. Then Sam led Mel through the inappropriately monumental doors. They walked through the car park, the white writing on blue signs, past the derelict outbuildings, through the Victorian gates and on to Wick Road. At the gates, Mel turned and wrapped her coat more tightly around herself. As the cold wind blew at her skirts, she looked at the squat, stone-built hospital.

She said, 'I don't know how you put up with it.'

Sam buried his hands in his pockets.

'It's all right,' he said. 'You get used to it.'

'It's got an atmosphere.'

'What kind of atmosphere?'

She rooted round in her bag and took out her cigarettes. She put one in the corner of her mouth and lit it with a disposable Bic.

'I don't know.'

He grabbed her wrist and tugged her in the direction of the road, but she hung back. He let go and she nearly lost her balance, going ankle-deep into a rotting pile of leaves.

'It's creepy,' she said, righting herself.

'It is not,' he said. 'It's a hospital. It's full of people who need help, that's all. It could be you or me one day.'

'Not bloody likely.'

'You'd be surprised. It happens to normal people, you know.'

'Janet's a mad cow,' said Mel. 'She's on Prozac.'

'There you go. Same thing.'

'She's *mad* though.'

'We don't call it that, Mel.'

Her eyes narrowed at the corners, as if this was a point hardly worth debating.

She said, 'Have you got any murderers?'

'It's not *Broadmoor*.'

'But you've got killers in there.'

'Only boring ones.'

'How can a murderer be boring?'

'You'd understand if you met them.'

'Can I?'

'Can you what?'

'Meet them.'

'No.'

He guided her by the shoulder along the road.

'Look, they're sad little men. They've all been fucked since Day One. Since before that – since conception. Sad cases. Substance abusers, wife-beaters. Alcoholics. Scared, depressed, violent little men.'

She linked her arm back through his, as if it wasn't funny any more, the thought of the cowed, blank-eyed rapists growing fat and still behind those foot-thick walls.

They walked silently to the café, an Italian on the corner with Lacey Road. At lunchtimes it was always frantic and full; office workers queued at the chrome and glass counter, shouting over the babble to describe whatever over-elaborate sandwich their status demanded. In the far corner were arranged five tables, like the face of a die. Mel and Sam pressed through the clamour of workers and squeezed into the single free table, closest to the window. They ordered cappuccinos from a passing, harried young waitress.

They studied laminated menus. The coffees arrived quickly and they took the opportunity to order food. The café's frantic pace hid an underlying efficiency and lunch arrived in a few minutes, unevenly heated as if in a microwave. Mel dug in. When she looked up, she had a tomato sauce moustache. Sam took a paper napkin from the chromium dispenser, crunched it into a ball and handed it to her. He pointed to his pursed lips to show where the problem was. Mel dabbed at her mouth until he gave her the all-clear, and left the crumpled napkin on the table.

'So,' she said. 'How is it, then? Apart from the murderers are boring.'

'I'm not even working with them,' he said.

'Who are you working with?'

'Just the general loonies.'

'So how are the general loonies?'

He smiled. 'They're fine. You'd be surprised how many of them are probably wandering round the supermarket right now.'

He nodded his head at the Tesco Metro across the road.

He drained his coffee and lit a cigarette. His sandwich lay in two uneaten halves on his plate.

He said, 'It's good to be back at work. You know how it is. It's been a long time.'

'Not that long.'

'It wouldn't seem like a long time to you, Melanie, no.'

'Life's too short.'

He agreed, nodding, and sipped coffee.

Mel froze.

'Oh God,' she said. 'It's just an expression.'

He smiled, to show he hadn't taken offence. He hadn't, but the smile felt wooden anyway and he let it fall. He rubbed his eyes.

'Christ,' he said. 'I'm so *tired*. I forgot what it was like.'

'You're bound to be tired, the first week back. First day of term.'

He ordered two more coffees.

He said, 'I hope I can find a more relaxing place to have lunch.'

Mel looked around.

'It's all right,' she said. 'It makes a change. I like it.'

'I can hardly hear myself think.'

'Nice lasagne though.'

She prodded the viscous, yellow and orange square as if she doubted her own words.

'It's a bit busy,' said Sam. 'Is all I'm saying.'

Mel pushed aside the remains of her meal and lighted a cigarette.

She said, 'I saw Jamie the other day.'

'Yeah? He didn't say.'

'He wouldn't.'

'Why not?'

'It was about quarter to eleven on Wednesday morning,' she said. 'He was sitting on a wall round the back of the Dolphin Centre. By the car park.'

'What was he doing?'

'Nothing. Playing with the GameBoy or something.'

'That's not what I mean.'

'Well, what do you *think* he was doing?'

'Jesus,' said Sam. He looked mournfully down at his sandwich. 'He's not been there a term yet. He's got to give the place a chance.'

'Don't be like that.'

'Like what?'

'You sound like Dad.'

'I do *not* sound like Dad.'

He forced himself to calm down.

'Fuck,' he said.

He puffed at his cigarette.

'Christ. What does he think he was *doing*?'

'I don't know what they call it now,' she said. 'Probably something American – *skipping class*? Anyway, that's what he was doing. He was knocking off.'

She ground out her cigarette and watched people come and go along Wick Road.

She said, 'He was all by himself.'

Something, a physical pain, lanced through Sam's stomach. He winced and kept his eyes closed for several seconds.

Mel said, 'Don't go off the deep end.'

'I'm not planning to.' He watched tiny bubbles pop in the frothy base of his empty mug. 'What did you say to him?'

'Nothing.' She looked distracted. She was watching the people pass heedlessly by, as if they were projected on a screen. 'I don't even know if he saw me. He probably didn't. He was playing *Pac-Man* or whatever. And I didn't want to embarrass him. So I just walked by on the other side of the road. I'd only popped out to go round the NSS to get some fags.'

Sam rubbed his eyes. 'What do I do?'

'Don't let on,' she said. 'Find out what's wrong. Speak to his form tutor or something.'

The second coffees arrived. Sam took a good, long swig.

The noise and bustle were oppressive, like background sounds clattering too loudly through cheap speakers. They finished their lunch in silence. Mel waited outside, stamping her feet, while Sam paid the bill.

He joined her outside.

He said, 'I didn't know Janet was on anti-depressants.'

'Has been for years. She's always bloody depressed. She's got no whatsit – self-esteem.'

His cheeks felt cold and raw.

'Then perhaps we should stop calling her Fat Janet.'

'We don't, not to her face.'

'Still.'

'She needs to sort her life out,' said Mel.

'Yeah,' said Sam.

'Mad as a spanner,' said Mel.

She walked with him to the hospital gates. The bus stop was just across the road. Its convenience had prevented Sam from getting round to buying a car. He needed to piss. He looked through the iron gates at the ugly, black stone building.

He said, 'I don't know what to do.'

She squeezed his upper arm.

'You'll be all right,' she said. 'You're a good dad.'

'You think so?'

'Brilliant.'

He wished he knew if she meant it. He could never tell, not even after all this time.

'Right,' he said, and glanced redundantly at his watch. He was fifteen minutes late.

He pecked her on the cheek and half-jogged through the gates, through the car park and through the heavy doors. Inside, it was warmer. He blew into his hands, then rested his weight on the ancient, cast-iron radiator. Molly looked on like an indulgent, secretly resentful Buddha. Slow heat spread through his arse and up his spine and down his legs and to his feet.

He wondered who would choose to be outside in such weather. He pictured Jamie, sitting alone on a car-park wall, huddled in his parka against the weather. Then coming through the door at 4 p.m., dumping his bag and coat in the hallway, his shoes in the living room, making himself a round or two of toast and jam, and lying about his day with every action and every breath.

Sam got home before 7 p.m. Jamie was watching TV. Sam sat heavily in the armchair. He still wore his overcoat and scarf. His face was ruddy with cold.

'What're you watching?'

Jamie clucked impatiently.

'*Simpsons*.'

'You eaten?'

'Toast.'

'What do you want for tonight?'

Jamie shrugged.

'Whatever.'

'I'm knackered. Do you fancy a curry?'

'Whatever.'

'Have you done your homework?'

'Haven't got any.'

'You hardly seem to get *any*. In my day, we had half an hour per night. Minimum.'

'In Jurassic Park, yeah.'

'So. If I phoned your form tutor – what's his name?'

'Ash Bandit.'

'No, it is not.'

'Mr Ashford.'

'If I phoned Mr Ashford, he'd tell me you had no home-work tonight. Is that right?'

'I don't know, do I?'

Sam unbuttoned his overcoat.

'Come on, mate,' he said. 'Give me a break.'

'Phone him then, if you don't believe me.'

The effort of unbuttoning the coat was too much. Sam sank further into the chair. The coat was wet, cold where it touched his cheek. He spoke to his chest.

The Simpsons began. He watched the opening sequence for what felt like the millionth time.

He said, 'So, have you decided what you want?'

Jamie looked at him.

'Do you want curry?' said Sam wearily.

'All right. Keep your hair on. Lamb Pasanda.'

Sam watched Jamie's profile for a long time.

Then he said, 'Chuck me the phone.'

Jamie dug the cordless phone from deep between the sofa cushions, where it was usually to be found, lurking in secret, malevolent fraternity with the remote controls, and threw it to Sam.

Sam went to the kitchen to make the call in peace. It was dark outside. When he switched on the light, he could see only his reflection, bounced back at him in the window. His eyes were dark hollows. He ordered the food, then he stooped, heel-to-haunch, and opened the freezer door. He dropped three ice cubes into a tumbler and poured himself a large whisky.

*

On Monday morning, he phoned Jamie's form tutor. After a moment's hesitation (he seemed to be consulting something), Ashford agreed to see him that afternoon.

Sam was ten minutes late for their appointment. (Sam was ten minutes late for everything.) Hurrying through the school gates, he felt himself hexed by *déjà vu*. Churchill Comprehensive was a large school with a broad catchment area. More than twenty-five years before, he'd been one of over two thousand pupils. That number had since been exceeded.

The main building was an interlocking series of steel and concrete blocks, like a sculpture of an engine component. It loomed before his long approach like a lowered brow. The huts – prefabricated classrooms – were to his right, blocking his view of the school fields. Through the windows, he could see pupils in white shirts, bent over desks, teetering on chairs, talking, staring into space. They might have been ghosts.

He entered through the main doors with a sense of transgression; they were not for the use of pupils – students, as they were now called. Sam had never passed through them. The doors swung closed and he was engulfed by the familiar scents of dust and floorwax and bodies.

He stood in the same foyer, on the same chevroned parquet floor. The assembly hall was directly before him. The Head Teacher's office stood at the end of a corridor that ran off to his right. From this corridor there emerged a slight, balding man in rolled shirtsleeves and floral tie, loose at the throat. He offered his hand.

'Mr Greene?'

'I'm sorry I'm late. The buses.'

'Gerry Ashford. Don't worry. I was held up too.'

There was an air of depletion about him, but he shook Sam's hand briskly enough. Sam followed him down the Head Teacher's corridor to the door of a room that abutted the School Secretary's office. Inside, it was like a doctor's waiting room: generic office carpeting, functional tables and chairs. Some effort had been made to decorate the walls with unframed watercolours – by students, he presumed. Some of them seemed quite good. Others did not. On a corner table there were basic tea-making facilities: two flasks, assorted novelty mugs.

Ashford asked him which he preferred, tea or coffee. Sam told him tea. He longed for a cigarette.

They sat facing each other. Ashford opened a blue folder. He knuckled a bloodshot eye. Then he pinched the bridge of his nose and seemed to gather his thoughts. His index finger was yellow as parchment.

He took a deep, shuddering breath then immediately brightened, like somebody walking on stage.

'So,' he said. 'You want to discuss Jamie.'

'Yes.'

Ashford smiled.

'What exactly would you say we're here to discuss?'

Sam looked at him askance. He thought it too defensive an opening gambit.

'Well,' he said. 'It's come to my attention that Jamie's attendance isn't what it might be.'

Ashford sat back, perhaps with relief.

'That's true enough,' he said.

Sam shifted in his chair. He made a pained face.

'How true, exactly?'

Ashford glanced at his notes. With his thumbs, he exerted pressure on his upper eyelids.

'Well,' he said eventually, 'there's no getting around it: Jamie's giving us cause for concern. We were just about to write to you, in fact.'

A shudder of unease passed through Sam. *In trouble with the teachers*. Ashford pressed his eyes again. Sam dug a knuckle into each temple. Two headaches in one room.

Ashford said, 'Can I ask how Jamie's been? At home?'

'In what sense?'

'Has he changed at all? Has he become moody and withdrawn? How does his current behaviour compare with that at his previous school?'

Sam spread his arms, helplessly.

'Where do I begin?'

Ashford scratched his scalp. A little tuft of hair stood erect on his crown.

Sam shifted in his seat.

'He's had a difficult year,' he said. 'His mother passed away.'

Ashford nodded but didn't comment. The officious way he scribbled a note seemed mannered and self-conscious.

'She used to be a teacher,' said Sam. 'Funnily enough.'

'I didn't know about Jamie's mother. Has he seen a counsellor?'

'No.'

'It might help.'

Sam smiled indulgently. He spread his hands again, this time in benediction.

'Look,' he said, 'I work in the mental health field. Believe me, Jamie's fine. Of course he's been upset – who wouldn't be? It's been a shock to us all. But he's coped well.'

'Except that he's not attending school.'

'That's it, you see,' said Sam. 'I think it's too easy to attribute his truancy to problems at home. Jamie's very *happy* at home. I'm not convinced the attendance issue is related to the upheavals in his life. I believe there's something else.'

'Such as?'

'Well, obviously I'm not sure.'

Ashford looked up from the notes. He was watery-eyed.

He said, 'Jamie seems like a nice lad – when he's here. He's polite, he's quiet. He can be quite funny, when he puts his mind to it. But he hasn't given us much of a chance, has he?'

Sam took a sip of colourless tea.

'I don't think he's got many friends,' he said.

'It's early days. It'll take a while to settle in.'

'So you think that's all it is? There's no particular problem?'

Ashford picked up his biro, twisted it through his fingers, then put it down again.

He said, 'The best thing we can do for Jamie is to make sure he walks through those gates every morning. Once we've got him into the habit, he'll settle down. I've seen it a hundred times. In its own way, it's perfectly normal behaviour.'

Sam looked at the pen. Its plastic end was chewed jagged.

'I'm sure you're right. Perhaps I should speak to him.'

'You haven't done that?'

'I wanted to speak to you first.'

Ashford nodded and made another note.

'I see,' he said.

He looked up and smiled, as if to ask was there anything more he could do.

The meeting seemed to have ended. Sam stood, gathered his coat and his bag, and once again shook Ashford's hand. He said, 'Thank you,' although he did not feel grateful.

Ashford escorted him to the main doors.

Sam listened to the sound of his adult heels impacting on that identical parquet flooring. When last he'd heard this sound, it was amplified by hundreds, thousands of rushing young feet, surging like a dam overflow through the corridors. He'd been lost, swamped by the numbers, a bobbing head, while certain children – men they had seemed – kept their hands in their pockets and walked slowly, the crowd parting for them. They had seemed kings of this place.

Later, a slamming door alerted him to Jamie's arrival. Without stopping to say hello, Jamie dumped his parka and bag in the hallway and stamped upstairs. Sam called after him.

An hour later, Jamie had still not appeared. Sam decided to wait in the kitchen until hunger drew him out. He made himself a mug of coffee and spread the *Guardian* on the breakfast bar.

Reading front to back, he'd reached page five when Jamie strode wordlessly into the kitchen. He opened the breadbin with some prejudice, removed two slices of white bread, dropped them on the worktop and began to spread on them a thick smear of peanut butter.

Without looking up, Sam said, 'If you're hungry, eat something decent.'

There was no response. Jamie folded each slice of bread crudely in half. He stuffed one of these rudimentary sandwiches into his mouth and chewed on it as he spread Sun-Pat on a third slice. Sam closed the newspaper and folded it, a sure sign that he wanted to talk. But Jamie ignored the signal.

Sam said, 'What's wrong?'

'Nothing.'

'Well, obviously something is.'

Jamie made a mouth of his hand and yabbered it at shoulder height.

Sam said, 'You seem pretty pissed off about *something*.'

Jamie spat moist shrapnel at him.

'What did you think you were *doing*?'

Sam was surprised by his sudden ferocity.

He said, 'What are you talking about?'

'I saw you. I had Chemistry. I saw you through the lab window.'

Suddenly, with a triumphant paradiddle, Sam's headache was back. He felt very tired.

'I didn't have much choice. They wrote to me.'

Jamie paused. Then he resumed slamming dollops of peanut butter on to the bread. It was ripped and stretched with the violence of his buttering.

'Wrote to you about what?'

'About what do you *think*? About your not going to school.'

Jamie stopped buttering and glared down at the worktop. He wiped his hands on his jeans and went back to the fridge. He took a series of drowning gulps from a carton of orange juice, left the sweating carton next to the destroyed slice of bread. He closed the fridge door, then marched out of the kitchen.

Sam half-stood, as if to follow. Then he changed his mind. He sagged and slumped on his stool. The headache had become so bad, it was difficult to move. He went to the drawer, found some Nurofen and dry-swallowed five of them.

He shuffled to the sitting room and switched on the TV. He turned over to BBC2, the snooker, and lay on the sofa. He pressed a cushion over his eyes and listened to the soft drone of the commentary until it became meaningless and soporific. He meant to go upstairs and talk to Jamie, once the headache had calmed a little. But instead, he fell asleep and woke, confused, in the early hours. The house was dark, flickering with the cold blue fire of the television. He sat up and tried to get to bed before waking irrecoverably. But by the time he climbed between the cold cotton, sleep had deserted him. He lay on his back and stared at the bedroom ceiling. In his mind there played a muttered, imaginary snooker commentary.

He woke in the morning, with no idea how long he'd slept.

He could hear Jamie in the kitchen. He pulled on a pair of tracksuit trousers and went downstairs. Barefoot and cold, he put the kettle on to boil.

Jamie was watching TV, shovelling milky cornflakes into his mouth. He'd used the last drop of milk.

Sam said, 'So, are you going to school today?'

Jamie rolled his eyes, as if this were the most stupid question he'd ever heard.

'Yes.'

'Good,' said Sam. He made a cup of instant coffee, strong, black, and lit a cigarette. Jamie wafted away the smoke with a regal hand. Sam smoked and looked down at his pale, veiny, hairy feet.

He said, 'Look, I know it can't be easy. It's a big place. You don't know anybody.'

Jamie turned up the television. Sam ground out the cigarette, then marched over and turned it off.

He said, 'Jesus, Jamie. I can't hear myself *think*.'

'When will you stop going *on* at me?'

'I'm not going on at you. Jesus Christ, they wrote me a letter! I can't just let you not go to school.'

'Why not?'

'It's the law! They'll take you away or something. They'll put you in care.'

He regretted it, the moment he said it. He heard the hectoring ghost of his mother.

Jamie looked at him with blank accusation.

'Is that what you want?'

Sam started to speak. Then he stopped, trying to calm himself. But his voice still went high with frustration.

'Of *course* it's not what I want. That's why we're *talking* about it.'

Jamie stood and carried the bowl of cornflakes, half-eaten, to the kitchen.

'You have to go to school,' said Sam. 'That's all there is to it.'

He followed him through the kitchen and then down the hall. He watched as Jamie pulled on his parka, then gathered his things.

Sam said, 'It's not even eight o'clock. Where are you going?'

Jamie stopped. His arms hung at his sides as if the whole business of conversation was simply too tiring.

'To Stuart's.'

'Right,' said Sam. 'And then on to school.'

'Change the record,' muttered Jamie, who probably had never seen one. He took some care not to slam the door behind him, as if the morning had been a contest of dignity.

Sam stood at the window and watched him stamp along the garden path, then down the pavement. He was followed by a broken trail of condensed breath. It was cold outside. Christmas was coming.

He thought about calling Stuart's house, then realized that he didn't have the number or even know the address. Instead, he called Jamie's mobile from his own, scrolling first through a list of redundant names. (Justine's mobile number was there, and her work number. He scrolled through the names of shared friends who'd deserted him, one by one, with such stealth he'd barely noticed until they were all gone.)

He thumbed the CALL button and reached Jamie's answering service. He re-dialled and got it again. Frustrated, he dumped the phone on the sofa. The headache had not entirely gone. There was a slow pulsing in one side of his head. He ran the shower too hot and too long and emerged from it red and gasping. He looked at his watch, propped on the cistern, and saw he was late for work. By the time he remembered where he'd left the mobile phone, for which he had little use anyway, he was even later. He dialled the local minicab firm. The car, a canary yellow Ford Capri, showed up ten minutes later than promised. It found Sam waiting at the front gate.

He sat in the rear passenger seat, his tatty briefcase clasped on his lap. He lacked the heart to be brusque to the driver, whose apology and general cheeriness seemed entirely genuine. But when they arrived at the hospital, Sam's neck was in spasm. He could barely move his head.

From the cab's steamy window, he looked at the hospital, squat and forbidding against a monochromatic sky. The dim, thundery light rendered the minicab pale mustard. Sam paid the fare and trudged through the gates, across the car park and through the doors into the psychiatric ward. Pinpoints of light danced in the periphery of his right eye. When Molly smiled hello, he smiled back and the world rushed away and he stumbled. Correcting his balance, he accidentally barged a passing cleaner. The cleaner helped Sam to steady himself. The right side of his head had closed like a clam. He imagined the lobes there shrinking like a salted slug, leaving behind only a vestigial, throbbing knot, a dry broccoli head.

He said, 'Molly, I've got a migraine.'

His voice was distant and muffled, but the exertion of speaking caused the tender flesh of his eye to shriek. Molly left the desk (he had never seen her except from the waist up: she had a tweed skirt and chubby, old-woman's ankles) and came over to help him sit down. He took one of the chairs in reception and sat with his spine rigid, breathing in measured, timed mouthfuls to counteract the nausea. Within a few minutes, two colleagues, Jo and Steve, had arrived. They led him through to the staffroom, taking his elbows. Jo rushed ahead and pulled the curtains against the fierce light. Sam curled foetally on the floor in the farthest corner, a hand clutched across his eyes. Steve covered him with a thin grey blanket. He and Jo left, quietly. A few minutes later, Steve returned: he passed Sam two large tablets and a plastic cup of water.

Sam swallowed the tablets. In the semi-darkness he lay on the floor, listening to the distant rattle and clashing of the hospital. The migraine beat time with his heart. He prayed for sleep.

Eventually it came. He woke to discover the migraine had gone, leaving behind a strange hollowness in one side of his skull, and a sense of dislocation, like being mildly stoned. There would be a floating, greasy smear across his vision for the rest of the shift.

He drew the curtains in the staffroom, letting in the thundery light, then shuffled to the male staff lavatory. He stood at the small sink in the corner and splashed cold water on his face. His hair was a mess. He wetted his hands and ran them through it. His right eye was violently bloodshot, like a cherry tomato. He pressed it, tenderly, with two fingers. He examined his tongue, scowled, and sucked it back into his mouth. In the staffroom, he drank several cups of icy cold water.

Steve poked his head round the door.

'You all right, mate?'

Sam spoke quietly, scared the pain might come back as soon as he opened his mouth. It had happened before.

'Much better. Thanks.'

'Christ,' said Steve. 'I thought you were having an embolism.'

Sam drank off another cup of water. He knew his thirst would be unslakeable. He poured another cup, pressed it to his forehead.

'Yeah,' he said.

'How often does it happen?'

'Never,' said Sam. 'Well, hardly ever. That's the first I've had in years. The first *proper* one, you know. I get warnings. But not the Full Monty.'

'You want to go home? We'll cover.'

He smiled and said no, he was fine. Steve worked hard to hide his relief.

'Are you sure you're all right? You look pretty shaky.'

'Really,' said Sam. 'I'll be fine. Just give me one minute.'

In three, he was on the ward.

He offered to make up the hours, but his colleagues knew he was a single parent and insisted he go home on time. He didn't suppose they'd be so tolerant if it happened again.

He stood at the bus stop with the wind puffing at his overcoat. He wished, irritably, for some proper weather, something to drive away the oppressive wintry fug that had settled over the city. The bus was late, and crowded. He perched on the edge of a seat on the lower deck and tried to read the paperback, by now much-travelled but still unread. Pages fell in clumps from its creased and fractured spine.

Even with the lights on, an unoccupied house obtrudes its emptiness. Before the key scratched the lock, he knew Jamie wasn't home. Entering, he said, 'Hello?' anyway, and hung his coat over the banister. The walls soaked up the word. There was not the faintest echo. He checked the answer machine. No messages. Again, he called Jamie's mobile. It was still switched off.

Shortly after eight, the phone rang.

'Hello,' he said, before the second ring.

It was Mel.

She said, 'Sam? Jamie's here. He wants to know if he can have his tea.'

'Jesus, Mel, it's gone *eight*. How long has he been there?'

'He's just arrived.'

'Then where's he been?'

Distantly, he heard:

'Jamie, lamb, your dad's asking where you've been.' There was a pause. Then Mel said, 'He's been at Stuart's.'

Second-hand, he couldn't be sure that Jamie was lying.

He sighed.

He said, 'Fine. Fine. Whatever. Tell him to come home when he's ready.'

He replaced the phone in its cradle, then returned to the living room and switched on the television. There was nothing on.

6

Two weeks before the Christmas holidays, the weather broke. The city was buffeted by powerful winds and heavy rain.

Sam thought the weather would drive Jamie to school. If he was still spending time on the streets, he would have come home soaked. If not, he'd be spending time with a friend — and, to Sam's knowledge, he had only one of those. A couple of times, Sam interrogated Stuart. But if Jamie was going anywhere, it wasn't to Stuart's house. Stuart's parents had made him so neurotically determined to do well in his GCSEs, he would not voluntarily miss a day's school.

So if Jamie had found somewhere to go, it was without Stuart. Although Sam knew it shouldn't, the thought came as a relief. Perhaps Jamie *had* made another friend. Perhaps, at this stage, friends of the wrong kind were better than no friends at all.

Sam bought a car, a twelve-year-old Rover estate. When he could, he drove Jamie to school in the morning, sometimes making a detour to pick up Stuart. Then he waited behind the wheel and watched them walk through the gates. He assumed it was harder actually to leave the school grounds than it was simply never to arrive, if only because teachers were on patrol for stragglers and truants. He watched until Jamie's head was lost in the surge of uniforms, then drove to work.

He asked Mel to coax from Jamie what he might want for Christmas. But Jamie had withdrawn even from her, and her attempts were futile.

He was sullen even when he turned up at her house, unannounced, expecting to be fed and looked after.

The week before Christmas, Mel came round to help Sam put up the decorations. He'd bought a tree from a street trader who was selling them from the back of a white Transit parked on a corner near the Dolphin Centre. On foot, he'd hauled the tree all the way home. In the wind and cold, his seasonal enthusiasm quickly deserted him. He became breathless and irritable and, when he finally arrived at the house on Balaarat Street, he forced the tree through the door with unnecessary violence. When Mel arrived, he was on his third whisky and ginger. The Christmas tree was propped against the banister in the hallway, surrounded by a mat of pine needles.

She squeezed past it and came into the living room. Her cheeks were red with cold. She dumped at Sam's feet a cardboard box full of old decorations. Then she removed her woolly gloves, and blew into her hands.

She said, 'Are you going to make me a drink, then?'

She fell into the armchair.

'Go on,' she said. 'I'm gagging.'

Reluctantly, he stood. He went to the kitchen and made her a vodka and tonic. First a handful of ice cracking in a long glass. Then half a lemon, squeezed over the ice, followed by a large measure of vodka, poured straight from the freezer. Then a splash of tonic and a slice of lemon. Mel never seemed to notice the care he took over her drinks. But he didn't mind.

Slightly drunk, they dressed the tree, draping it with threadbare tinsel and decorations from which the dye had faded, the glitter had fallen and the paint had chipped. Sam discovered the fairy, hidden by a broken snowman in the bottom corner of the box. He remembered it from his early childhood. The paint on the fairy's face was long gone, her wand was missing and the coarse net of her voluminous skirt was faintly musty with the smell of attic. Through force of habit, he surreptitiously glanced up her skirt.

He was on tiptoes, hooking the fairy on top of the tree when the door slammed and Jamie walked in.

Mel and Sam had learnt their lesson. Neither responded to Jamie's arrival. Sam stretching up and Mel was on her knees, rooting through the box of decorations. They tensed, but continued about their business. They exchanged a look, the kind of glance that, as children, they had shared across the dinner-table when a parental argument became imminent.

Jamie looked at the tree. They continued to ignore him. They played a stupid tug-of-war with the last piece of tinsel. It was little more than a foil-fringed length of string. But there was much laughter and hand-slapping. Jamie radiated disgust. It was a relief when he went upstairs.

Sam had been to Woolworth's to buy some fairy lights. He and Mel wrapped them round the tree. He plugged them in and dimmed the lights, then linked arms with his sister. Drinks in hand, they wished each other a Merry Christmas.

They enjoyed a shared moment of acute loneliness.

Sam kept the lights dimmed, made them fresh drinks. Alone on the sofa, they watched a repeat of *Only Fools and Horses*. In the corner, the twinkling fairy lights cast shifting shadows on the tatty decorations that had been with them every Christmas since they were children. Since before they were born.

From habit, Sam woke early on Christmas Day. And from habit, he lay in bed and waited for Jamie to come and wake him.

But Jamie didn't come and wake him. And neither did Justine.

He stared at the ceiling. It was a matter of hopeless pride not to be up first. It would be a terrible kind of defeat, an acknowledgement that something between them had changed for ever.

He was still in bed when Mel arrived. She rang the bell once before letting herself in. He pulled on his dressing-gown and went downstairs. She was wearing her best clothes. Dressing up on Christmas Day was another family tradition. She had with her a Woolworth's carrier bag that bulged with the corners of wrapped presents.

She was flushed and happy.

She said, 'Aren't you *up*?'

He smiled sheepishly and told her he had a hangover.

She rooted round in the carrier bag and withdrew from it a CD badly wrapped in Wallace and Gromit paper.

She said, 'You lazy sod. Merry Christmas.'

He kissed her cheek and thanked her. They wandered into the kitchen. Mel turned on the radio. To the accompaniment of carols from King's College, he made them each a buck's fizz with Asti spumante and fresh orange juice. They touched glasses and said, 'Cheers.'

Mel went to watch TV while Sam cooked breakfast. He made three plates of poached eggs, toasted wholemeal bread and ham, a pot of tea and a pot of coffee. He and Mel ate breakfast on their knees, the plates balanced on holly-decorated paper napkins. Jamie's went cold in the kitchen.

As soon as breakfast was finished, they began to prepare lunch. Sam opened a bottle of wine. He was still barefoot in his dressing-gown and hadn't cleaned his teeth or shaved. His feet were cold on the tiled kitchen floor. Mel poured herself the first of several Bailey's Irish Creams on ice. In the kitchen they weaved expertly around each other, opening drawers, extracting kitchen knives or pots and pans, a familiarity born of many years and many such Christmas meals.

By the time the vegetables were prepared and the turkey was in the oven, they were singing Motown Christmas songs. But when Mel pointed out that Jamie was still in bed, Sam's jolly face went taut. He looked at her blankly.

'Leave him,' he said. 'He'll be down when he's hungry.'

*

Unka Frank arrived in time for the Queen's speech. Mel greeted him at the door. They exchanged a hug that lingered just too long to qualify as platonic.

Then Frank came in. For several minutes, he did nothing but complain about the wet and the cold. Sam poured him a whisky – half an inch of Laphroaig in a heavy tumbler, no ice, no water – and pressed the glass into his still-gauntleted hand. Unka Frank swallowed the whisky and set the tumbler down heavily, like a gavel. Then he wished Sam a Merry Christmas and offered his hand. Sam shook it, then he and Unka Frank hugged. His leathers were shockingly wet and cold. Sam yelped and retreated.

'I told you it was bloody freezing,' said Unka Frank, removing the gloves. He took off his army-surplus rucksack and, after removing from it his rolled-up sleeping bag, he searched round inside. Eventually he discovered three dog-eared Christmas cards, a bottle of champagne and a pack of slim panatellas. Then he unzipped and removed himself from his leathers, dumping them in a pile in the corner of the kitchen. Underneath, he wore torn jeans and a leather waistcoat over a grey, much-faded *Jaws* T-shirt. His arms were sinuous and ropy with muscle.

Five minutes later, Jamie came downstairs. He wore track-suit trousers and the T-shirt he'd slept in. His hair needed cutting and washing. He wished Frank a Merry Christmas. Frank ruffled his hair and wished it back.

They opened their presents in the front room, with the Queen's speech in the background. Jamie seemed by several orders of magnitude more excited by the ten-pound record

token Frank gave him than the mountain bike Sam had hidden
in the cupboard beneath the stairs, and taken a long morning to
wrap.

Frank was embarrassed and praised the mountain bike too
fulsomely. Even then, Jamie was able to generate little interest
in it. He fiddled with the derailleur and the brakes and said
he'd go for a ride when the weather was better.

Sam scratched the back of his neck and topped up his wine
glass.

They sat down for lunch at four, and made it last two hours.
At Frank's suggestion, Jamie carved the turkey. Like Frank, he
asked for dark meat. They pulled crackers and wore paper
hats. Jamie was allowed two glasses of wine. It quickly made
him tired. He left the table and curled up on the sofa, in front
of the TV. Soon he was asleep.

Unka Frank lit a panatella and blew smoke through his
straggly, salt-and-pepper moustaches. He sat back in his seat.

'He's not himself.'

Sam rested his forearms on the table. It was a wasteland of
half-empty plates, torn crackers and joke-scrolls, exploded
party-poppers. He belched, sipped wine.

'He's having a few teething problems at school.'

Frank tipped a dogtooth of ash on to the edge of his dinner-
plate.

'Have you talked to him?'

Mel loosened a button on her skirt.

'He's tried,' she said. 'Believe me.'

Sam acknowledged her with a dutiful smile.

'We've both tried,' he said.

Frank flicked a trailing lock of grey hair from his bony shoulder.

'You be careful,' he said. 'Keep a close eye on him. Don't forget what it's like, being a boy.'

Sam grunted a monosyllable. He stood and began to gather dirty plates, scraping greasy remains into the gaping turkey carcass ('Oh, *gross*,' said Mel, and looked away.) He carried the stacked plates to the cool of the kitchen. Rain drummed on the windows. He slotted the plates in the dishwasher, then opened the kitchen door and stood there for a while, on the threshold, letting the wind and the rain blow the fug from his eyes.

He swallowed a couple of painkillers and took a healthy swig from an almost-empty wine bottle.

He returned to the dinner-table to find Frank topping up Mel's glass, cackling at something or other. His gold tooth shone in the Christmas lights.

Mel twiddled one of the earrings that had been her gift from Sam.

'We should drink a toast,' she said.

Sam looked down at the remaining chaos on the table.

'To what?'

'To family.'

Sam smiled.

'To what family?'

'To us,' said Mel. 'We're a family.'

'I suppose we are,' said Sam. 'After a fashion.'

Unka Frank raised his glass. His eyes locked with Mel's.

'To family,' he said.

They stood and clinked glasses over the table.

Sam lifted the glass to his lips and glanced at his sleeping son. Jamie's eyelids were flawless, like daisies, a vestige of the perfect baby Sam had once wanted to crush with the ferocity of his love, whose first, gummy smile had made him weep with elemental joy and sadness and terror. That seemed like a long time ago, in a different life.

7

During the Christmas holidays, Jamie rarely went outside. Once or twice, at Mel's request, he ventured to the chip shop. He and Sam seemed to exist in worlds that ran parallel and never bisected, like ghosts from different eras haunting a single house.

Unmentioned and untouched, Jamie's new mountain bike stood propped in the hallway. Slowly, it gathered articles of clothing. By January, it was hung with coats and carrier bags and sweaters. Eventually, Sam forgot it was there.

Jamie went back to school a week into the new year. Sam was on the early shift and was getting ready to leave as Jamie came downstairs.

'Eat breakfast,' he said.

Jamie looked at him.

'I'll be back by teatime,' said Sam.

Jamie looked away. Through the window, he seemed to be

following the progress of a distant jet. Sam fought an urge to grab him by the shoulders, to shout something into his face. Instead, he laid a half-eaten slice of buttered toast and Marmite on a crumby plate and drained his big mug of milky tea.

'Well. Have a good day.'

Jamie muttered something.

Sam slung his briefcase over his shoulder. He stood in the doorway, as if waiting for something. But whatever it was, it didn't come. He smiled for the futility of it and went to work.

Three weeks into the spring term, as it was promisingly called, Sam took another call from Jamie's form tutor.

'Mr Greene?'

'Yes?'

'It's Gerry Ashford. We spoke a few months ago about Jamie.'

'I remember.'

'Do you think you could come in? As soon as possible?'

Sam and Ashford made the arrangements, then Sam said goodbye, turned off the mobile and sat with head in hands. He opened the staffroom window and lit a cigarette, grinding it out eventually on the windowsill. For the rest of the afternoon he was distracted and of little use. At 3 p.m., he sneaked off the ward and called Mel. He asked if she could be at Balaarat Street to meet Jamie when he got home from school.

He met Ashford in a horse-brassed local pub at 5 p.m. It was already filling with the after-office crowd – people who, for whatever reason, didn't want to go home, people who would rather spend yet more time with the people they spent all day with, all week. The sight of them depressed him – the gelled hair and the Next suits, the cheap cufflinks and shoes.

One wall of the pub was lined with booths, in one of which he found Ashford. On the bench next to him were a series of bulging carrier bags, full of folders and papers. On top of that, he'd laid his grey tweed jacket, frayed at the cuffs. His shirt-sleeves were rolled up. He rested his elbows on the table; his forearms were matted in coarse, black hair. He held a cigarette in one hand and a pint of lager in the other. A large whisky chaser waited in a chipped tumbler. For such a pale, slight man, his five o'clock shadow seemed very heavy.

He looked up, saw Sam and made a courteous stab at half-standing. Sam dismissed him; offered his hand and they shook across the lager-pooled table-top. Sam removed his overcoat and scarf, dumped them on the bench opposite Ashford.

'What can I get you?'

Ashford looked at the whisky, the pint glass.

'Stella,' he said. 'Please.'

'And another of those?'

Sam nodded at the whisky.

Ashford stubbed out the cigarette on the edge of the over-spilling ashtray, and said, 'Why not? Thank you.'

His forced jauntiness belied his exhausted appearance. He reminded Sam of a wearied, resting firefighter.

When Sam returned from the bar, the ashtray had been replaced. He never saw who replaced it. He and Ashford bade each other good cheer, which was sufficiently ironic to make Sam smile. He supped the head from his pint, then drank off half of it, slaking a thirst he didn't know he had.

He inspected Ashford and tried to imagine his life. But there was nothing there, no clue. Sam couldn't see family or the absence of family in his bruised-looking eyes; neither heterosexuality nor homosexuality; neither house nor flat. He looked at him through adult eyes, but saw only a teacher. He could imagine no habitat for him beyond the indurate 1950s architecture of Churchill Comprehensive.

He said, 'I appreciate you seeing me like this.'

Ashford drained the final half-inch from his pint, set aside the glass and supped the cold head from the second.

'You're welcome.' He slid a Benson & Hedges from its packet.

'So,' said Sam. 'How bad is it?'

Ashford lit his cigarette, took two shallow puffs and exhaled. He tugged at the upper arch of a small, neat ear.

'Look, first things first. This conversation is off the record.' He indexed Sam's worried expression and laughed. 'By which I mean simply that it's unofficial. I'm not going to deny speaking to you or anything like that. I'm not being Deep Throat here. But there are certain matters about which the school will shortly be in contact—'

'Such as?'

'Such as Jamie's continuing poor attendance.'

Sam groaned. He closed his eyes.

Ashford tilted the whisky down his bristly gullet. He winced, perhaps somewhat theatrically, and set the glass resoundingly down on the table.

He said, 'Mr Greene.'

'Sam, please.'

'Sam. Has Jamie ever mentioned a boy called Liam Hooper?'

'He hasn't mentioned *anybody*. He hasn't spoken three words since Christmas. So, is this kid leading Jamie astray or what?'

Ashford made a sour face and washed it away with lager.

'Not as such. Liam Hooper is what we used to call a problem child.'

'In what sense?'

Ashford went quiet. He looked at the table with an expression Sam couldn't read. There was something bitter in it, humour perhaps, or irony. And something like melancholy, the rehearsal of an old, private joke.

He looked into Sam's eyes and said, 'Do you know Stuart Ballard?'

'I do. He's a friend of Jamie's.'

'Well, Stuart's also in my tutor group. Last week, he took me aside after registration to have a word with me. About Jamie and Liam Hooper.'

Sam's hands and feet were cold.

'What sort of word?'

Ashford scratched the side of his nose. 'Here you are,' he said. 'You see? This is the bit I really shouldn't be saying. I shouldn't be discussing Liam Hooper with you, not least because Churchill runs a "no blame" policy, which by implication I'm breaking. So I can't discuss Liam Hooper with you. But I think you should discuss Liam Hooper with Jamie.'

Ashford's eyes flitted to the table. Sam saw that he'd torn a beer mat to shreds, each of which he was now laying in parallel lines across the table-top. The shreds were bloated and flaccid with spilt lager.

Sam said, 'Is he being *bullied*?'

'Look, I can't say – not only because I shouldn't, but because I genuinely don't know, not for sure. All I know is that Stuart Ballard was sufficiently worried about Jamie to come to me, and Stuart's not the kind of boy to do something like that lightly. Jamie's a nice lad, you know. He's not had an easy time of it.'

'Isn't there something you can do?'

'There's been no official complaint. My hands are tied.'

'But you *know* about this boy.'

'Everybody knows about this boy.'

Ashford took a long draught of lager.

In a different tone, Sam said, 'What's he doing? What's he doing to Jamie?'

'I don't know.'

'Christ. Is he *hurting* him?'

He stood.

'*Christ*,' he said, and walked to the bar. It was crammed three-deep. He lowered his head and barged his way to the front. Nobody seemed inclined to try stopping him. He ordered three double whiskys and carried them back to the booth. He sat down, pushed one whisky towards Ashford.

Gently, Ashford pushed it back to him.

'Driving,' he said.

It was clear that Ashford was already over the limit, but that hardly seemed worth worrying about. Sam downed a second whisky; lit another cigarette. He felt the smoke rush through him.

'I don't believe this. Tell me about this boy.'

It was like asking his wife to describe her lover. He waited while Ashford's reticence drew Liam Hooper in monstrous proportions.

'There's not much I can tell you. What can I say? He's a problem.'

'Has he done this before?'

'Done what?'

'Bullying.'

'There's not much he hasn't done.'

Ashford looked yearningly over the table. Clearly, he regretted refusing the whisky. But it was too late. Sam had downed the second and was already sipping at the third, a bit more steadily. His eyes looked hooded and dangerous and shone with a dull light.

Ashford lit another cigarette. He tapped its filter end on the edge of the blue ashtray.

Sam bit down on his lip.

'How old is he, this boy?'

'Year Nine. He's fourteen, fifteen?'

'Is he big?'

'In what sense?'

'Is he a big lad? Is he bigger than Jamie?'

'That's not really the point.'

'But is he?'

'Well. I suppose so.'

'You suppose so.'

'Yes.'

'What is it about him? What does he do to cause so much misery?'

'Look, I think you'd better speak to Jamie about that. Like I said, we'll be sending out a letter shortly. You'll have to come in to discuss Jamie's future.'

'*Jamie's* future?'

'He's a persistent truant. The school has to take some action.'

'But if he's truanting because of this other kid . . .'

'You or Jamie can make an official complaint.'

'And what will that achieve?'

'Off the record, very little in all probability. As I say, we have a no blame policy. We must be seen to be meeting our responsibilities to Liam's special needs.'

'And Jamie's special needs don't count.'

'Jamie doesn't have special needs.'

'He needs an education!'

'I'm talking about in the eyes of the school. Liam Hooper has special educational needs. Jamie Greene is a persistent truant. Jamie has access to various welfare services, including a counsellor with whom he can discuss his problems confidentially. But it's up to Jamie to make use of those services. Until he does that, he's simply a truant, whose behaviour has to be dealt with through the normal channels.'

'But he's truanting because of Liam Hooper!'

'We don't have official notification to that effect. While that's the case, the school is powerless to take any remedial action. We have to meet our responsibilities to all our pupils, even when those responsibilities seem by their very nature to conflict. You're a psychiatric nurse, aren't you?'

'Yes.'

'Then you of all people should understand what it's like—'

'What *what's* like, specifically?'

'Exercising a duty of care,' said Ashford. 'To those for whom you have nothing but contempt.'

Suddenly, Ashford's life was revealed to Sam. It was empty. When he went home, when he stepped through the doors into the partial security of whatever aggregation of bricks and mortar he had exhausted himself to pay for, he ceased to exist. There was nobody there, nobody at home. There was nothing inside. And when he emerged in the morning, freshly shaved, his thinning, greying hair showing the wet striations left by a plastic comb, it was as if he had winked into existence. His shadow was thin and short at sunrise. He sat at the wheel of the black Polo with the dented driver's wing, the vinyl seats that smelt of cigarettes, Glacier Mints and alcoholic sweat.

'What do you teach?' said Sam.

Ashford blew smoke through his nostrils. He tipped the pint down his neck.

'English,' he said.

'Aha,' said Sam, as if that explained everything.

Sam didn't know he was drunk until he willingly engaged the minicab driver in conversation. The minicab driver had several children, who (by all accounts) were a source of unending joy and permanent security in old age. Sam leant forward in his seat.

'What would you do if your boy was being bullied?'

The driver glanced in the rearview mirror. His reflected eyes were intermittently obscured by the beaded religious good luck charm that hung from the mirror.

'I would take the bully,' he said, shaking a clenched fist, 'and I would make sure he leaves my son alone. You understand?'

Sam understood.

He sat back and watched the suburbs go by.

'And if he don't listen,' said the driver, whipped into a fury, 'I break his stupid neck. I do time, no problem.'

Sam extracted coins from his pocket and counted them into the driver's palm.

'No problem,' he said. 'Cheers.'

He staggered from the taxi. He slammed the front door too hard, unintentionally. He cringed, as if it were 2 a.m. He looked at his watch and was surprised to see that it was only eight o'clock. He tiptoed into the sitting room.

Mel was watching TV. *Heat* magazine was open on her lap. There was a tub of Ben and Jerry's and a half-bottle of wine on the floor at her ankle. As he entered, she muted the TV – *EastEnders* had just finished – and placed the remote control on the arm of the sofa.

'Blimey,' she said. 'I can smell you from here. Where have you been?'

'Parent-teacher meeting.'

'In the pub?'

'In the pub. Is the boy home?'

'Upstairs.'

'How is he?'

'Who can tell?'

'I think he's being bullied.'

Mel picked up the remote and turned off the television.

'Who by?'

'Some kid.'

'How badly?'

'I don't know how badly. Bad enough to turn him into—'

He gestured vaguely, upstairs.

'—that.'

Mel sat rigid on the edge of the sofa and blinked.

She said, 'Poor baby.'

'He's not a baby, Mel. Remember?'

Mel hesitated.

Sam met her eyes. He saw an unspoken warning.

'What?' he said.

'You be careful how you treat him,' said Mel. 'Put yourself in his shoes. Imagine what it must be like for him.'

He clicked his tongue.

'Christ, Mel,' he said, 'Give me a break.'

'Talk to him in the morning.'

'I want to talk to him now.'

'Well,' she said, 'don't. Wait until morning. Give yourself time to think about what you're going to say.'

'I know what I'm going to say.'

She ran a hand through her messy frizz of curly hair.

'What I'm trying to say is: don't talk to him while you're pissed.'

'I'm not pissed.'

'Oh, I think you are.'

He followed her eyes down and saw that his fly was unzipped. A trailing hank of blue shirt protruded through the gap like a magician's handkerchief. He tucked it in and zipped himself up. Then he sat on the sofa and lit a cigarette.

It was still early, but he felt drained, already hungover. He offered Mel a bed in one of the spare rooms. She told him she'd think about it, so he said good night and left her in front of the TV. At the foot of the stairs a wave of giddiness passed over him and he clung to the banister.

He was too fatigued to clean his teeth or undress. He went to urinate, left dark wet splashes on his thighs, then fell on the clean bed, fully clothed.

In the morning, he could tell by the precise quality of the stillness that Mel had gone home. He'd always been sensitive to presences in houses. She must have walked back after watching the late-night film. He knew he'd find an empty wine bottle, an unwashed glass and a dirty ashtray ranked on the kitchen worktop, next to the sink.

He rolled on to his back. There was a gentle pressure behind his eyes, as if they were being squeezed like supermarket fruit. He ran a dry tongue over furred teeth and wished he'd eaten something before going to bed.

He was under the shower, letting the jet of water massage his shoulders and scalp, when Jamie walked in. He wore a pair of boxer shorts and one sock. He nodded unspecific acknowledgement to his father, then took a piss.

Reaching for the shampoo, Sam looked at him.

He said, 'What's that?'

'What's what?'

'That mark. There – on your ribs.'

Jamie looked down.

'Dunno.'

'It looks like a bruise.'

Jamie stopped pissing. He went to the sink and wiped a port-hole on the steamy mirror. He jutted out his tongue.

'Well,' said Sam. 'Is it?'

'Is it what?'

'A *bruise*.'

Evidently in equal parts mystified and irritated, Jamie looked down again. He prodded the mark with his index finger.

'Dunno.'

'How did it get there?'

'I don't *know*.'

The boy squeezed Aquafresh on to his toothbrush and began to clean his teeth. After a few horizontal strokes, he turned and faced Sam, his lips foamy white. The sock was half off his foot and trailed wetly on the tiles, like a jester's shoe.

'*What*?' he said.

'Nothing.'

Sam squeezed shaving gel into his palm and massaged it into his coarse, greying-blond stubble. Menthol and tea-tree fumes stung his eyes. He stretched the skin on his neck and began to shave. From the corner of his eye, he watched as Jamie cleaned his teeth.

He said, 'How's school?'

Jamie had his head bent to the cold tap. He rinsed, spat, rinsed again.

'It's all right.' He replaced the toothbrush in the holder. 'Are you going to be long?'

'Two minutes. You can wait.'

Jamie sat on the lavatory. He removed the single wet sock. Then he crossed his legs and began to pick at his toenails.

Sam smiled. For a reason he couldn't name, it was a good moment.

He stretched his upper lip between thumb and forefinger, shaved the difficult scoop beneath his nose. He rinsed the razor under the shower head and replaced it in its cup. He held out a hand. Jamie threw him the conditioner. Sam massaged it into his scalp; closed his eyes and rinsed it away.

'You need a haircut,' said Jamie. 'It's going fluffy round the bald bit.'

Sam stepped from the shower. He rubbed at his crown.

'Do you think?'

'Yeah. You should get it cut short.'

'I like it long.'

Jamie shrugged.

'Whatever.'

Sam wrapped the towel round his waist, bent at the sink to clean his teeth. He paused, looked up.

Jamie seemed to be waiting for something.

'What?' said Sam.

'I'm waiting for you to leave.'

'Oh,' said Sam. 'Right.'

He hurried to finish cleaning his teeth, then stepped on to the landing. The bathroom door closed behind him. He heard the lock engage, then the sound of the shower.

He stood, kilted in a blue bath towel. Then he hammered on the door.

From inside: 'What *now*?'

'Do you fancy breakfast?'

'What breakfast?'

'Bacon sandwich?'

'Go on, then.'

Sam hurried to the bedroom. He pulled on a clean pair of jeans and an unironed T-shirt and, barefoot, he hurried downstairs. He wanted to have the bacon frying when Jamie emerged from the shower. It seemed a vital component of preserving the delicate but good atmosphere of the morning.

He was cutting the sandwiches in half when Jamie came down. He wore grey school trousers and a plain white shirt, untucked. He pulled up a stool to the little-used breakfast bar for which Sam had entertained such hopes. Sam set the plate down before him, followed by a squeezy bottle of tomato ketchup.

Sam had opened the kitchen window and an early spring breeze was freshening the room. The extractor hood hummed. The kettle boiled and steamed. Jamie squeezed loops of ketchup over still-sizzling bacon and crushed the sandwich flat. He took a bite. Bacon fat and ketchup oozed down his chin.

Sam set down two mugs of strong tea, then pulled up a second stool. He ketchup-ed his own sandwich, made appreciative noises. No radio played and the TV was not on. There was the faint, ascending whine of a car reversing on a nearby road.

Love fluoresced in Sam's guts like sunlight.

He watched the movement of tendons in Jamie's neck.

Jamie said, 'How's work?'

Sam shook his head.

'I'm sorry?'

Jamie chewed, swallowed.

He said again: 'How's work?'

'Oh,' said Sam. 'Good. Fine. You know.'

Jamie left the crust on the side of his plate and set about the second sandwich.

'I don't mind,' he said, 'if you want to go out. If you want to go to the pub with your new mates, or whatever.'

To give himself a moment, Sam lifted the mug of tea and took a tiny sip.

He set down the mug and said, 'What do you mean?'

'You didn't have to come home early last night. And Mel didn't need to babysit. I'm thir*teen*.'

'I'll bear that in mind. Next time.'

The silence fell easily between them, as if some longstanding but unspoken difficulty had been resolved. Jamie ate the remaining sandwich with an air of concentration.

Sam watched him, stroking the tender contours of his freshly shaved throat.

Then he said, 'Who's Liam Hooper?'

Jamie stopped eating. There was an uneaten, doughy ball of half-masticated, ketchup-y bread in his mouth. His expression did not change.

He said, 'Who?'

Sam pushed his plate to one side.

'Why don't you tell me about him?'

Jamie's brow furrowed. The lines there were new and unaccustomed. When he gathered himself they were erased completely, like footprints in sand. He met Sam's eye; looked away. He lifted his mug of tea in both hands, blew across the surface. A kind of displacement activity. He took a considered sip, then put the mug down.

He said, 'I can deal with him.'

'What do you have to deal with?'

'You know. I'm a new kid. It'll stop, sooner or later.'

That was the moment when Sam's heart broke.

'What'll stop? What's he doing to you?'

'It doesn't matter.'

Sam reached out to take Jamie's hand. Pretending not to notice, Jamie avoided his touch by picking up the mug.

Sam withdrew his hand.

He said, 'Of course it matters.'

Jamie regarded him evenly.

'It's just school, Dad.'

Sam stopped.

Frank was right. He didn't know any more what it was like to be a boy. He felt big and ursine and helpless. He wanted to hug Jamie, to tell him it would be all right.

And he wanted to kill Liam Hooper.

He said, 'You don't have to put up with it.'

Jamie smiled, too sad and too wise.

'It won't last.'

'We can stand *up* to him.'

'No, we can't.'

'Yes, we can. You don't have to be scared. This isn't the Dark Ages. And I'll always be here to look after you. I love you more than anything in the world. Do you understand that?'

Jamie looked down. Embarrassed or tearful, Sam couldn't tell.

Sam wiped at his eyes with the heel of his hand.

He said, 'That's it. We'll go to the school.'

An expression of tenderness and pity passed over Jamie's face. It allowed that Sam could never understand the world he lived in.

He said, 'Dad, if you do that, Liam will kill me.'

Sam looked down at his uneaten bacon sandwich.

He said, 'Look, if you're unhappy you need to tell me. I can't do anything about it, if you don't *tell* me.'

'I'm all right.'

'If you're old enough to be left alone in the evenings,' Sam said, 'then you're old enough to discuss your problems like an adult. Do you understand that? *Talk* to me. God, what did you think – that I'd be angry?'

Jamie shrugged.

'What can you do?'

Sam thumped the breakfast bar.

'That's what we need to talk about,' he said. 'That's what talking's *for*. So we can decide what to do. Do you want to go to another school?'

What colour was left in Jamie's face drained away.

Quietly, he said, 'Don't move me again.'

Self-contempt twisted in Sam's guts.

He said, 'I won't do anything without discussing it with you first. But you have to talk to me, too, Jamie. I'm still your *dad*.'

'But Dad, there's nothing you can do. So what's the point? He'll leave me alone eventually.'

Sam shook his head.

'What's he doing to you?'

Jamie pushed back his stool.

'He found out Mum was dead.'

Sam said, 'What?'

Jamie dumped the sandwich crusts in the swingbin and put the plate in the dishwasher.

'He found out Mum was dead.'

'And he's bullying you for that?'

His back turned, Jamie shrugged again.

'Jesus,' said Sam.

His voice sounded smaller than he wanted it to. He cupped a hand across his mouth.

He said, 'Hit him.'

Jamie straightened. Sam couldn't see his face, but there was dignity in his posture.

'He's big, Dad. He's really big.'

'Right,' said Sam softly.

Jamie left, to finish getting dressed. Sam found a pack of cigarettes and stood in the garden, smoking, the concrete patio cold and damp against his bare feet. The cigarette was smoked nearly to its stub when Jamie called him.

Sam turned. Jamie stood in the kitchen doorway. He was in full school uniform, with the fat end of his tie tucked inside his shirt. He wore his blue parka, and had the Adidas sports bag slung across his chest.

Sam dropped the cigarette. It lay on the concrete, smouldering.

'Are you off, then?'

Jamie nodded.

'Do you want a lift or something?'

Jamie shook his head.

'Your car's at work,' he said. 'You took a taxi home.'

'So I did,' said Sam. He looked at his feet. He said, 'You don't have to go through this.'

Jamie shrugged one shoulder.

'I'll be all right,' he said. 'I'll see you later.'

Sam couldn't watch him leave. He stood without moving until he heard the front door close. Then his shoulders sagged. He looked around for something to kick, but the garden, like the house, was practically empty. Everything in it was new. Jamie would see any damage he did, and he'd know the reason why. And his feet were bare and breakable.

He walked inside and felt his son's absence like a pain.

8

Before leaving for work, Sam called Ashford's mobile number, and again got through to an answering service. He looked at his watch and supposed that, by now, Ashford would be talking about *Julius Caesar* or *Jude the Obscure* to thirty bored and hostile adolescents. He wondered if Jamie was among them, counting down to the terror between lessons.

Ashford returned his call at 10.45, during morning break. By now Sam was on the ward. He felt the mobile trilling silently in his hip pocket and hastily excused himself. He rushed from the ward without actually running and paced up and down the car park, in his shirtsleeves, puffing a cigarette.

Ashford asked what he could do for him.

Sam said, 'I want to talk to Liam Hooper's father.'

There was silence on the line so extended that Sam checked

the reception. It was fine. He made a face and put the phone back to his ear.

He said, 'Are you there?'

'I'm here,' Ashford said. He sighed. 'Look,' he said. 'I've met Mr Hooper . . .'

Sam could almost see the contemptuous twist of the lip for that necessary Mister. 'And?'

'And – well. Look, how can I say this? I'm not sure talking to him will be of much benefit.'

Sam lit a fresh cigarette from the still-burning coal of the first.

'What harm can it do?'

There was another long pause. Then: 'I can't give you his home address, but I can tell you where he works. But if somebody were to ask – it wasn't me who told you.'

'That's fine,' said Sam.

He took the cigarette from his mouth and was surprised to see the pulse flickering in his wrist, rapid and shallow.

That afternoon, he offered to swap his Friday shift.

The mother of a colleague, Jo Hancock, had fallen and broken a hip, causing the cancellation of her Golden Anniversary cruise. Instead, Jo's father had arranged for a surprise family party to be thrown in Cardiff that weekend, which Jo's mother would be attending in a wheelchair. In order that she could drive to Cardiff on Friday morning, Jo spent the morning attempting to inveigle her colleagues into swapping their weekend shifts with her.

With affected grace, Sam succumbed. Jo kissed his cheek and stood on tiptoes to hug him. Everyone was grateful. He'd liberated them from Jo's passive-aggressive wheedling. In this way he made partial amends for the migraine and his recurring lateness, which he continued to blame on the poor bus service.

It also meant that, on Friday morning, he was free to visit Liam Hooper's father at work.

Dave Hooper worked at the slaughterhouse, with which Sam was excellently acquainted. It stood just beyond the edge of town.

Sam knew the route from childhood. He'd drive through the Merrydown Estate, past Mel's house, then turn on to Sturminster Road and pass the Dolphin Centre. Eventually he'd reach the edge of the estate, where there was an inexact tessellation of countryside and grubby concrete, like foreign limbs inexpertly grafted.

Then he'd have to drive past Farmer Hazel's property. For generations, it had been widely known that Farmer Hazel would take a shotgun to any schoolboy or courting couple discovered trespassing on his land. Farmer Hazel was known to be an old, old man when Sam was a child. By now he would be impossibly ancient, a leathered agrarian mummy. But one morning, while passively eavesdropping on Jamie and Stuart, Sam learnt that Farmer Hazel's murderous injunction was still current. Young boys still cycled quickly past his land.

Hazel's farm bordered the slaughterhouse, about which a great many stories had also been told. Generally, these tales concerned the ingredients that went into the plant's secondary meat products: pie-fillings and sausagemeat. It was common knowledge that beetles, rats, domestic pets and aborted foetuses often found their way on to the production line. So too had at least one human being. During the summer holiday of 1974, Jason Brannen got drunk on cider, soaked a vagrant with petrol and burnt him to death. Later, the tramp was fed into the slaughterhouse's industrial mincing machine. He emerged as sausages – the kind of sausages, moreover, that were destined to be served up by the malevolent dinner ladies at Churchill School.

Jason Brannen was a slight boy with slow eyes, a hasty, jagged smile and hair like David Cassidy. Sam avoided him in the school corridors. Jason Brannen's father worked in the slaughterhouse. The boot of his white Ford Anglia was thought to have been the vagrant's final transport. Sam and his friends imagined him, still living, scratching feebly at the inside lid of the boot.

Nobody really believed it, not even when they were fourteen and sincerely wanted to. They didn't believe it even when Jason Brannen denied the story in a satisfied manner contrived to imply it might be true. The police never came, and nothing appeared in the papers or on the local news.

But who would miss a vagrant? When Sam left town, several years later, Jason Brannen was still known as the kid who burnt the tramp to death.

From the brow of the hill, the slaughterhouse resembled a disused airfield. It was a gated and fenced concrete enclosure, a vastly expanded shower block. At night it was luminous as a POW camp, its walls and walkways thrown into achromatic, intersecting planes of light and shadow. By day it lay muffled in heavy, dour air.

Approaching the plant as an adult who was no longer afraid of the dark, Sam could feel his childhood self, half-eager, half-terrified, peering over his shoulder from the back of the car. They had never dared to investigate the abattoir, imagining their worst desires realized. How would it be, actually to see a blackened tramp's body unloaded from the back of a rusty Anglia? How would it be to cycle headlong into unlit B-roads and dark lanes while someone, something, slavered in pursuit?

At the main gates he found a permanently manned guard's office and a security barrier marked *Authorized Vehicles Only*.

Sam pulled up and uncranked the window. He thought he detected a rich, thick odour on the air. He made a visor of his hand and squinted at the security guard.

He said, 'Hi. I'm here to see Dave Hooper.'

The guard clicked his tongue and referred to a clipboard, to which was attached a page of A4 paper that, for all the world, appeared to be blank.

'Name?'

'Sam Greene.'

'Do you have an appointment?'

'No.'

'Then what's the nature of your visit?'

Sam scowled into the sun.

'It's a personal matter.'

The guard gave him a good, hard look. Sam wondered if he looked like a militant vegetarian. Finally, the guard instructed Sam to back up and park on the grass verge, alongside the perimeter fence. As he did so, the guard lifted the desk-phone and made a call. He turned his back as if further concerned that Sam might be a lipreader.

Eventually, led by his belly, the guard returned to the car.

Contemptuous in his politesse, he said, 'Mr Hooper will be out shortly.'

Sam thanked him with an insincere smile, then wound up the window and lit a cigarette. He took a few, nervous puffs and turned on the radio. He watched spring clouds scud across the low hills on the horizon. As he waited, three slat-sided lorries arrived and halted, throbbing, at the gate. Each driver spoke briefly to the security guard, then disappeared with a diesel roar through the gates, towards the concrete and stainless-steel secret at the heart of the complex.

Sam didn't see them leave. He supposed the drivers were breaking for a cup of tea and a cigarette, while elsewhere their living cargo, mortally terrified, was penned and lined up and executed.

He unwound the window and chucked out the cigarette. He saw that a man was approaching. He supposed it must be Dave Hooper. Sam hadn't known quite what to expect, but he'd anticipated at least a filthy, bloody apron. But this man wore clean, white Nikes, indigo 501s and a brown and cream, two-tone bowling shirt that, to Sam's untrained eye, did not look cheap. Thinking about it, he supposed the slaughterhouse was run under strict hygiene regulations. That was presumably why Dave Hooper had taken so long to emerge; perhaps in order to leave the complex, he had to shower and change. It didn't occur to him that Dave Hooper might not be directly involved with the slaughter of livestock.

Hooper wasn't a tall man, but he was solid and handsome,

like a retired footballer, and he moved with a particular, familiar assurance.

Sam got out of the car. He left the door open and the keys in the ignition. Hooper approached him along the grass verge. His expression was neutral; not unfriendly.

Sam licked his lips.

Hooper stopped several feet away and crossed his solid arms. He said, 'All right?'

Sam swallowed and hoped his voice wouldn't shake.

He said, 'Hello.'

Hooper uncrossed his arms. 'You're Sam Greene.'

'That's right. Have we—?'

'We were at school together. Well, not together. I was two years below you.'

'Oh,' said Sam. 'Right.'

'You're Mel's brother.'

'That's right.'

'You used to go out with that Lisa Kilmer.'

Sam laughed now.

'That's right,' he said, distracted from his purpose. 'Jesus. Lisa Kilmer.'

He hadn't thought about her in many years. But there had been a time when his life was rendered meaningless by her decision to dump him for Simon Marshall. Simon Marshall was seventeen, had highlights, and drove a Ford Capri. Sam was surprised that, even now and in this strange context, there was a stab in his guts: the sense-memory of pain endured long ago. He had assumed it to be neutrally assimilated, the stuff of self-deprecating comedy.

Then he remembered what Simon Marshall had done with that Capri: he'd sent Lisa Kilmer through its windscreen.

More than a year after the accident, more than two since she dumped him, Sam saw her on the street. Lisa's face was crazy-paved with purple rhomboids, like a tattoo of scales, and she averted her gaze when they spoke.

He supposed he was eighteen by then, preparing to leave. Putting it all behind him.

'Jesus,' he said again, and ruffled his hair. 'Lisa Kilmer.'

Then Dave Hooper said, 'I was there when you had that scrap with Whatsisname. Lee Harris. The one on the school field.'

Hooper didn't need to elaborate. In his life, Sam had engaged in one fist-fight. It was a defining event of his early life.

He didn't even know what it had all been about. He remembered only that an enmity had been ripening between him and Lee Harris for what seemed like for ever. Then he and Lee Harris faced each other on the school field and punched seven bells of shit out of each other. More than the blows, Sam remembered the claustrophobia of the pressing, chanting crowd. He remembered the wide-eyed girls, blank-faced and thrilled. There was no rolling round in the mud, no pulling hair, no kicking or biting. Lee Harris and he stood toe-to-toe and exchanged blows like bare-knuckle boxers. Like they imagined men did.

In truth, few blows were landed. But it felt like a hundred, and the number had multiplied with each retelling. Sam clouted out Lee Harris's front teeth. He still had the scars across his knuckles, little half-moons that never tanned. And Lee Harris broke Sam's nose. Sam remembered the loud, wet crack. By then the fight was over anyway: teachers had rushed on to the field and Sam and Lee were tugged apart by the bastard Welsh sports master whom Sam detested and whose name he had long since forgotten. They were dragged first in the direction of the Headmaster's office, then – when it became clear that both boys were hurt – to the school nurse. An ambulance arrived and took them to Casualty. It was this that really impressed their audience, stamping the fight into the parochial collective memory.

In Casualty, embarrassed by the presence of their parents (shocked mothers and sensible, secretly approving fathers) Lee and Sam faced each other again. They couldn't shake hands because Sam's wrist was in a sling. But they nodded courteously, their differences, whatever they were, having been honourably settled.

Sam and Lee never became friends. But, although their respective social standing was massively increased by the fight, neither wanted to risk repeating it. So thereafter, they bade each other a grave and courteous hello whenever they passed in the corridors. The Fourth Year timetable ensured that they sometimes passed each other this way ten or eleven times a day. Should they meet at the local, or in town, they would always stand each other a drink. This assumption of adult civility made them feel like men; dealing with a serious issue in a mature, principled manner.

Sam recalled that fine feeling. He scratched at his head and smiled with pity for his lost self.

'Yeah,' he said. 'Lee Harris. Whatever happened to him, I wonder.'

'Anyway,' said Dave Hooper.

Sam was startled into the present.

He said, 'Sorry. I was miles away.' He looked around himself. 'It feels a bit weird, talking here,' he said. 'At the edge of a field.'

Hooper shrugged.

'Well, that depends on what you want to talk about.'

Sam sucked his cheeks to gather some spit.

'It's about your son,' he said.

Hooper barely paused. Nor did he break Sam's gaze.

'Which son?'

'Liam.'

Slowly, Hooper folded his arms again.

'Right. Liam. What's he been up to now?'

'I don't know,' said Sam. 'Not exactly. But I think he's been giving my boy some problems.'

'What sort of problems?'

'Like I said, I don't know – not exactly. But he's giving him a hard time.'

Hooper shrugged.

'What do you want me to do about it?'

Sam laughed, as if he was joking.

'I thought – you know – that maybe you could have a word with him? I think it's upsetting Jamie more than Liam realizes.'

Hooper unhooked one of his hands and scratched at the fold on the back of his neck.

'I doubt that.'

He gave Sam an ingenuous, challenging stare.

Sam pinched his nostrils and pretended to think.

'So,' he said, 'you don't think that speaking to Liam will do any good.'

'Best thing is,' said Dave Hooper, 'if your boy's having trouble with Liam, let them sort it out between them.'

'Oh come on,' said Sam. 'They're *kids*.'

Hooper shrugged, as if to communicate the degree of his helplessness in the matter.

Sam said, 'Come on. You're joking. You're just flat saying no?'

Hooper scratched his eyebrow.

Sam looked at the ground. He toed a pebble from the black, moist soil.

'Right,' he said.

Hooper spat on the ground, between the white shell-toes of his trainers.

Sam wanted to meet his eyes, but he couldn't. He couldn't think of anything to say.

Hooper stood there, arms crossed, waiting for him to leave.

'Look,' said Sam. 'We're talking about my *son*.'

'Your son's not my problem.'

'Then whose problem is it?'

'I'm going to tell you this once,' said Dave Hooper. 'All right? I'm not going to stand here, arguing with you.'

Sam felt very tired. He felt himself sag.

He shook his head, bewildered, and looked at Dave Hooper's bullish intransigence.

'Fair enough,' he said, and waved it away like a trifle. 'Whatever.'

Sam got in the car. His movements were awkward and self-conscious and he tried three times to engage the seat belt, and twice to start the engine. Dave Hooper waited for him to leave.

Pulling away, Sam didn't look at him. But he watched him in the rearview mirror, as he spat again and wandered back through the gates to the slaughterhouse, pausing to exchange a joke with the security guard whose presence had not increased Sam's sense of safety even fractionally.

Sam drove without thinking about where he was headed. He felt light, as if only his hands, locked around the steering wheel, kept him anchored to the seat. Round the first corner, out of sight of the slaughterhouse, he pulled over and lit a cigarette. He smoked it to the stub before U-turning and heading back to the Merrydown Estate. His route took him past the slaughter-house again. He passed by at carefully measured speed, but without glancing at it, just as he had when cycling past as a child.

He was late for work.

His shift finished at 10 p.m. An hour before leaving, when it was quiet on the ward, he went to the staffroom and phoned Mel to tell her all about it.

She waited, making sure he was finished. There was a silence. She drew breath.

He imagined her closing her eyes.

She said, 'What did you expect? Of course he was like that! You went and saw him at work. Imagine how that would make *you* feel.'

'Where else was I supposed to see him?'

'Christ. A hundred places. The pub?'

'What pub? How am I supposed to know where he drinks?'

'He drinks in the Cat and Fiddle.'

Sam frowned.

He said, 'Mel, do you know him?'

'Of course I know him. He's a nice bloke, as it happens.'

'He's a fucking *ape*.'

'No, he's not. He's a nice bloke.'

He put his forehead against the cool wall.

Mel said, 'This is your fault, Sam.'

He sighed and mumbled something.

'Look,' she said. 'Come to the Cat and Fiddle on Sunday. Buy him a drink and say sorry.'

He looked at the phone as he might a spider in the bed.

'Say sorry for *what*? I thought he was going to kill me.'

'Do you want to sort this out or not? If not, don't bother phoning me to complain about the mess you've got yourself in. It wasn't me who got on their high horse and drove out to the slaughterhouse demanding to speak to him. Jesus, Sam. I can't even believe you did that.'

'I didn't demand anything.'

'That's not what it sounds like.'

'To whom?'

He thought about it.

He said, 'Mel – Jesus – did you already know about this?'

'Of course I knew about it. I've got friends who *work* there. What did you expect? Once it got round, they couldn't wait to get on the phone and tell me what a prick my brother had made of himself.'

He burnt with dishonour and humiliation.

He said, 'Oh, for fuck's sake. This is mad. I only wanted to talk to him about his bastard *son*. Is that too much to ask?'

'There's asking and there's asking. You put him on the spot. Of course he acted defensive.'

'I couldn't have been nicer. And he didn't act defensive. He acted like Mike fucking Tyson.'

'Put yourself in his place. How would you feel?'

'That's different.'

'Different how?'

'My son isn't hurting his!'

'That doesn't mean he doesn't love him. He wants to protect his son, the same as you want to protect yours.'

'What's that supposed to mean?'

'What's *what* supposed to mean?'

'Do you think I'm not looking after Jamie well enough? If not, just say so. I'd like to hear you say that.'

There was a much longer silence.

Mel said, 'You're twisting my words because you're in the wrong. You always do that. It drives me mad.'

'Drives *you* mad? I'm not the one who accused you of not looking after your son.'

She put down the phone.

He stood there, shaking and embarrassed, wondering who might have heard. He could tell by the dryness in his throat that he'd raised his voice. He rubbed his sweating palms on the seat of his jeans and lit a cigarette. He was still shaky and distracted when he went back on the ward, ten minutes later.

Still angry, he stopped off in the pub on the way home.

It was crowded and noisy, moist with sweat and breath. He pushed himself into the mixed throng at the bar and demanded a Guinness. The harried barmaid accepted his boorishness with blank, tired censure and pulled the pint in a single draught. He didn't mind. He dropped a sweat-damp five-pound note into her palm, then pocketed the change without bothering to count it. He carried the pint to the non-smoking corner, where it was a bit quieter, propped himself against the wall and watched the Guinness settle and separate. He took artful, sidelong looks at the other patrons. It seemed to him that each of the faces was distantly familiar. He wondered how many of them had gone to his school. How many of them had never really left home?

He thought about Lisa Kilmer and her crazy-paved face. Was she married now? Probably. She would be a mother whose scars her children never thought to question. That their mother had once been an unharmed and adored child was a concept beyond their conceptual gift. She was their mother, unguessable and infinite, a sphere without centre. Was Lisa divorced and struggling, perhaps living on the same estate, dropped from view? The old scars, grown white, would be linked by the first wrinkles of middle age, a web of ancient impact. He saw bright girl's eyes in that busy mess, that jaggedy scribble.

He knew the truth might be different. Her potential lives

were beyond number, each of them beyond his capacity to imagine.

He felt claustrophobic, angry at himself, uncomfortable in his skin and clothing. It became a sense-memory of boyhood. He remembered the low, encompassing atmosphere of Christmas Day, being surrounded by a family who (he thought) sought only to patronize and embarrass him.

He drank the Guinness. A craving swelled in him for another, but he couldn't bear the proximity of those half-familiar strangers.

He was not this man. He was the man who spooned like a comma to the soft warmth of his sleeping wife, the man who took a picnic to the annual Fleadh in Finsbury Park, the man who bought his kitchen table at Heals.

There was an empty taxi at the lights. He jumped in the back seat and was home in fifteen minutes.

He slammed the front door behind him and stamped past the living room, where Mel and Jamie were watching *Frasier* on satellite TV. He went to the kitchen, poured a tumbler a quarter-full of whisky and emptied it in three gulps. Then he knelt at the freezer, the whisky like lava inside him, and threw aside frozen lasagnes and fish fingers and sausages until he came across a serviceable ice-tray, from which he twisted and agitated four ice cubes. These he dropped into the base of the glass before pouring himself another drink. He kicked the freezer door closed.

When he entered the living room, something went tense. He thought of birds about to take flight. Mel and Jamie ignored him. He sat in the armchair and glowered at the TV, the whisky clasped in his fist. When Mel could bear it no longer, she drained her wine glass, then stood and pulled on her coat, which had been draped across the back of the sofa.

She said, 'Look after yourself, Jamie,' and let herself out.

Jamie said, 'See you,' without taking his eyes from the screen.

His shaggy hair hung in his eyes like a pony's mane. His arms and legs looked puny. His mother's limbs. The graceful length of neck belonged to Justine. Watching TV, he looked girlish and petulant, with pouting, bee-stung lips. Sam wanted to slap him.

Abruptly, Sam stood. Jamie tensed and withdrew, as if from a blow. Sam paused, incredulous, then marched to the kitchen. To justify the action – he had simply wanted to move, there was an angry restlessness in his limbs – he topped up the tumbler again. The bottle of Johnnie Walker, opened this evening, was nearly half-empty.

He listened. Jamie went upstairs without saying good night.

Sam lit a contemptuous cigarette and took another mouthful of whisky. He was disgusted that Jamie could be afraid of him, he who had never raised a hand in anger.

He sat at the breakfast bar, replaying the events of the day until his shame had become a dignified victory. He told himself he'd seen the fear in Hooper's eyes. Shortly before he passed out, face-down on the bed, he had managed to convince himself this was true.

When he woke the next morning, hungover, it wasn't true any more.

The house was silent and empty. He could hear a lawn-mower, some kids playing. On the floor next to the bed was a glass of water and two paracetamol. A thin film of dust had gathered on the surface of the water.

Disgust pressed him to the mattress and kept him trapped in the knotted, sweat-sodden bedding. It was disordered and tangled by the twisting of his forgotten, intoxicated nightmares.

9

At work that morning he was bungling and penitent.

His constant apologies carried little weight. He got the feeling his colleagues were talking about him. Conversations stopped when he drew near, and started again when he moved on.

During his lunch-break, he went to the car park and called Mel to apologize.

She claimed to accept it readily enough, but he was long-familiar with the quality of Mel's mercy. Often, it was contingent and partial, sometimes mulishly so. Mel was capable of maintaining a coating of frost, a reserve no stranger could have detected, that was yet imperishable and permanent, a distance never to be crossed.

Sam knew it hurt her to maintain this distance. Sometimes he could *see* it hurting her. But that didn't stop her.

The following Sunday was his day off. He went to Mel's via the petrol station and knocked on her door, clutching a wilting fistful of daffodils.

Mel was blue round the eyes. She wore a white dressing-gown and enormous, fluffy-bunny slippers. She looked haggard, much older than he imagined her. The thought was painful and he cut it short.

He handed her the flowers. She took them in her hand and shook them, like a child with a new rattle. Their yellow heads shivered, as if on broken necks, and one or two buttery petals fell on the sparkling concrete of the garden path. They stood and watched them fall.

'Come in, then,' she said. The undercurrent of resignation jabbed at his guts.

He followed her into the front room. Shoes, jackets, trousers, skirts, tights, ashtrays, paperbacks, magazines, newspapers, make-up, small mirrors, lighters and matches lay on every available surface. Framed photographs were ranked on the mantelpiece and low bookshelf: Mel and Sam as fat-kneed toddlers, looking serious with bucket and spades on the beach at Dawlish Warren. Mel and Unka Frank's wedding day. A portrait of Mel taken by Frank during their much-celebrated cross-Europe motorcycle trip – Mel's hair, longer, blows in the breeze as she gazes across the Danube.

Sam cleared a space on the sofa and sat down. Mel went to the kitchen. He heard her rattling about, the clink of teaspoon on mug, her loose, phlegmy morning cough that lasted these days until early afternoon. She came in with mugs of tea and half a pack of plain chocolate HobNobs. She sat and crossed her legs. On the blade of her shin was a faint purple scar, about an inch long.

He asked where she'd been to give her such a hangover. She told him that a workmate of Janet's had thrown a hen-party last night. They stayed in some restaurant drinking Tequila slammers until they got thrown out (it didn't sound like any restaurant Sam had ever been to). Then they went to a Seventies night at a nightclub whose name he didn't recognize.

Mel fixed him with a bloodshot eye.

'It used to be the Studio.'

He remembered the Studio.

Feeling oddly priggish, he said, 'Did you have a good time?'

She stared at him half a second too long.

'It was all right,' she said. 'Nothing special.'

'Right,' he said.

He picked up and began to read the previous Monday's *Sun*.

Mel smoked a cigarette, then took her tea upstairs. He heard the shower running. She was gone a long time. Sam kicked back and fell into a doze from which he was awoken by the climactic drumroll of the *EastEnders* omnibus. This was followed by a Technicolor Western he didn't have to the energy to turn over. He dozed off again.

He woke to find Mel rooting round in her handbag, searching out her keys. She was showered and dressed. The water had blasted the hangover away like soot from an old building. She smelt of shampoo and perfume and the cigarette she was smoking. She found her keys, replaced them immediately in the handbag, then went and fiddled with her hair in the hallway mirror.

She said, 'Are you coming or what?'

He stood and followed her out of the house. His mouth was gummy with sleep and he wished he could clean his teeth. Four houses down, they knocked on Janet's door. Nothing had blasted away Janet's hangover. Her pie-face was doughy and mottled. She wore a long, shapeless cardigan and a pair of purple leggings that were baggy at the knees and taut across the vast half-globe of her arse.

Sam was possessed of a transitory but childish and cruel anxiety. He didn't want people to link him romantically to Janet.

'Oh Jan,' said Mel. 'You look rough, love.'

Janet tucked a lock of hair behind her ear and smiled, bravely.

'Fucking hell,' she said. She looked at Sam. 'You should have seen your sister last night. What a piece of baggage.'

'All right, Jan,' said Mel. 'That's enough.'

Janet winked at him, and smiled and waggled her head. Then she went inside to get her keys and handbag.

Mel crossed her arms.

'She's exaggerating.'

'I'm sure she is.'

'Yes,' said Mel. 'Well. Whatever.'

The Cat and Fiddle wasn't far away, just the other side of the Dolphin Centre, but Janet wasn't a fast walker, so they ambled at a leisurely, Sunday pace that belonged to better weather. Mel and Janet were discussing something very, very funny in a language that only superficially resembled English; it was composed of hurried, low murmurs, punctuated by horsey snorts and sudden bursts of laughter. He envied the easy way they linked arms and bent double with laughter, without even breaking pace. He felt excluded and prissy, too cumbersomely male, and he hung back slightly, smoking and making no attempt to join in the conversation.

They stopped off in the NSS to stock up on cigarettes. Round the corner, at the junction of Lacey Road and Robinwood Road, he saw the Cat and Fiddle. He thought it might be the ugliest pub in Britain: low-rise and brick-built like an open prison, it sat centrally in a concrete car park and backed on to a pitiful strip of green upon which had been erected a rusty yellow climbing frame, which Sam would have feared to go near, let alone permit a child to play on. A few kids sat on the low wall, kicking their heels and gobbing on the pavement. They might have been there for twenty-five years.

The sight of them made Sam want to go home. He longed for the shifting, alienating kaleidoscope of London; ever-changing and never-changing: all those millions of people glimpsed briefly and never seen again. The Cat and Fiddle was the acme of changelessness. All that he had once sought to escape.

He looked at his admired sister, who'd been coming here for a drink every Sunday afternoon since they were children, and who was happy, and he didn't know what to think. In unlit shop windows he saw his flitting shape: a grotesque version of the boy he had been, half-glimpsed and ugly, like a gargoyle hanging behind these happy women.

His heart began to flutter too rapidly.

He stopped in the street.

He said, 'I can't do this.'

They didn't hear him – he had spoken so quietly – so he said it again.

Unconcerned, Mel looked over her shoulder.

'Course you can.'

'Mel,' he said.

She drew to a halt, her arm still linked with Janet.

'Sam,' she said, 'he won't hurt you. Not in broad daylight, not in front of witnesses, not when you haven't really *done* anything. It would make him look bad. Just do what we agreed, OK? You go in, you say sorry, you tell him you were out of order and you buy him a pint. Bob's your uncle.'

He swallowed. The world was bending in and out of focus, like a mask being inhaled and exhaled.

'Christ,' he said, and put a hand to his sternum.

He sat down on a low garden wall. Behind him, he sensed movement: the house's occupant moving to the window to see what was going on. Janet waved over his shoulder and mouthed the word *sorry*. He sensed the occupant retreat, satisfied. Somehow, that made the gathering rush of panic worse. It was about to erupt in his chest, massive as an orgasm.

He squeezed his knees and tried to breathe.

He was homesick. He yearned to be in bed next to his wife (his Justine), whom he loved and who loved and understood him. Sunday mornings had been wonderful. He pale pink, she butterscotch, his knees tucked behind hers, her arse nuzzling warmly into his belly, the sleep-musk like perfume on her skin, while their tiny son hummed and purred and cooed and clattered and played with oversized Lego bricks on the carpet next to the bed. The gentle murmur of the radio and the summer outside.

He wanted Justine so much he feared his heart might actually break, crushed like a cider apple. He looked again at the kids kicking their heels on the pub wall. It seemed that he had yearned for the past so powerfully that, by some terrible cosmic over-compensation, he'd gone back too far. He'd gone back twenty-five years, or thirty. He'd seen himself, a child, kicking his bored heels on the low wall outside the Cat and Fiddle, waiting for something to happen that never did.

Mel and Janet waited there, worried. Eventually he looked up and smiled, feebly.

'Sorry, girls.'

Janet said, 'Are you all right?'

He nodded. It made him dizzy and he corrected his balance.

'It's just . . .' he accepted and lit a cigarette. The blue smoke blossomed and rolled and faded, deep down inside him. 'It just happens,' he said. 'You know. Sometimes.'

Janet's compassion was tender and undisguised, edged with habitual curiosity.

'Poor love,' she said.

She extended her hand and rubbed the crown of his head, like he was a sick old dog.

He thought himself contemptible: the worst kind of snob, a secret snob, and he could see that Mel knew it too. He avoided her narrow gaze.

Mel said, 'Jan, why don't you go ahead and get us a table? Get a round in, while you're at it. I'll have an Archers and he'll have—'

'A Guinness.'

'A Guinness. Pint. Go on ahead. We'll be five minutes.'

Janet lingered.

'Are you sure?'

'Yeah,' said Sam. He waved his hand decliningly. 'Thanks, Jan. But I'm all right. Honestly.'

'Go on,' said Mel. 'Get us a drink in.'

Janet didn't want to go. She was anxious for his well-being. And she wanted to see what happened next, too.

With an air of reluctance, stoicism and deep concern, she sighed, 'OK,' and waddled slowly down the road.

Mel squatted, hands on knees.

She said, 'Christ. Should I call a doctor or something?'

He laughed, then saw her face and wished he hadn't.

'No,' he said. 'Honestly. I'll be all right in a minute. It's just an anxiety attack.'

'That Caroline down the road used to have them,' said Mel. 'The one who had her house repossessed. The one with the husband. She had pills.'

He said, 'I'm fine. Honestly. Honest to God. It happens every now and again. Since Justine.'

Mel unclasped her handbag and removed her cigarettes.

She said, 'You don't have to go through with this.'

'Through with what?'

'Seeing Dave Hooper. It's not worth it, if it's just going to make you ill.'

He counted down from ten, gave up at four.

'It's got nothing to *do* with Dave Hooper,' he said. 'I'm not worried about Dave Hooper. If Dave Hooper touches me, I'll break his fucking neck. All right? It's about *Justine*. It's been happening ever since Justine died.'

'I know,' said Mel.

'That's *right*,' he said, with emphasis.

'You don't have to prove anything,' said Mel. 'I'm your sister. I don't want you to put yourself through a situation you can't handle, on my behalf.'

'What do you mean, can't handle? Do you think I can't handle Dave Hooper?'

She paused; not for long, but long enough.

He shook his head in disgust.

'Well,' he said. 'Fuck you, then.'

He stood, puffing out his chest.

He said, 'Come on.'

'Come on where?'

'The pub.'

She tugged at his sleeve.

'Sam,' she said. 'Why bother?'

'Why not? You told me there'd be no trouble.'

'You nearly passed out. You might be having a heart attack or something.'

'I'm fine.'

He promenaded off.

At the car-park entrance, he already regretted his petulance. But it was too late. Mel took his elbow and escorted him through the car park (his legs weak beneath him), her heels clicking purposefully on the concrete, and then she was ushering him through heavy, double doors and into the Cat and Fiddle.

The doors were varnished black and soundproof. As they entered, he was taken aback. The bar was almost full. All the tables and chairs seemed to be taken, and everybody was shouting. At one end of the long bar, a widescreen television had been erected, showing a European soccer match. A group of young men had gathered before it and were half-watching the game, half-engaged in mutual, possibly friendly ridicule. The air rolled at him in buffeting waves that crashed and split over his head. There was a micro-climate of cigarette smoke and human effluvium.

He was relieved not to recognize the bar staff – a middle-aged husband and wife and a young barmaid, pretty, chubby, probably their daughter – which was enough to relieve him of the notion that nothing had changed. Little else had. The fruit machines, close to the toilets, were modern, computerized and louder; there was no longer a ball-tipped arm to yank down. The cigarette machine was newer and sleeker. It was positioned at the far side of the bar, next to a bright yellow payphone, surely itself redundant: a large number of people were jabbering into mobile telephones, or composing or reading text messages, or showing text messages to laughing friends.

The bar itself had been replaced; it was longer, extending into what had once been a separate poolroom, and had a brushed aluminium surface. At least once in the last ten years, the interior had been cosmetically redecorated; in places the carpet was sticky underfoot and fag-burnt, but it wasn't the same carpet. One Oasis song on the jukebox segued into another. Sam didn't know the name of either. Even that, even

Oasis, seemed trapped in time, something that happened a million years ago.

He paused in the doorway, aware of the evaluating eyes. Possibly some of them recognized him. He set this possibility aside and scanned the room, as neutrally as he might scan the horizon from a high and lonely cliff. Eventually, he saw Janet in the corner by the blue-baized pool table. She sat behind her handbag, a black pint and two long glasses on a round table close to the window. She half-waved and patted the stool next to her. Sam was relieved to see her. He waved back, and weaved through the crowd at the bar, casting his eyes as low and unspecific as he was able. He sat and said hello. Janet asked if he was all right. He gave her his saddest eyes and said, 'I'm fine,' and smiled sadly, bravely. Mel was a few seconds behind him. She told them to budge up and put a stool down next to his. He sat with his thigh pressed into Janet's.

'There he is,' said Mel.

'Where?'

She nodded towards the far end of the bar, where Dave Hooper stood, in the company of five or six other men. Hooper rested an elbow on the bar and kept his head low, listening to a younger man's anecdote. He wasn't looking in their direction. Either he hadn't noticed Sam's entrance, or he was ignoring it.

Mel said, 'Do you want me to come over with you?'

Sam glared at her as if offended. The answer to her question was yes.

'No,' he said. 'Don't be stupid. I'll be fine.'

'He's a nice bloke,' said Janet. 'I like Dave.'

'So I hear,' said Sam. He sipped his Guinness. He could feel

Mel and Janet, expectant, to either side of him. So he slapped his thigh and said, 'Well. No time like the present.'

But he didn't move.

Mel nudged his shoulder.

'Go on.'

He lit a cigarette and smoked half of it in three long puffs. Then he stood. The cigarette felt awkward in his hands and he crushed it in the ashtray. His body felt unfamiliar, as if he had returned to adolescence. With his fingertips, he rapped out a paradiddle on the edge of the table.

He said, 'Right.'

It was a long way across the busy pub, and it would be disastrous to nudge a shoulder and spill someone's drink because the necessary apology would devalue whatever he then went on to say to Dave Hooper. So he took the expedition slowly and carefully, measuring the weight, timing and direction of each step.

Eventually, he reached the corner of the bar. Its curve reminded him of an aeroplane's wing. Dave Hooper wore a checked, shortsleeve shirt untucked over his jeans. His back was turned, with the same ambiguous intent. Perhaps by ignoring Sam he was simply trying to prevent any further embarrassment. Sam hoped so. The span of Hooper's shoulders seemed immense, like a shire-horse. Sam imagined him as an anti-stud; a bull employed to kill cattle.

Hooper was now in muted discussion with four other men, all younger. Three were dressed like Dave, the fourth wore an estate agent's suit and a bright tie in a fat Windsor knot.

Sam spread a hand on the bar.

Hooper continued to act oblivious, cackling at whatever joke he'd just been told.

Sam cleared his throat and said Hooper's name.

There fell no heavy, awkward silence. Dave Hooper glanced simply and naturally over his shoulder. He registered Sam's presence and smiled. He turned, pint in his hand, and leant an elbow on the bar. He reached into his breast pocket for a golden pack of Benson & Hedges. He lit a cigarette and offered the pack to Sam, who shook his head.

Dave Hooper said, 'All right?'

'Yeah,' said Sam. 'I'm good. Thanks.' He looked around and said, 'It's a few years since I've been in here.'

Hooper joined him, looking round the pub.

He shrugged, minutely.

'It's still a shit-hole.'

Sam held back a forced laugh that he feared would be honking and patronizing.

Instead, he said, 'Look. I'm sorry about the other day. I handled it all wrong.'

Hooper shrugged again.

'Don't worry about it. It's forgotten.'

'It's just . . .' said Sam.

'It's forgotten.'

It was an assertion, more than an observation.

Sam said, 'Can I get you a drink?'

Hooper looked at his glass, then drained it and set it heavily on the surface of the bar.

'Go on,' he said. 'Cheers. Pint.'

Sensitive to the minutest signals of tension, the barmaid had been loitering close by, washing glasses, so at least the service was prompt. It seemed necessary to Sam that he order himself a pint, although his Guinness stood undrunk, back at the table. The drinks took a while to pour and they waited in silence. Then Sam raised his glass to Hooper and said, 'Cheers.' Hooper said 'Cheers' in return. That was the end of the conversation. Hooper turned his back again and Sam wandered back to his seat.

'See?' said Mel, making space for him. 'He's a nice bloke.'

Sam hated him.

'Yeah,' he said, and supped the head from the pint that had been waiting for him, slowly warming.

Janet went off to put some money in the fruit machines. Mel spotted some friends at the bar and waved them over. They were called Anna and Alison. Alison was thin and wan, Sam's notion of a junkie, but he learnt that she was Deputy Manager of a small Gap outlet in town. Anna was black North African, elegant, with close-cropped hair and bootleg jeans.

Within five minutes, Mel had made it clear to Sam that Anna was single. Within ten minutes, she'd made it clear to Anna that Sam was single, too.

Sam could feel the unfamiliar lunchtime drinks hissing at the base of his skull like an untuned radio and he avoided Anna's inquisitive gaze. She laid a hand on the back of his and told him not to be shy. Then she looked at Mel and Alison and all three of them laughed.

Sam wanted to go home. But solitary egress was not possible. It would look conspicuous, as if he'd come to the Cat and

Fiddle simply to grovel to Dave Hooper. It was some comfort that he made for only passing sport to the women. Surreptitiously, Alison pointed to somebody across the bar (another woman, he presumed). The three women joined in a huddle and began to exchange intelligence about her.

Sam examined his mobile phone. Earlier in the week, he'd spent a bus ride to work clearing its memory. Now only four numbers were listed in his personal directory: two were work-related. One was Mel's mobile. The fourth was Jamie's.

Jamie answered on the third ring.

'Dad?'

'All right, mate?'

'Yeah.'

'What're you up to?'

'Nothing. Stuart's round. We're watching a DVD.'

'Nothing saucy, I hope.'

(Briefly, the women broke off their conversation and looked at him. He didn't notice.)

'Course not. We're watching – what is it, Stu?'

'*Scream Three*,' said Stuart, as if from a considerable distance.

'*Scream Three*,' said Jamie.

'Fair enough,' said Sam. 'Wouldn't you rather watch *Attack of the Clones* or something?'

'*Dad* . . .'

'All right. I don't know. *Gladiator* or something.'

'I've already seen it like a gazillion times. I haven't even *seen Scream Three* yet.'

'All right,' said Sam. 'But I'm telling you now – there's no sleeping with the lights on.'

'Ha ha,' said Jamie, for Stuart's benefit. 'Dream on.'

'Anyway,' said Sam. 'I'll be back in a minute.'

There was a pause.

'What? Right now?'

'What's wrong with now?'

'Duh. It hasn't even started yet.'

Sam looked at his watch.

'All right,' he said. 'All right. I'll see you a bit later then. About teatime.'

'Whatever.'

Sam terminated the call and pocketed the mobile.

Mel had been keeping half an eye on him. She broke off from whatever Alison was saying and said, 'Is he all right?'

'Fine,' said Sam. He gave her an encouraging, martyred expression and urged her to continue with her conversation.

He lit a cigarette and tried to join in, but it was a half-hearted attempt. Gossip was of greatly reduced appeal when it involved strangers. Nevertheless, it was a fruity story. It featured a woman called Jenny he would be interested to meet.

Taking grim pleasure from his own selflessness, he went to get in another round. At the bar, he cast several glances at Dave Hooper, who was engaged in the same conversation with the same four men. Hooper was interrupted every few seconds by someone saying hello on their way to the lavatory.

He seemed unaware of Sam's presence. Sam found this greatly irritating.

It was clear that Hooper was drinking too much. At one point he offered up a great yell, such that the entire pub paused for a second and looked his way. Hooper was clambering on his mate's shoulder, holding up a twenty-pound note like an Olympic torch, trying to get the barmaid's attention. He got it.

Sam's contempt darkened. Taking great care, he balanced the drinks on a circular tray which he carried back to the table. Everyone was too involved in their conversation to thank him properly. Only Anna took the proffered glass, raised an eyebrow and briefly touched his upper arm.

The Guinness, five pints of it by now, pressed against his bladder. He'd delayed going to the lavatory because he'd have to pass Dave Hooper to get there, bidding him a courteous acknowledgement. If Sam broke that protocol, sanctions might be applied. These would be followed by a renewed peace agreement that would require greater reparation, and more profound public humiliation.

Even worse was the possibility that Dave Hooper might wish to visit the lavatory at the same time as him.

He imagined Hooper doing a quick, copper's squat at the urinal, untucking his cock from its lair. Should Dave Hooper occupy the urinal next to him, Sam knew that he wouldn't be able to piss. It had happened before. If it were the wrong kind of pub lavatory – two urinals, and only one cubicle – he might find himself in real trouble. If the cubicle was occupied, he could find himself trapped at the urinal, desperate to piss and quite unable. An unending queue of men would see only Sam's back and his bald spot, as he waited with gritted teeth at the urinal, mentally rehearsing the $13 \times$ table, waiting for the train that never comes.

Whenever it was possible this might happen (which was whenever he visited a new pub) Sam would not go to the lavatory until he was drunk, or until discomfort had matured into pain. Whichever was first.

He stood. The weight against his bladder sent a cramp across the wall of his stomach, down to his anus. He excused himself, then walked fearfully in the direction of the door marked *Gentlemen*.

There was a laugh.

The young man talking to Hooper glanced briefly at Sam, and said something into Hooper's ear. Hooper laughed and looked sideways. He cuffed the younger man round the back of the head. Sam was close enough to see, but not hear, him mouth the word *behave*.

He pretended not to notice. But as Sam approached, the lull in Hooper's conversation deepened. Soon it had become a derisive silence. Hooper stayed propped at the bar, looking at Sam with blank disinterest. His companions paused, then parted, allowing Sam to pass.

Sam fought to keep his expression impersonal. His penis twitched. He feared to piss himself.

He nodded hello to Dave Hooper and passed by. The small group of men closed in his wake.

With an open hand, Sam pushed open the lavatory door.

He heard Hooper laugh behind him.

In the lavatory, there were four urinals and three cubicles, only one of which was unusably stuffed with shit-smeared wads of paper. He passed it, gagging, then hurried into the farthest cubicle and locked the door behind him. He scrambled to unzip his fly. He waited for a few moments, in some discomfort. Then he pissed for longer than seemed possible. When he was done –

and there were several false starts – he pulled a few sheets of paper from the roll, just to make the right noises, and pulled the flush. He stepped into the tiled lavatory, adjusting his belt.

One of Dave Hooper's companions stood at a urinal. It was the young man who'd spoken into Hooper's ear when Sam approached, causing him to laugh. He was good-looking, in a sporty way, in his late teens or early twenties. He was looking at the ceiling, whistling as he passed a hot parabola of pale beer-urine against the aluminium splashback.

Sam passed by him, and stopped to wash his hands. (He knew that flush handles, touched by numberless faecally-smeared hands, were the dirtiest part of any public lavatory. Second came the taps, which were touched by many (not all) of those same shitty hands. And further, he knew it was unnecessary to wash one's hands after urinating: the skin of the penis was no dirtier than the neck or the cheek or the ankle, and the hand was not contaminated by touching it. Yet he could never bring himself to leave a cubicle without flushing it, and washing his hands afterwards.)

As he washed, the young man sighed and zipped himself up. He joined Sam at the wash basins, but only to check his hair in the mirror.

He caught Sam's reflected eye.

He said, 'All right?'

Sam nodded, rinsing the soap from his hands under a trickle of cold water.

'All right?' he said.

He turned and began to dry his hands on a damp loop of thin, blue towel that hung from a battered dispenser.

The young man said,

'Are you Jamie's dad, then?'

Sam straightened.

He faced the wall for a few seconds, the filthy, wet towel limp in his hands.

Then he turned and faced the young man.

He said, 'Are you Liam?'

The young man nodded in a manner that suggested *of course* he was Liam. Everyone knew that.

Sam spoke through his teeth.

He said, 'Leave my boy alone, you little bastard.'

Liam made a show of patting flat the crown of his gelled hair.

He said, 'I haven't *touched* your fucking son.'

The casual obscenity, with his child as its object, slapped Sam with the cold force of blasphemy and he trembled when he spoke.

'You coward,' he said. 'Look at the size of you.'

Liam's smile was beautiful.

He laughed.

'Fuck off,' he said.

Before Sam could answer, the lavatory door swung open. In the mirror, Sam watched Dave Hooper enter and stop behind them.

'What's going on?'

Liam Hooper laughed again.

'Mr Greene's having a word with me.'

Sam faced Dave Hooper.

Dave Hooper said, 'If you want to have a word with someone, have a fucking word with me.'

He punched Sam in the face.

Sam's head struck the towel dispenser. He and the dispenser's metal cover fell to the floor. It whirled and rattled on the wet tiles like a spun coin.

Sam lay in the wet, looking at the scuffed nubuck suede of Dave Hooper's Caterpillar boots. Hooper drew back a foot. Then he paused, put it flat on the floor.

He said, 'Twat.'

He held the door open for Liam to leave, and followed his son back into the pub.

Sam got to his feet, using the washstand to steady himself. His jaw felt broken. He examined it with tender fingertips. Then he looked at himself in the mirror.

Abruptly, he turned to face the far wall. He saw that the only window was heavily barred. The bars were thick with old coats of white gloss paint and they hardly budged when he reached up to tug on them.

He didn't believe he could walk out of this lavatory and go past Dave and Liam Hooper. Not with his arse and back still sopping wet, and blood on his face. But the longer he delayed his exit, the worse he knew it would be.

With resigned anger, he slammed his way through the swinging door. Dave Hooper and what Sam now supposed was his family were waiting for him. They made a silent half-moon of Ben Shermans. Sam tried to keep his head up, but it was not possible. Scorn radiated from them like heat and he passed them with his gaze lowered. The boy, Liam, moved into his path, specifically to shoulder-nudge him.

Sam didn't pause. The Hoopers watched him make his way across the pub, back to the table. It seemed infinitely familiar. He sat down. Alison and Anna were gone. Mel was alone.

She looked at him.

'What happened to you?'

He tried to speak.

'Christ,' said Mel. 'Did he hit you? Did Dave hit you?'

Before he could restrain her, Mel stood. The Hoopers were still watching.

Mel caught Dave Hooper's eye.

Across the now quiet pub, Dave called, 'All right, Mel?'

Mel gripped the edge of the table. She bellowed, 'You fuck-ing animal, Dave Hooper. You fucking *coward*.'

The assembled Hoopers raised their glasses and cheered. Dave Hooper cheered the loudest. Then he muttered some-thing to Liam, who laughed.

Everybody else looked at their tables, out the windows, into their glasses, at the coal of a cigarette.

Mel took Sam's elbow.

'We're not scared of you,' she said. 'You're just fucking ani-mals. All of you.'

The Hoopers beat out a tribal rhythm on the surface of the bar as Mel ushered Sam from the Cat and Fiddle. When the heavy doors swung closed, the jeering seemed to stop. But behind the door, Sam knew it continued.

They stood on a bright, painty smear of sunshine that fell on the concrete. Mel fumbled with a cigarette. She inhaled five or six angry, pecking puffs.

She said, 'Are you all right?'

'Yeah,' said Sam. His brow was furrowed. He was thinking about something else.

He said, 'Mel. You shouldn't have done that.'

'Fuck them,' she said. 'I'm not scared of them. What happened?'

He told her. He described being punched and she pursed her lips. She looked old and pale and furious. She stamped off down the street, slightly unsteady on her heels. He followed, shambling, ashamed, like a scolded Old English sheepdog. Already he needed to piss again.

On the corner by the Dolphin Centre, Mel's mobile rang. It was Janet. She'd been in the toilets chatting to Anna and had missed everything. Already she'd heard several versions of what had happened. In the worst of them, Sam had been glassed and had run from the pub, one eye dangling free of its socket.

Curtly, Mel let Janet know what had happened. Then she told her to stop worrying and stay in the pub. She'd see her later.

Sam stopped off at Mel's house, to clean himself up. Mel applied a sticking plaster to his cut, bruised cheekbone. Sam drank several mugs of coffee. He didn't want to sleep. He dreaded the waking moment, when today's events would charge at him and shame would rush through him like sunlight.

When he left, Mel was still withdrawn. She seemed to be furious with him, as much as Dave Hooper.

'Mel,' he said. 'There was nothing I could do. It happened so fast. And there were so many of them.'

'I know,' she said, and turned on the TV.

He stood there, fussing with the blood on his shirt. Then he said goodbye and walked home.

He arrived to discover that Stuart hadn't left yet. So he called hello from the hallway and went straight upstairs to bed.

The house, new wood on an old frame, remained indifferent to his presence.

10

The next morning, he stood at the bathroom mirror, applying a borrowed cover-up stick to the ripening bruise on his cheekbone. It left a pale, disfiguring smudge.

He patted his pale, solid, hairy belly.

Whenever he thought about the Cat and Fiddle, he endured a debilitating thrill of shame. It distracted him from his work. He was inattentive to patients and brusque to colleagues.

Eventually, Barbara summoned him to her office. He sat like a schoolboy on a beige Ikea chair while she took her place behind the desk. She glanced at some notes spread before her. Then she looked up and told Sam that she was concerned about him. She knew he was a talented, dedicated nurse – after all, Isabel Beaumont wouldn't have recommended him so highly if that were not the case.

She told him she knew he had a lot on his plate. But during

this, his trial period, he had never seemed quite happy and it was beginning to affect his work – which she knew (she reminded him) could be excellent even in situations that were far more demanding than they enjoyed at Agartha Barrow. As his line manager (and, she hoped, his friend), she had a responsibility to him. But she also had a responsibility to his colleagues – and their collective responsibility lay with the patients in their care. She could under no circumstances allow the quality of that care to be compromised by the problems of an individual member of staff.

She asked if there was anything he'd like to say. He told her no, and held her gaze for a difficult second. She dismissed him.

All he wanted was to sleep.

Variously during the distracted day, he'd thought about taking Jamie on a long holiday, moving him to a private school, finding a job on the continent, or perhaps America. He thought how Jamie would enjoy America. As fantasy segued into fantasy, he felt more deflated and trapped.

He finished his shift without speaking to anybody, and without anybody speaking to him, and he caught the bus home. Stepping into the hallway, he barely had the strength to remove his coat. He hung it on the banister like a soldier returned from the trenches and dropped his bag in the very place he reprimanded Jamie for leaving his.

Jamie was on the sofa, watching TV in the dark. Blue, flickering cathode flickered and lashed at his face. Sam said hello and dumped himself in the armchair. Jamie didn't respond. Sam said hello again.

Then he caught himself and sat forward. Jamie's face was smeared and wet. In the cold blue light he looked brutalized.

Sam said, 'Jamie? Mate? What's wrong?'

Angrily, Jamie wiped his nose on his hairless wrist. He tried to speak, but the words caught in his throat and all that emerged was a hound-like whimper.

Sam knelt before him and held out his arms. But Jamie pressed himself further back into the sofa and Sam let his arms fall to his side. He stayed there, wondering what to do.

Jamie said, 'How could you?'

'How could I what?'

Jamie stood. He looked down on his kneeling father. His upper lip was smeared with snot and his eyes looked swollen and tender.

His voice broke.

'You let him *hit* you.'

For a few moments, they were frozen like that, cold blue in the cathode rays.

Then, wearily, Sam got to his feet.

'Jamie,' he said, 'you don't understand.'

He reached out to put a hand on Jamie's shoulder.

Jamie shied from his touch.

'You fucking wimp,' he said.

He went upstairs.

That night, Sam dreamt the cabin crew of a 747 en route to California were urgently insisting that he was the aircraft's missing pilot. Despite the fact that he wore sandals, a Hawaiian shirt and, inexplicably, no trousers, he was required in the cabin. Then the soft, spongy chair from which he could not rise to go and fly the plane became a bed, and he lay awake.

He felt welded to the mattress. He forced himself to rise only because he needed to speak to Jamie. He moved in weary, befuddled circles, searching out his discarded clothes. Downstairs, he made a pot of coffee and sat at the breakfast bar, where he found a pack of eleven cigarettes. Only two were left when Jamie walked into the kitchen, showered and dressed for school. He registered his father's presence, then went to the fridge and poured himself a long glass of orange juice.

Sam stubbed out his cigarette.

'Jamie,' he said.

'What?'

'Let me explain.'

Jamie held the glass to his chest.

'Explain what?'

This the delighted, pink, warm, happy child whose nappy he had changed so many hundreds of times.

'Explain what happened.'

Jamie wiped his eyes.

'I told you not to *do* anything,' he said. 'I told you.'

'I know,' said Sam. 'Look—'

'Dad, you've made it worse. All right? You stuck your nose in, and you made it worse.'

'I didn't stick my nose in,' Sam said. 'I'm your *dad*.'

'And now everyone's *laughing* at you,' said Jamie. 'All right? Everyone at school knows you're a wimp. Lying on the floor and crying.'

Sam jerked as if prodded.

'Hang on,' he said. 'It wasn't like that.'

Jamie shook his head.

'You fucking wimp,' he said.

'Hang *on* a minute,' said Sam.

'And you're a liar,' said Jamie, more quietly yet. He stood there, dependent and repelled.

Sam could find no words. He looked at the crushed cigarettes in the ashtray.

Jamie slammed the front door hard enough to shake the teetering pile of junk mail from the telephone table. It lay scattered like playing cards across the stripped wood of the hallway.

Sam stayed in the kitchen for a long time. The house hissed with emptiness, like a seashell put to the ear.

Sometimes when he was alone, he heard somebody creeping around upstairs and wondered if it might be Kenneth.

Kenneth was the imaginary friend of his early childhood. Sam had been so at ease in Kenneth's company that his parents became disturbed and took him to a child psychologist, who pronounced him in every way normal. But, normal or not, nobody was keen to be alone with Sam when Kenneth was around. Even now, mention of Kenneth's name was enough to bring Mel out in goosebumps.

Perhaps Kenneth had sensed his renewed need. Perhaps he'd come back.

Would he still be a child?

Sam phoned in sick. Barbara sounded neither angry nor surprised. Nor was she moved by Sam's entreating, repeated apologies. He was irritated that she patronized his insincerity. When he had safely replaced the receiver, he swore at the phone.

He knew his colleagues had anxieties of their own. Marriages were fracturing. Flirtations flickered at the edge of infidelity. There was blood in the stools, a lump in the breast, a loose knot of gristle where once there'd been a proud erection. There were elderly parents who refused to be rehomed. He was aware that his absence would only add to the sum of that anxiety.

But he didn't care.

He went upstairs, to see if Kenneth were there. But he wasn't, and Sam laughed at his folly. The obscure series of clicks and creaking stopped the moment his foot touched the stairs. Whoever was there, they left when they heard him. Perhaps it was Justine, trying to make herself known.

With sudden, tearful fury, he hoped not.

He ran the bath and enjoyed the rumble of the taps, the unfolding bloom of steam. All at once, he noticed the bath was full. Several minutes had passed without his knowledge. He knew that such episodes, like leaving one's car keys in the fridge or forgetting why one had entered a room, came at the minor end of the scale of epilepsy. Temporarily, his mind had been voided by a little fit. He was frustrated by the phenomenon's elusiveness. He wanted it to happen again.

The bath was too hot and burnt his assessing foot. He ran the cold tap, then forced himself in. Water spilled over the edge. His testicles withdrew from the damaging heat.

Gradually, as the water cooled, he lay back and soaked his hair. Floating, it tickled his shoulders like weeds. He washed and shaved and walked naked and dripping to his bedroom. It smelt of new pine, new carpet and sour old bedding. Other than two lonely socks dropped several feet apart and rolled into strange shapes, the room was empty. Still wet, he lay on the bed. He could smell the sweat of his troubled sleep. He rolled over and turned on the radio. It was 11 a.m. He lay back with a pillow over his eyes and kept the radio's volume low, so it was little more than a companionable hum.

But there was no possibility of sleep. Shortly before midday, he went naked downstairs and got the whisky. He poured a glass and turned on the TV. He was on the third glass when something occurred to him, an idea. He thought it over for a while, then went to find his mobile phone. He called Ashford's private number.

Ashford was on lunchtime playground duty, patrolling the gates and fields in an attempt to thwart truancy. He sounded tired. He confirmed that Jamie was not at school today. Then he asked, with lowered voice, how Sam was feeling.

Sam went cold. It seemed that Jamie was not exaggerating. The story of the bitch-slap in the Cat and Fiddle lavatory had spread and grown. He wondered how superb his humiliation had become in the local mythology. He imagined Liam Hooper's extravagant school-corridor swagger. Dave Hooper, pausing to smile privately before installing a bolt through the shrieking head of a pig.

Sam told Ashford he was absolutely fine, thank you, and hung up.

He'd smoked the last cigarette. He poured himself another drink. When only an inch remained in the bottle, he went upstairs and dressed. Then he cleaned his teeth and rinsed with mouthwash.

He drove with overstated, drunken caution (losing concentration only once, on a zebra crossing) and was outside the school gates by 3.30 p.m. At 3.40 he heard the bell ring. It was the same bell. Its familiarity made him grimace, and he gripped the steering wheel hard. Within a few seconds, the first pupils had appeared at the exit gates. Soon they had become a surge, an inundation of shapes and sizes and ethnicities, similarly dressed. Navy-blue with yellow shirts for the girls. Black blazers and white shirts for the boys. A great variety of training shoes. As he watched, several of the kids piled into waiting parental cars. Most did not. The school run had not yet been fully established in this part of town.

Sam had not supposed the sudden horde would be so overwhelming. He despaired of sighting Liam Hooper. He got out of the car. Standing on the pavement, waiting, he felt furtive and strange. He suspected that certain of the waiting parents, grim at the wheel of their Renault Espaces, had already marked him out as a potential paedophile.

He wished he had a single friend among them and knew he never would.

When the tide had diminished to a sporadic trickle, he spotted Liam Hooper. He looked much younger. Hardly more than a boy. He strutted alone through the gates, bag slung over one shoulder.

Sam lit a cigarette and leant against the car. Liam came scuffing down the street, chewing gum. Sam stepped out in front of him.

At first, Liam didn't recognize him. His passing confusion, edged with fear, was disarming. Sam saw how much bigger he was than the boy, and how much stronger. He felt he could reach out and rip Liam's head from his shoulders and rend the limbs from their sockets.

He said, 'Get in the car.'

'What?'

'You heard me. Get in the car.'

'No fucking *way*.'

'I'm not going to hurt you.'

'Too fucking *right* you're not.'

Liam tried to barge past. Sam blocked his way.

'Look, Liam. I just want to talk.'

'You heard what Dad said. Talk to him.'

Sam set his mouth.

'Right,' he said.

He opened the boot, and threw in the car keys. Then he slammed the boot closed.

'There you are. Proof. We're not going anywhere. So, please. Just get in the car and hear what I have to say.'

Liam looked at the boot.

He said, 'You're fucking mad in the head, mate.'

'Probably,' said Sam.

Assorted pedestrians – parents, slow-moving pensioners, and straggling schoolkids – were beginning to pay attention to them.

'Come on,' said Sam. 'For God's sake. Just get in the car. Leave the *door* open if it makes you feel better. Sit in the back with the door open. I just want to talk.'

Liam responded to a challenge, not an invitation: he met Sam's eyes for too long and walked round the car with an air of defiance, an insolent swagger. He sat on the front passenger seat (leaving the door very slightly ajar) and removed a cigarette from a ten-pack of Benson & Hedges kept in the breast-pocket of his blazer. He lit it, exhaled at the ceiling.

Sam took his place in the driver's seat. He made himself small and hunched, nervous about making the kind of physical contact that might be misread.

Liam said, 'What?'

Sam took time to light his own cigarette, fresh from the stub of the first.

He said, 'What would it take to make you leave my son alone?'

Liam turned in his seat until he was facing Sam.

'I haven't *touched* your precious son. I haven't fucking *touched* him.'

There was a silence.

Sam could hear Liam's breathing, shallow and outraged. Sam looked dead ahead, as if the car was in motion.

'All right,' he said, at length. 'Fair enough. What would it take to make you stop whatever it is you're doing?'

Liam drew twice on his cigarette.

'I don't even know!' he said. 'I don't know what I'm sup-posed to have done. It's not my fault if Jamie's a—'

'If Jamie's a what?'

'A mummy's boy.'

Sam looked at his hands, tight on the wheel of the stationary car.

'Jamie lost his mother,' he said. 'She died.'

Liam shrugged.

'So?'

Sam didn't risk looking at him. He thought Liam's defiance had a belligerent, wounded quality — perhaps the aggressive self-justification of one who knows himself to be in the wrong.

'So,' Sam said, 'it doesn't help if you go on about it all the time. Jamie's much younger than you, and he's new here. Give him a break. Just, you know. Find another target.'

'He's not a *target*.'

'I accept that,' said Sam. 'But please. Even if you don't *mean* what you say, think about the effect it has on Jamie. It might be fun to you, and it might not even mean much. But it means a lot to Jamie.'

Liam found the ashtray and tapped into it a few centimetres of ash.

'It's not my fault if he can't take a joke.'

Sam closed his eyes, turned it into a long blink. His hands gripped the steering wheel tightly. His fingers were pale, livid round the knuckles. He relaxed them. Felt the blood flow.

'It's not a joke to Jamie. That's the point.'

'That's his problem.'

'Look,' said Sam. 'I'm appealing to you here, man to man. I'm asking you to understand the *effect* you're having. I'm sure that if you understood, then—'

'Is this all you wanted to say?' said Liam.

He pushed open the door.

'Wait,' said Sam.

Liam glanced over his shoulder.

Sam searched his pockets. He found and lit another cigarette.

He said, 'Money.'

'What?' said Liam.

'I'll give you money.'

Liam's weight was still on the open door.

'What *for*?'

'To leave Jamie alone.'

Liam closed the door and sat back in the car seat.

'How much money?'

'How much will it take?'

'Are you joking?'

'No,' said Sam. 'I'm not.'

Liam waved his hand below his nose.

'You're just *pissed*,' he said. 'It stinks like a fucking brewery in here.'

'That has nothing to do with it,' said Sam.

'You're talking bollocks. It's pathetic.'

Sam rested his forehead on the steering wheel.

'Be that as it may,' he said, 'please try to understand. I'm treating you like an adult, so try to behave like one.'

He glanced sideways. Liam appeared to be listening.

'Look,' said Sam, 'if you want to know the truth, I wish you didn't exist. I think the world would be a better place if you weren't in it. But you *do* exist, and you're hurting my son. And the funny thing – the thing that's a real laugh – is that I can't stop you. There's nothing I can do. When you're older, when you've got kids of your own, you might understand how ridiculous that is. At the moment you don't, because you're young and you think the world revolves around you. Do you understand any of that, Liam? Is there another way to stop you? Because if there is, I'd like to know what it is.'

Sam couldn't read Liam's expression. There was contempt, and some embarrassment. It occurred to him too that Liam was a little frightened. That thought made him unutterably weary.

He said, 'So. What do you think?'

'You're going to pay me money to be nice to Jamie?'

'You don't have to be *nice* to him, if that's too hard for you. All you have to do is stop giving him a hard time. I don't know. Find someone else to pick on. Whatever it takes.'

'How much money?'

'Five hundred pounds.'

'Fuck off. Are you taking the piss?'

'Sadly, no. Five hundred pounds. Cash. In your hand.'

'Have you got it on you?'

'Of course not. I can meet you on Monday – if you agree.'

'What if I don't agree?'

Sam continued to rest his head on the steering wheel. He felt a smile stretch his lips.

'Well, Liam,' he said. 'Then I'll have to kill you, won't I?'

'Yeah,' said Liam. 'You and whose fucking army?'

Sam lifted his head and turned to face him.

'I don't know,' he said. 'This way seems much easier.'

'All right,' said Liam. 'I'll do it. For five hundred quid.'

He offered his hand. Sam thought he must be joking. Then he realized that, having been exhorted to, Liam was trying to behave like an adult.

Sam extended his own, hairy-backed hand. They arranged a place and time to meet. Then he watched Liam Hooper swagger down the long curve of Blackstone Road, and wondered how hard he had to work not to look over his shoulder, or run away to exercise the unexpected thrill of victory.

He drove home more carefully still. At a red light, his attention drifted and he entered again that timeless fugue state. He was awakened from it by the driver of the white van in his rearview mirror, leaning on the horn. Sam held up his hand in apology.

It was prematurely dark. As he walked into the house on Balaarat Street, rain began to spatter on the kitchen windows, the sound of uncooked rice shaken in a plastic bottle. He turned on the downstairs lights.

In the living room, he flicked through some new CDs, but there was nothing he wanted to listen to. He had lost the ability to enjoy new music. Music had become an exercise in nostalgia, a mortification for which he had little stomach. There was nothing on television that he could bear to watch. The radio was chirpy and irritating. He went through the freezer drawers, looking for something to eat. He put a small boulder of lamb mince in the microwave to defrost.

He listened to the microwave's comforting, domestic hum. Then he gathered about himself all the ingredients for a spaghetti Bolognese, which had long been his speciality, the thing he cooked best. Or, at least, it was the meal his family had claimed to like the most.

His family.

He smiled bitterly as he rifled through cupboards, seeking

out a tube of tomato purée and then the garlic he knew was in there somewhere. He laid out the ingredients on the chopping board. The silence and the rain were oppressive. He returned to the living room and put on a Motown compilation CD. It was like the memory of sunshine.

When Jamie got home the air was rich with the familiar, garlicky smell of Bolognese. But it didn't matter. Jamie was a series of sense impressions – the key in the lock, the rustle of a parka being removed, the slamming of the door; hurried footsteps on the stairs. Another door banging.

It might as well have been Kenneth.

Sam was patient. He knew the candid appeal for love seldom won it. He cooked and drained the spaghetti, tonged it on to two plates, on to each of which he spooned two dollops of sauce, sprinkled with fresh parmesan shavings. Not without some pride, he stood back and examined what he'd done, while the wind and the rain battered harder at the walls and windows.

He uncorked a bottle of wine and poured himself a large glass, which he downed like Ribena. Then he went to the foot of the stairs and called Jamie down.

A stiffening at the deep heart of the house let him know that Jamie had heard, but he didn't say anything, and he didn't come down. Sam gave up calling him. He sat at the breakfast bar, listening to the rain, and ate his Bolognese alone. Sipping more wine, he spooned the remaining sauce into a Tupperware container, and the container into the fridge. Jamie's meal he scraped into the swingtop bin.

When he rose, early the next day, Jamie had already dressed and gone.

Not to school, he supposed.

He wondered how it had come to pass that, sometime
between the death of Justine and the move to Balaarat Street,
he had lost his son. He had been replaced by an unfamiliar
creature he did not greatly like. Perhaps he and Jamie were
simply ghosts of each other: they had joined Kenneth,
become three imaginary boys, haunting the same house.
Perhaps like ghosts or old photographs they were fading.
Perhaps one day they would simply become invisible to one
other.

On Monday morning, he was on the corner, ready to meet
Liam on his way to school. He felt like an illicit lover, a ped-
erast, a drug dealer. The engine was idling, the radio blared
jaunty inanities. He watched people go past. Eventually he saw
Liam in the rearview mirror and leant across the passenger
seat to open the door. Liam got in and sat next to him. He
smelt of hair gel and cigarettes and brand new trainers.

Liam said, 'All right?'

Sam opened the glove compartment and reached inside.
Although it seemed a bit theatrical, he'd put the money in a
Jiffy bag. Liam upended it into his lap and ostentatiously
counted through the notes, all twenties. Then he restuffed the
Jiffy bag and slipped it into his Puma schoolbag.

Nothing remained to be done and there was nothing to say,
but Liam didn't seem ready to leave. Sam felt the weight of
silence that trapped both of them.

To break it, Sam said, 'That's it, then. You'll leave him
alone.'

Despite himself (Sam thought) Liam glanced down at the bag. He seemed weighed down by its contents.

'It seems stupid, really,' Liam said. 'When you think about it.'

Sam laughed.

'Yes,' he said. 'Well. Don't be late on my account.'

Liam shrugged. He'd never cared about being late before and he wasn't going to start now. He checked the zip on the sports bag and got out of the Rover. Outside, he ducked his head to light a cigarette.

Then Sam put the car into gear and pulled into the traffic.

When he arrived at work, it seemed unfamiliar. The people inside seemed artificial and badly lit. Their words seemed flat and expressed without true emotion. It was as if they were actors who had been waiting until he arrived before commencing their roles. He spent the day as if being watched by hidden cameras. He spoke to the Skinhead, and to Kenny and Byron and Christina Box and Ted Bone and the others. They all patiently and quite madly expected tenderness of ministration, gentle wisdom, and for Sam to know what he was doing, and why. He pitied them their misapprehensions. He wished there was somebody to watch over him, too. But there had only ever been Justine.

Later that evening, Mel phoned for the first time since the Cat and Fiddle. It was clear she had little desire to discuss Sam's problems, or even Jamie's.

She barked, 'Have you been calling me?'

He was taken aback by her sharpness.

'No,' he said. 'Why?'

'Somebody's been calling me. When I pick up the phone, no one's there.'

'Have you dialled 1471?'

'Of course I've dialled 1471. The caller has withheld their number.'

'Have you spoken to BT?'

'Oh,' she said. 'There's no point. It's probably nothing. It's probably a frigging call centre or something.'

He agreed, although he suspected it was not.

'They use automatic dialling machines,' said Mel. 'Sometimes they get stuck. It's just that, it doesn't *feel* like a call centre. Do you know what I mean?'

He did.

He said, 'At the very least, you'd expect a call centre to answer when you pick up the phone.'

'No,' she said. 'That's the thing. Sometimes they get stuck on automatic redial. They just keep calling and calling, even though nobody's on the end of the line. But it's only the *computer* doing it.'

He held his breath and silently counted to ten.

'But you don't think this is a call centre,' he said.

'No. When I pick up the receiver, I can – well, it sounds to me like I can hear stuff in the background.'

'What sort of stuff?'

'I don't know. Background noises. Unspecific stuff. You know – stuff that makes it sound like a proper phone call.'

'But nobody speaks.'

'No.'

'And there's no heavy breathing, or anything like that?'

'No.'

'It's probably nothing.'

'I know that. I was just calling to make sure it wasn't you.'

'Why would it be *me*?'

There was no answering such a question. It was clear to him that Mel had phoned not to check if he was calling, but to let him know she was frightened. But she would never admit that.

He said, 'Don't worry.'

'I'm not.'

'OK. Good. But if it happens again, give me a call.'

He thought.

'Look,' he said, 'why don't you just turn off the landline? Unplug it from the socket. Tell whoever you want to they can contact you on your mobile. That way, whoever it is – if it is somebody – they'll get bored and go away. All right? How's that?'

'That's a good idea,' she said. 'Spoken like a true—'

She stopped.

'True what?'

'Father.'

She was right. Since the first day of fatherhood he'd been aware that outside, the storm raged and the wind blew, that predators gnashed their slavering, bloody jaws and circled their place of safety on spindly shanks, on broad, loping paws.

He said, 'Look, it's a good idea. They'll just get bored. It's the best way to deal with it.'

'But if they get bored,' she said, 'what'll they do next?'

'Mel,' he said. 'It's all right. Trust me.'

She told him that she did. And in a way, he supposed that was true, too, because that evening she arrived at his doorstep with a suitcase. Janet had dropped her off in the Fiat Oh, No.

He looked at her, clasping the suitcase like an evacuee. He smiled, for all that the sight of her made him sad. The suitcase and her rain-wet hair and the short silence between them seemed to necessitate some formal acknowledgement of her presence.

He said, 'Come in,' and stepped aside to allow her to enter.

She told him, 'I've double-locked everything. The neighbours are keeping an eye on the place. They've all got your number. They'll call if anything happens. Jan's got a set of keys. She said she'd go and check the mail every lunchtime, on her way back from work.'

As she unpacked her toiletries in the bathroom, he spread the duvet on the guest bed. And later, when it was dark and Jamie sulked upstairs, he glanced over at her, curled on the sofa watching TV, and was glad she was there.

Shortly after 11 p.m., the phone rang. They glanced in its direction and waited, without speaking, until the answer machine engaged. Nobody left a message. Sam didn't wait for the phone to ring again. He strode into the hallway and tugged the lead from the socket with enough violence to break it. Then he went and sat down. Mel didn't look at him or acknowledge what he'd done.

He asked her to turn up the TV.

Later, he followed her up to bed. On the landing, he turned and looked down. The hallway was dark, lit only by the ambient glow of streetlights. It was as if black floodwater licked halfway up the stairs. He stared into the darkness until he could almost see the lapping wavelets, almost hear them slapping at the banisters.

Gently, he knocked on Mel's bedroom door. She was already in bed. She was propped on one elbow, reading *Cosmopolitan*.

He said, 'Good night.'

She whispered, 'Good night,' in return and went back to her magazine.

Then he looked in on Jamie. He was a shape under the duvet, which he'd pulled fully over his head. It was how he liked to sleep. Somewhere there would be a small aperture through which he breathed. The room smelt ripe, slightly foetid: overused and underventilated.

He left off the light in his own bedroom. There was no need of it. There were few objects to negotiate and anyway there was a streetlight right outside, which cast the room in a gaudy liquid illumination. It was never really dark in there. One day, he would have to buy a heavier pair of curtains. But tonight he was pleased by the light, the honey-coloured glow that protected him from the dark, cold waters below.

11

Over breakfast, he could tell that Mel wanted to say something. She waited until Jamie had left for school and Sam had pulled on his own coat and was hunting out the long, tatty scarf, then his house keys. She leant in the doorway with a cigarette in one hand and said, 'Of course, we could ask Frank for help.'

Sam paused in the act of winding the scarf round his neck. They looked at each other uncomfortably. It was as if a protocol had been transgressed. Something that had gone unspoken, like an ancient and filthy family secret, had casually been alluded to. He let his hands fall to his side.

'There's no need.'

'I'm not saying there is. What I'm saying is, if there was a need, then – well. We could call Frank.'

'And Frank would know how to sort it out, would he?'

She shrugged one shoulder.

'I don't know. But he'd know someone who could.'

'Mel,' he said. 'This isn't Kosovo. We can't just call in a peace-keeping force.'

'I'm not talking about a *peace*-keeping force,' she said. 'I'm talking about the fucking Hell's Angels or something.'

'Frank's not a Hell's Angel.'

'But he knows them.'

Sam shook his head.

'Mel,' he said. 'I can't believe you're even saying this.'

'I'm not saying anything,' she said. 'All I'm saying is, if push comes to shove, Frank could help us out. That's all. God. Sorry for breathing.'

He wrapped the scarf round his throat and jingled the keys in his palm. He glimpsed himself in the hallway mirror, all bundled up against a winter whose worst was past.

'Anyway,' he said. 'I've sorted it.'

The cigarette paused on the way to her lips.

'That's news to me. What did you do?'

He mumbled a response and turned to go. Mel made him repeat it.

He said, 'I paid him.'

'Paid who?'

'Hooper.'

'You gave Dave Hooper *money*?'

'Not Dave.'

She dropped the cigarette. She screamed and batted at the fireflies that danced on her legs and feet. She bent to pick up the cigarette and looked at him.

'You did what?'

He heard their mother in her voice. He could hurt her by telling her that.

'Look,' he said, 'there was no alternative, all right? I wanted the little fucker to leave Jamie alone, and nobody was helping me do it. Do you think I'm over the moon about giving protection money to a fucking fourteen year old?' The strength left his voice, and he finished the sentence with a broken quack. 'I had no choice.'

Mel didn't move.

'I don't believe it,' she said.

'I don't believe it either. Jesus. What do you want me to do?'

'Be—'

He cut her off.

'Be a *man* about it? What does that even mean, Mel?'

'That's not what I was going to say.'

'Isn't it? It bloody sounded like it from where I'm standing.'

'Be *careful*,' she said. 'I was going to say "be careful".'

'Be careful about what? I told you – I already gave him the money.'

She massaged her brow. She looked haggard and apprehensive.

'Then who was phoning last night?'

'I don't know. Dave Hooper, probably. But he's just trying to scare us. I'm not worried about him. He'll get bored and move on, if we don't rise to it. This is it. This is the end of it.'

Mel laughed.

'What?' said Sam.

'What happens when Liam's spent the money?'

They faced each other down the length of the hallway. Him

in his winter clothes; she in her white dressing-gown and fluffy-bunny slippers and her frizzy, curly hair and her long nose and the purple scar on her shin.

'We'll cross that bridge when we come to it,' Sam said, and he left to go to work.

12

Sam had that Saturday off.

Jamie still didn't want to know him. He wouldn't even eat the food Sam prepared, preferring the martyrdom of a diet consisting wholly of toast, marmalade and peanut butter. So, because it was a fine morning, Sam took Mel to the café that served the Merrydown arcade, the shops local to Balaarat Street.

Luxuriously unbathed and unshaved, he went first into the newsagents and stocked up on newspapers and cigarettes. He and Mel took a table in the café's small, walled garden, thick with ivy on three walls, in which there bumbled a few early bees. The sunshine was a silky weight on their shoulders as they read the papers and smoked and drank coffee. When breakfast arrived, full English for Mel, scrambled eggs and smoked salmon for Sam, they swapped newspapers across the table.

They were home by lunchtime. Sam looked around the empty house – he supposed that Jamie had gone to Stuart's – and suggested they go into town to do some shopping. Mel was excited and ran upstairs to shower and put on her make-up.

They spent most of the afternoon window-shopping. Mel bought some clothes while Sam tried to linger inconspicuously in the corner by the changing rooms. She agreed only reluctantly to go with him to the Virgin Megastore. Here, because Saturday night maintained some residual significance, he bought a couple of DVDs for them to watch with a takeaway and some bottles of wine.

They got home during the Saturday dead-time. It was still too early to prepare anything to eat, and there was nothing on TV. Pleasantly tired, they slumped in the armchairs and read sections of the newspapers that had been omitted that morning. Sam tried to engross himself in the *Travel* and *Personal Finance* sections of the Saturday *Guardian*.

At 6.30, Mel opened a bottle of wine and brought them both a glass.

Sam thanked her and took a sip.

He said, 'I had a nice day today. I enjoyed it.'

Mel lit a cigarette and sat back with it in one hand, the wine glass in the other.

'God,' she said. She looked at the ceiling and blew smoke at it. 'I need to get a life.'

So did Sam. He folded the *Personal Finance* section and laid it on the floor.

The sun was going down. Somewhere, somehow, Saturday

night was beginning. It hardly seemed possible.

At a few minutes past eight o'clock, they heard Jamie's key turning in the lock. By now they were on to the second bottle and were watching a gameshow whose rules were too arcane for Sam to grasp, and too sadistic for him to believe.

They shared a conspiratorial glance.

Mel called out to him, 'Come in, we're going to watch a video in a minute.'

'DVD,' said Sam.

There was a non-sound: Jamie pausing in the hallway.

'I heard that!' said Mel.

Muffled by the door, Jamie was sullen.

'Heard what? I didn't even *say* anything.'

'I heard your lips move.'

'Don't be stupid.'

'I did. I read your lips.'

'What did I say, then?'

'You told me to fuck off,' said Mel. 'You cheeky little monkey.'

'I did *not*.'

'Jamie Greene. Don't make it worse by lying to your auntie.'

On the other side of the door there was another, longer suspension of movement. It seemed to Sam that Jamie was fighting a smile. He looked at Mel and saw that she thought so, too. But Jamie didn't come in. He went to the kitchen to make himself some toast, then straight upstairs. Sam didn't mind. He knew by the quality of Jamie's silence that things were going to get better.

*

Half an hour later, the telephone rang.

They ignored it.

An hour later, it rang again.

There was giggling on the answer machine.

Just before midnight, Sam heard something. Male voices, raised in song.

He saw that Mel's eyes had been drawn to the window. Her brow was knit. She caught his eye and they laughed too loudly at each other's uneasiness. Sam slapped his thighs and stood. He went to make sure the front door was properly locked and secured.

He ignored Mel's gaze and increased the volume on the television.

But they heard it again anyway, in the pauses between adverts. It was so faint it sometimes faded to the edge of imagination. A wind-borne football chant.

Sam couldn't sit down. For lack of anything else to do, he walked to the far corner of the room, by the window. He crossed his arms and watched TV without seeing it.

'It's probably nothing,' said Mel. 'How would he even know where you live?'

'Christ, all your friends know where I live. And they all drink in the same fucking pub as him.'

She looked at him for a long time, without speaking. Then she laughed without any humour and said, 'We're like a couple of kids, scaring each other round a campfire. Relax. It's nothing.'

Sam said, 'Nothing my arse. It sounds like the invasion of Poland.'

She laughed, properly this time. They stopped to listen. They heard nothing.

They made faces at each other and began to relax.

Then they heard the sudden, shrieking wail of a car alarm. It was eerie and ominous, like a night ghoul's lamentation.

The stupid grin fell from Sam's mouth.

He said, 'Go upstairs and check on Jamie.'

'Sam—' said Mel.

'I'm not joking, Mel. Go on.'

She made a performance of rolling her eyes at his foolishness. But she went upstairs quickly enough.

Sam turned off the TV. Then he turned off all the downstairs lights – in the living room, the hallway, the kitchen – and stood in the darkness, waiting. His breath seemed very loud.

On the street, somebody called his name.

It seemed so absurd, he wondered if he'd imagined it. There was a long, dark stillness.

Then he heard it again.

Sam!

A fizzing, weakening thrill raced from his stomach to his limbs. He crept up the stairs. Halfway up, hysteria mushroomed inside him. He stopped and waited until it passed. He took a series of long, slow breaths.

On the street there was movement, an obscure series of scuffles and rattles. Giggling.

Entering Jamie's room, Sam looked calm and brisk.

Mel was on the edge of the narrow bed. Jamie was sitting up, the duvet pooled at his waist. He looked confused, as if uncertain he was awake.

Sam knelt at his bedside.

'Jamie,' he said, 'don't be worried, but get up and get dressed, right now. Quiet as you can.'

In the gold-tinged darkness, Jamie's skin was flawless. He jumped from the bed and pulled on the jeans and T-shirt that lay on the floor. Putting on his trainers, his fingers slipped and fumbled at the laces. Sam bent down to tie them, as he'd not done since Jamie was eight years old.

He told Jamie to sit down, to keep still and quiet. He sat alongside Mel.

To Sam, she said, 'How many of them are there?'

'I don't know. I haven't looked yet.'

'What are they doing?'

'I don't know. I can hear them whispering, I think.'

'What are they saying?'

'I've no idea, Mel. They're *whispering*.'

'Shall we call the police?'

Jamie inhaled sharply and drew his knees up to his chest.

Sam wanted to call the police more than he'd ever wanted anything. But he saw Jamie's alarm. He knew that calling the police would result in months of unendurable mockery. Perhaps worse.

He said, 'There's no need for that. We'll be all right.'

He ushered them towards the window. They crouched low, as they might in a building under sniper fire.

Mel said, 'Maybe they'll just go away.'

'Maybe,' said Sam.

On the street, a voice called out.

'Bring out your boy!'

This was followed by muffled laughter.

Jamie said, 'Dad,' and scuttled into Sam's arms. Sam hugged him. He placed the palm of his hand on the crown of Jamie's head.

'Ssshhh,' he said. 'It's all right.'

'What are we going to do?' said Mel.

Jamie pressed himself harder into his father's chest. Sam found Mel's eye and made a furious face that commanded her to silence. She glanced at Jamie and cringed. She clapped a hand across her mouth.

They waited.

Mel lifted the hem of the curtain and peeked out.

She said, 'It's all the Hoopers, I think. About five of them.'

Jamie lifted his face from Sam's chest.

'Is Liam there?'

'Yes, darling,' said Mel. 'Don't worry. It's all right.'

She looked at Sam.

'They're lashed out of their minds. They're staggering all over the place. One of them's pissing in next door's garden. I don't think they know what to do, now they're here.'

Sam wondered if they might soon tire. Perhaps they would simply set off in pursuit of more alcohol. And if they didn't, if they hung around on the street, then perhaps one of the neighbours would call the police. The Merrydown Estate wasn't the kind of area where people waited long before reporting such a breach of the peace. They had property to protect. Sam was surprised to discover a secret contempt for his unseen neighbours.

There was a sound like a cannon. Reverberations rippled along the hallway.

Somebody had kicked the front door.

Outside, there was more laughter, some slow hand-clapping.

Fiercely, Sam kissed the crown of Jamie's head and released him.

Jamie said, 'Where are you *going*?'

'To sort this out,' said Sam.

Mel got to her feet.

'Don't be a fucking idiot.'

'I can't just cower here while they kick the door down.'

'Then call the police.'

'I can't do that.'

'Yes, you can.'

'But what if they kick the door down before the police arrive, Mel?'

Jamie ran to protect his aunt, and be protected by her. All three of them were standing now. It occurred to Sam that, gradually, they were following each other around the room.

Mel said, 'Now you're frightening Jamie.'

There was no answering that.

Jamie said, 'I'm not scared.'

Sam crouched and put his face close to Jamie's. The boy didn't flinch from him and that was good. Sam could smell his night breath, as personal to Jamie as his fingerprints, and more intimate.

'It's all right to be scared,' he said. 'Of course you're scared.'

Somebody kicked the door again.

Somebody else, further away, called Jamie's name.

'Jay-mee . . .'

Sam took Jamie's face in his hands and kissed his forehead, a promise.

The same voice called out Mel's name, the same sing-song tongue breaking the words into syllables

'Yoo-hoo, Mel-an-ie . . .'

Sam recognized the voice. It was Dave Hooper.

Dave Hooper, drunk. Not the tattered, fox-eyed spectre of his worst imaginings.

Mel's temper broke. She stamped to the window, yanked aside the blinds, opened the window and stuck out her head.

'Why don't you just fuck off, Dave Hooper?'

Her derision was met with snuffling male laughter and a couple of half-hearted cheers.

Sam wished she hadn't done it. He knew how easily humiliation could turn into violence. That was the mundane alchemy at the heart of so much misery. But he looked at Mel, arms crossed over her breasts, glowering magisterially from the bedroom window, and he was proud of her too.

He left Jamie with her and closed the door behind him. He took the stairs slowly. With each step, he negotiated with God to provide a police car and a number of uniformed young men and women to bundle the Hoopers, bent and headfirst, into the back of a white van with wire-mesh windows.

But it was Saturday night. God and the police were busy elsewhere.

Somebody kicked the door again. Sam saw it jump in its frame.

Outside, the Hoopers cheered.

Sam knew that doors didn't collapse like they did on television. But his imagination was powerful. He imagined that one more kick would see it sagging broken from its hinges.

He approached the door, gathering pace as he drew near. He could sense the presence of a man on the other side. He could see movements cast in shadow. And he could hear the gravelly scuff of trainers.

In a single, unbroken movement, Sam disengaged the Yale lock and hauled open the door.

There was a man on the doorstep. Jeans and trainers and an Adidas sweater. His back was turned. Perhaps he was seeking his father's approval.

Sam grabbed the man's wrist and twisted it. Then he jerked the hand up between the man's shoulders.

The man screamed and bent double, away from the pain. He smelt of CK1.

Sam marched him towards the gate. His face was set like it was when he took out the rubbish.

Halfway there, he gave Hooper's son a shove that sent him stumbling to his knees on the pavement.

Dave Hooper's eyes were blank. In one hand, he held a can of Stella Artois. He knelt down at his son's side. Then he stood to face Sam.

With the house behind him, and with his son's expectations focused on him, Sam felt buoyed and capable. But he could think of very little that would compel him to take a step further.

Upstairs, Mel switched on the bedroom light. The 100-watt glow erupted behind him. Its beam fell parallel with the garden path and lit the edge of the lawn. It threw Dave Hooper's shadow away from the house and into the road.

Hooper and his sons stood there, ranked and silent. At the edge of the group, Liam looked disengaged and sullen.

Sam made no attempt to move. Neither did Dave Hooper. They stared at each other.

If Sam took another step, he would be attacked. He was big enough to hurt them, he knew that now, with his house and his sister and his son behind him. And if Dave Hooper and his sons hurt Sam badly enough, they'd do time for him. A scrap of life for each blow.

The attention of the neighbours had been drawn to them. Sleepy-faced men and throat-clutching women stood at bedroom windows.

Sam said, 'Just go home.'

Dave Hooper looked up. He looked at Mel, backlit in the bedroom window. Then he looked at Sam.

One of his sons ripped the aerial from Sam's car. Sam didn't mind. The son waved the aerial around for a few seconds, like a conductor's baton. Then he chucked it in next door's garden. The light winked from it as it tumbled and fell. Sam's eyes followed its trajectory. So did Dave Hooper's. It landed silently, on a cushion of lawn in the darkness.

'Stay away from my property,' said Sam.

'And you,' said Dave Hooper. 'You fucking watch yourself. You know what I mean.'

Sam tilted his jaw to show how the threat rolled from him.

There was a perilous, unbalanced moment. Nobody knew what direction to move in.

Then Dave Hooper turned and led his sons towards home.

Still bathed in radiant light, Sam watched them go. Then he went back inside. He stood in the hallway for a few moments, to listen for their singing. But he heard nothing.

13

Sam closed the door and became afraid. It occurred to him that he'd been very foolish. Had there been two men at his door, not one, by now he could be lying in the garden beaten and tooth-less, while the Hoopers tore apart his house.

A sequence of fantasies brought him to a standstill.

When Mel came downstairs with Jamie behind her skirts, Sam was standing with one hand on the lock, staring at the door.

Mel said, 'Are you all right?'

She had to repeat the question.

Sam nodded, slowly.

'Yeah. Fine.'

He snapped back to the present.

'How are *you*? Are you all right?'

'We're fine.'

'And Jamie? How are you, mate?'

Jamie seemed nonchalant. Sam might have been fooled, had he not clung to Mel's heels on the way to the kitchen. Sam turned on the lights and the naked glass bounced their reflections back at them. Their sightlessness, the knowledge that a dark garden lurked behind their bleached reflections, spooked them all simultaneously and, without a word, Sam pulled down the blinds for the first time since they were fitted, rendering the kitchen subtly unfamiliar.

Jamie said, 'Dad? Do you want a cup of tea?'

A cup of tea was the last thing he wanted.

'Yeah,' he said, 'tea would be good.'

'I'll put in extra sugar.'

'Why?'

Jamie shrugged and opened the cutlery drawer.

'I don't know. It's supposed to be good for you.'

Dutifully, he scooped two heaped spoonfuls into the mug and put the kettle on to boil. As the water began to grumble and hiss, he said, 'Do you think they'll come back?'

Sam was lighting a cigarette. He exhaled a long rope of blue smoke.

'No, Jamie. They're not coming back. They were drunk, is all it was. They're just bad losers.'

'How come?'

'Just trust me.'

'But what about Liam?'

'Liam won't touch you. Not any more.'

Jamie looked at him with wide and faithful eyes.

'What did you do?'

Sam's sadness was a physical pain. He wanted to rush over and bury his head in Jamie's hair, to savour the last remnants of little-boy about him.

'Never you mind,' he said.

'Tell me.'

Sam tapped his nose with a forefinger.

'Mel,' said Jamie. 'What did he do?'

'I don't know,' said Mel. 'Don't bother asking me.'

'Tell me,' said Jamie.

But nobody would.

Eventually, Jamie made them all a cup of tea and they sat together at the breakfast bar to drink it. Their excited, relieved conversation died away and they stared into their mugs.

Sam could tell that Mel wanted to talk. He knew she wanted to tell him that it was far from over. Dave Hooper wouldn't be back that night, or the next. But if he chose to, he could make their lives impossible.

Mel had seen it done to others. She'd even joined in jokes about it, down the Cat and Fiddle, when the Hoopers took it upon themselves to drive an incoming Romany family from the estate. The family was multigenerational and large, and had something of a history. They were what the council described as 'difficult to house'.

At the time it had seemed just and hilarious that the Hoopers did what the Council and the police couldn't do, and protected the community from that family of inbreeds and thieves.

Eventually, Jamie fell asleep on the sofa. Mel draped her coat over him. By then, she and Sam had relaxed. They sprawled in exhausted torpor.

There was a lot to say, but neither seemed capable of saying it. They just stared, glassy-eyed, at late-night crap on the TV. Each was waiting, without telling the other, for the telephone to ring.

Shortly before 4 a.m., they roused Jamie just enough to get him up the stairs and they slouched in his wake to their respective beds.

When they woke, it was Sunday. Saturday night might have happened long ago, to different people.

Sam woke refreshed and, before showering or cleaning his teeth, he pulled on a pair of tracksuit trousers and went to get the papers. It was a bright, crisp morning and he decided to walk to the Merrydown arcade. And that's why he didn't notice until he got home that, during the night, somebody had stolen his car.

Eventually, he managed to get inside. But he was still too apoplectic to speak. The house smelt of frying bacon and fresh cigarette smoke. The blinds in the kitchen were still lowered, but Mel had opened the windows behind them, letting in the fresh air. The wooden edge of the blinds clattered on the sun-fluorescent windowsill.

Sam thought he was having a heart attack.

Mel asked him what was wrong.

Wheezing, he pounded on his chest.

'Fuckers,' he said.

Mel's eyebrows drew in. She opened the door and peered

out. Then she went outside and examined the garden, the hedge, the gate. She went back to the house, crossing her arms because it wasn't as warm as it looked. She stared at the house. Then she tilted her head and stared at it again. Finally, arms still crossed, she shrugged and came back inside.

She stood in the hallway, the door open behind her, and said, 'What?'

Logically, Sam couldn't be angry with her.

He said, *They took my fucking car.'*

Mel went outside again.

'Oh yeah,' she said.

'What do you mean?' said Sam. '"Oh yeah"?'

Mel closed the door.

'I hadn't noticed,' she said. 'Isn't that funny?'

'No, it's not fucking *funny*.'

Jamie had been sleeping late. Fuddled and bed-headed, he came downstairs to see what was happening.

He said, 'What's going on?'

'They took the car,' said Sam wearily.

'Fucking hell,' said Jamie.

Mel and Sam looked at him.

'There's no need for that,' said Sam. 'Thank you very much.'

'You do it all the time.'

'Yeah, well. I'm an adult.'

'So?'

Even in more felicitous circumstances, Sam knew this question was unanswerable.

So he said, 'Can we just concentrate on the matter at hand, please?'

Barefoot in pyjama trousers, Jamie opened the door.

'What are you doing?' said Sam.

'Looking.'

'Looking at what? The car's not there.'

Jamie stuck his tongue into his lower lip.

'Duh,' he said. 'Obviously, Einstein.'

'Then what are you looking *at*?'

Jamie closed the door.

'Just checking.'

Sam could almost hear the arteries popping in his head.

'Just checking *what*?'

Jamie gave him a mystified look.

'Well, *I* don't know, do I?'

Sam turned to Mel for support and found none.

She said, 'It's no good shouting at Jamie. He didn't nick your bloody car.'

'I'm not shouting.'

'I think you'll find you are.'

'Jesus,' he said. 'Who can blame me?'

'Oh, come on,' said Mel. 'Stop being such a drama queen. You got off lightly.'

'Lightly how, exactly?'

'I don't know. They could've put bricks through the windows. They could've torched the place. Don't think they're not capable of that. All they were doing was giving you the finger. Blowing you a raspberry. Let them get on with it. Get a new car.'

'I just got *that* one!'

'Sam, it's only a car. You don't even *like* cars. You'd rather get the bus so you can have a pint on the way home.'

'That's not the point.'

'Then what is?'

He kicked the skirting board and mumbled something outraged and defeated.

'Look,' said Mel, 'it was a piece of shit. You'd've had to replace it by Christmas, anyway. If it lasted that long.'

'It's a good car!'

'It's a pig. Call the police, get it registered as a crime, claim the insurance. The police are too busy to go looking for it. They know, and you know and I know, it's burnt out round the back of Farmer Hazel's fields somewhere. So make a claim and put the money towards a better car. And that's that. All over. Nobody's hurt and everyone's happy.'

'Dad,' said Jamie.

'What?'

'Can we get a Chrysler PT Cruiser?'

Mel put her head on one side.

'Is that the one that looks like a taxi?'

'Whatever,' said Jamie. 'Dad,' he said. 'Can we?'

'We'll see,' said Sam, meaning no.

'Yeah,' said Jamie, 'but *can* we?'

'We'll see,' said Sam, still meaning no.

'Cool,' said Jamie, and raced upstairs on the balls of his bare feet.

Disconsolate, Sam followed Mel into the kitchen. He leant on the worktop and took a can of Coke from the thin blue carrier bag he was still carrying. He opened it and took a series of long swigs.

Mel put the bacon back on the heat. Next to her was a plate stacked with pre-buttered white bread. With her back to him, she said, 'Buy him the car.'

Sam hissed urgently in her direction.

'Christ,' he said. 'Be quiet. He might hear you.'

'I don't care if he does. Buy him the car.'

'Mel, those things cost fifteen grand without extras. I haven't got fifteen grand to throw round on a fucking Batmobile.'

'Yes, you have.'

This, the second unanswerable statement of the morning.

Huffily, he said, 'You don't buy your son's love.'

'Whatever,' said Mel. She passed over a small plate on which there weebled three perfect tomatoes. She asked him to slice them. She made sure he used a serrated knife in the way their mother had taught them, a few miles away and many years before.

Sam took his sandwich to the breakfast bar and called the police. The officer he spoke to didn't sound particularly alarmed by this malfeasance. He told Sam they'd send some officers round.

Sam asked him, 'When, exactly?'

He was told, with some emphasis: 'As soon as possible.'

They came round late in the evening and stayed for about six minutes.

Sam was frustrated that nobody seemed to care about his car and he let the police officers know it. They stared at him impassively. In the heat of anger, Sam told them he knew the thieves. Mel shot him a warning glance. But the police officers still weren't interested. One of them said, 'And do you have any evidence to that effect?'

'Yes,' said Sam. 'A stolen car.'

A slow, weary blink.

'Did you see the car being stolen – in which case we'll have to take an immediate statement? Or did you perhaps take some photographs? Or better still, did you video the thief as he went about his business?'

The officer's frosty, bored eyes told him that of course he hadn't, because he was an idiot. The police officer's frosty, bored eyes had seen a lot, and they would forget Sam Greene and his stupidity the minute the door closed behind them.

On a matter of abstract principle, Mel had no love for the police force. But it was she, apologetically, who showed them out.

Sam sat on the sofa, quietly wrathful. He decided that, to prove a point, he would buy the Chrysler. He wasn't altogether sure what point he was making. Nor was he sure to whom he was making it. But the decision provided him with immediate, grim satisfaction, as at an unpleasant job well done, and he went to bed strangely content.

To maintain the impulse, he used the Internet to locate the nearest showroom the next morning and, during his lunch-hour, he paid it a visit. He wandered round with his arms clasped regally at the small of his back.

Despite giving every pink-eyed impression that he was of Anglo-Saxon stock, the youthful salesman had the perfect post-colonial name of Monty Cashmiri. Sam liked Monty for his cordial desperation to close a sale, even at lunchtime on a Monday.

He told Monty what he was looking for and Monty led him to a Chrysler PT Cruiser that stood resplendent on a low, white plinth. Monty caressed its shining Batmobile curves and confided in Sam that he was able to offer him preferential finance. Sam was interested. He sat at a pale wood desk opposite Monty, while Monty tapped on a filthy keyboard that seemed at odds with the otherwise gleaming surroundings.

Perhaps stupidly, Sam wished he'd worn better shoes and trousers.

During that moment, looking down at his unsatisfactory footwear, it occurred to him that he was actually going to buy this car, in part because he liked Monty and didn't want to disappoint him. He accepted the proffered sheaf of A4 print-outs that detailed the various terms offered, and stuffed them in the teacher's briefcase with the broken clasp.

He thanked Monty. Monty looked moist-eyed and hopeful.

Sam paused at the sliding glass door by the glass showroom walls and turned to wave a cheery goodbye. Then he wandered through the ranked muzzles of second-hand cars in the forecourt, waxed and polished and each priced as a once-in-a-lifetime deal. At the bus stop, he unfolded his newspaper and fought with the wind to be permitted to read it.

The rubbery imprint of a trainer sole was clearly visible just below the lock on the front door of the house on Balaarat Street. Last night, he'd considered presenting it to the police as corroborating evidence. But then the police would ask him why a car-thief should try to kick down his front door. So he decided against it.

Passing it now, he realized the perfect, unsmeared imprint would be there for ever. Neither he nor Jamie – and still less Mel – would ever get round to cleaning it off. This thought filled him with a strange, summery contentment. Somehow, the slight damage had familiarized the house. He all but patted the doorframe as he entered.

In the front room he found Anna, who he'd met in the Cat and Fiddle. Her legs were crossed, one elbow rested on her knee. In her hand was a cigarette. Mid-laughter, she and Mel looked up and paused when he entered. He got the impression he was being talked about.

He said hello to Anna and took a cigarette from Mel's pack. He sat on the floor with his back to the sofa.

He said, 'Where's Jamie?'

'Out,' said Mel.

'Who with?'

'Stuart.'

She didn't add *of course*, because she didn't need to.

Mel went to the kitchen to open a bottle of wine. It seemed obvious that she wanted Sam to flirt with Anna, but he didn't know how. While Mel was gone, he asked Anna a few carefully weighted questions. She worked for an insurance company down town. It was boring, but it was all right. She was about to tell him how she'd met Mel – her eyes had narrowed to crinkles at the edge and she was smiling as at some memory she had yet to articulate – when Mel came back in.

'What?' Mel said.

'Nothing,' said Anna.

Mel topped up Anna's glass.

'What?' she said again.

Sam stood.

He said, 'We were talking about you, Melanie. Not *to* you.'

He went up to take a shower and change his clothes. He could hear Mel and Anna laughing about something he hoped had nothing to do with him. But he thought it probably did.

Sam had to wait some weeks before the Chrysler was delivered, so his insurance company arranged a courtesy car. It arrived on Tuesday, a blue Honda that had been valeted to within an inch of its life.

On Wednesday, it was Sam's birthday.

Mel and Jamie got up early to cook him a birthday breakfast, which they took up to him on a tray. Two fried eggs, two sausages, black pudding, bacon and two fried slices. His mouth flooded at its hot, oily crumble.

They sat with him while he ate, then presented him with gifts. Mel had bought him a CD and Jamie gave him a Swatch with a transparent face that showed the clockwork mechanism.

Sam put on the watch and turned his wrist this way and that, examining it under the dim morning light.

Mel said, 'Jamie's been saving up.'

'I love it,' Sam told her, for Jamie's benefit. 'I needed a new watch.'

'Yeah,' said Jamie. 'The old one was a bit naff.'

Sam smiled to hide the silly hurt he felt on his watch's behalf. He'd owned it for so long – and his father had owned it for so long before that – that it had developed a soul, like a much-loved toy.

He said, 'This one is much better.'

Nobody at work knew it was his birthday, but then nobody at work was speaking to him. He didn't really care. The Skinhead who shouted 'England!' when he came in was unusually quiet, moving chairs to follow the fall of shadow in the ward. Kenny and Byron were playing Happy Families. Everyone else was quiet, as if something embarrassing had just happened. But nothing had. For several weeks, there had been no incidents on the ward. Probably one was brewing. But it was a quiet day, without a single call put in to Ted Bone from Mick Jagger, the Pope or Kris Kristofferson.

He left on time (to the rolling of eyes) and caught the bus home.

Mel had told him to expect a birthday dinner. He opened the door to find her and Jamie waiting for him in the hallway. Mel was holding his suit, which had been dry-cleaned and was still wrapped in polythene. Jamie held a new shirt, still wrapped.

He stood in the hallway with the door open.

'What's going on?'

Mel linked arms with Jamie.

'You've got a date.'

Sam started to laugh. He stopped himself.

'A what?'

'A date.'

'What are you talking about?'

'Anna's taking you to dinner,' said Mel.

Jamie rushed forward and stuffed the new shirt into Sam's hand.

'Do you like it? We chose it.'

Sam examined the shirt.

'Well,' he said. 'It's very *blue*.'

'It'll match your eyes,' said Mel.

'Jesus,' he said. 'I don't want things to match my *eyes*. What do you want me to look like?'

He thought this might sound illogical, so he added: ' I can't go on a date.'

'Why not?'

'I don't even know this woman.'

'That's what dates are for.'

'Duh,' said Jamie.

'Look,' said Mel. 'She's pretty. She's single. She likes you.'

'She's *paying*,' said Jamie.

'What's to worry about?' said Mel. 'We've organized everything. All right? It's no big deal. Anna's a grown-up. She's met bigger and uglier men than you, believe me. She won't bite.'

He held up the shirt, like evidence in a courtroom.

'I can't do this,' he said.

'You'd bloody better,' said Mel. 'We've been planning it for weeks.'

She nudged Jamie's shoulder.

'Haven't we?'

'Yes,' said Jamie.

Sam looked at them.

'Where are we going?'

'Some place called Ottavio. In town. Anna's choice.'

His shoulders sagged.

'OK,' he said, and back-kicked the door closed. He ambled upstairs to the sound of cheering.

In the bathroom, new toiletries had been laid out for him. To each was adhered a handwritten sticky yellow label. A new can of shaving foam and a new razor stood on the sink, labelled USE ME!

Mel came in to see him when he was dressing. He sat on the edge of his bed, drying off his feet with a sprinkle of her talcum powder. Mel leant against the door and crossed her arms.

She said, 'He's downstairs, trying to iron your shirt.'

Sam pulled on his socks. Dressed only in these and boxer shorts, he examined himself in the mirror: muscular, solid of belly. Hair too long, thinning at the crown.

'The labels were his idea,' said Mel.

Sam gathered his hair in a short, punishing ponytail that stretched and narrowed his eyes. When he let the hair go, his face took a second too long to settle properly over his skull. He found its liquidity disturbing.

He tested the muscles in his arms.

'Is he all right?'

Mel sat on the bed.

'He's getting there.'

'Has he been to school?'

Mel shrugged.

'What shoes are you going to wear?'

'I don't know. The loafers, do you think? Or the lace-ups?'

'How can I put it? Not the loafers.'

He opened the wardrobe. His lace-up shoes, long unworn, waited there, lustrous. A sticky label adhered to one toe. It read WEAR ME.

'He hid the other pair,' said Mel. 'Just in case.'

Sam removed the shoes. Jamie had made a good job of polishing them. He set them parallel with the bed and began to free the suit of the dry-cleaner's polythene. He pulled on the trousers.

'Do you think he'll be all right?'

Mel had rested one foot on the opposite knee and was minutely examining her big toenail.

'What about?'

'Tonight.'

'You're going to dinner,' she said. 'Not getting married.'

He experimented with the trousers' fastening and concluded that he would not be requiring a belt that evening.

'I know,' he said. 'But you know how it is. Kids see things differently.'

'He's not a kid. And put some gel in your hair.'

'Do you think?'

'Yes. Come here.'

She stood, walked over to him, and produced a comb which she ran haltingly and painfully through his hair.

'Ow,' he said.

She left the room to get some hair gel. She returned with it smeared over both hands and rubbed it vigorously into his hair. For a few seconds, he looked like a mad scientist. Then the hair wilted.

'The best thing you can do for him,' she said, 'is enjoy yourself. He worries about you.'

He looked over his shoulder.

'Does he?'

This had never occurred to him.

'Duh,' said Mel, and went to get a hair-dryer.

Jamie was waiting for him at the foot of the stairs, holding up the poorly ironed shirt. Sunlight shone through it as if through stained glass. Sam took the shirt and thanked Jamie as he buttoned himself into it. Mel helped him into the suit jacket and told him to leave the lowest button undone.

While all three of them stood in the hallway, admiring him, the minicab arrived.

He arrived late for 8.00 p.m., and learnt that Mel had lied about the time of the reservation. It was for 8.30.

He was irked and touched that she knew him so well.

Ottavio was an Italian restaurant of blonde wood and crisp white linen. The waiters wore wine-red shirts and dove-grey waistcoats.

Sam lit a cigarette and scanned the drinks menu. He decided to order a Martini. He didn't particularly like them – to his cigarette-brutalized palate, they tasted like nothing so much as a bucket of cold, neat gin – but he wished to cultivate at least the aura of proximate sophistication. He lingered over the drink and lined his stomach with a few olives.

Exercising a complex psychological prerogative, Anna arrived at 8.45 p.m. Sam looked up when the door opened. She wore an ankle-length leather coat that added a degree of theatricality to her entrance. Her hair – he thought – was freshly cut, softer and combed forward round the hairline. She smiled hello as the waiter took the coat.

He admired the way she avoided the potential awkwardness of greeting (to kiss or not to kiss?) simply by taking the seat opposite him, crossing her legs and popping an olive in her mouth.

He said, 'Well, you look great.'

She looked down, brushed something from her chest.

'Thank you.'

She reached forward and popped another olive into her mouth.

'And you look very smart.'

Without knowing it, he mirrored her, brushing at his lapel with his fingertips.

He said, 'I can't accept any praise. This is all Mel's doing.'

Anna said, 'Isn't it just?' and she laughed and leant forward and opened her handbag, producing a fresh pack of menthol cigarettes.

'Do you mind?'

'Not at all.'

She broke the seal with a painted nail and lit the cigarette with a gold lighter, took one puff, then tapped it on the edge of the ashtray.

The waiter arrived at their table. Sam left the half-drunk Martini and followed her into the restaurant. It was busy enough. The waiters made elaborate entrances and flouncing exits via the swinging door to the kitchen. To this carnival the huddled customers seemed wholly oblivious.

After they'd been seated (the waiter's fussing put Sam on edge), there followed a short debate concerning who should choose the wine; Anna and Sam batting the burgundy leatherette wine-list back and forth between them. Eventually, Sam accepted responsibility. Once that was done, he could begin to relax. He could feel the Martini, warm in his blood.

He unfolded the crisp napkin on his lap.

He said, 'This isn't the kind of place I'd expect to find somebody who drinks in the Cat and Fiddle.'

She laughed and gave him a look. She told him she didn't go there often. She owned a small apartment in the dockland redevelopment. But her mother lived round the corner from Mel, and Anna had made a point of keeping in touch with Mel and two or three other schoolfriends. It was important to maintain the kind of friendship they were now too old to originate.

She was interrupted by the arrival of the wine. Sam endured the tasting ritual ('It's fine, thank you'), then sat back, exasperated, as the waiter made a meal of his expertise in pouring. Anna's glass first.

Sam watched him hurry away.

'It's weird,' he said, 'I don't think I remember you from school.'

'You must have been blind.'

'Did you look very different?'

'Come on,' she said. 'How many black kids were even *at* our school?'

He blushed and looked away, feeling in some way caught out.

She laughed.

Sam ran his forefinger round the rim of his wine glass.

He said, ' I don't know. You forget so much. Do you know what I mean? Year by year, the cast of thousands diminishes, until all you can remember is a few names. Does that sound stupid?'

She smiled, more gently.

'I know what you mean,' she said.

The starters arrived. They fell silent for a few moments, making nodding, appreciative faces across the table.

Then Sam said, 'So what do you do, exactly?'

She pointed her fork at him.

'I think I told you; I'm in insurance. But I don't want to talk about it, because it's very boring.'

'I'm sure it's not.'

'To me, no. To you, yes.'

'How can you be sure?'

'Do statistics interest you?'

'Not conspicuously.'

'Well, statistics are my job.' She speared limp asparagus. 'You see my dilemma.'

He put down his fork, dabbed at the corner of his mouth with the napkin and placed it again in his lap.

'But you must have lots of stories about fraudulent claims, that kind of thing.'

'Not my department, I'm afraid. And anyway – you're the one with the interesting job.'

'Not really.'

'Oh, come on.'

He smiled.

'The mentally ill aren't as much fun as they're cracked up to be. Especially when they're taking their medication.'

'But you must have seen a few things in your time.'

'I'll give you that,' he said. 'But not the kind of thing you'd really want to talk about over dinner.'

'You see? Now I'm intrigued.'

'All right,' he said. 'I once had to restrain a young man who was well into the process of castrating himself with a blade he took from a safety razor.'

Anna made a gagging sound.

'All right,' she said. 'I'm not intrigued any more.'

He laid his hands flat on the table.

He said, 'Look, I'm really sorry.'

She flapped her hand at her mouth.

'That's all right,' she said. 'Honestly. I asked for it.'

He picked up the fallen napkin and flattened it on his lap.

To ease his discomfort, she said, 'In a way, I deal with mad people too.'

'How so?'

'Everyday madness,' she said. 'The psychology of risk. People tend to exaggerate tiny little risks, and to minimize great big, whopping ones.'

'Such as?'

'Such as, following a train crash, the death toll increases on the roads. People are freaked out by the train crash, which is a rare occurrence and unlikely to happen again any time soon. More people die every day on British roads than die annually on the railways. But rail crashes are newsworthy. After a crash, nervous passengers take to the roads. The roads are a great deal more dangerous than the railways. And the more congested the roads are, the more dangerous they are. Simple really. But people don't think about it like that.'

'No,' said Sam.

'See?' she said. 'You're bored.'

'Not in the slightest.'

'People worry about the rising crime rate,' said Anna, 'but they continue to smoke. Or they worry about what pesticides are going to do to them, and continue to eat junk food, and fail to take any exercise.'

'And that affects the way your industry operates?'

'Not always directly. But, of course, it's always preferable – for us – to insure against the unlikely.'

'That's pretty cynical.'

'It's a job.'

He said, 'You see, I think you're underestimating people. People understand things better than your industry gives them credit for.'

Anna bit her lower lip and smiled at him.

She laid down her cutlery.

She said, 'During the OJ Simpson trial, the defence team employed a man called Alan Dershowitz to act as consultant. In an article in the LA Times, he argued that fewer than one in a thousand women who are abused by their spouse go on to be killed by them. So it was a thousand to one against that OJ did it. This seems to have impacted on the case.'

He felt he was being effortlessly outmanoeuvred.

'That seems fair enough,' he said. 'If it's true.'

'Aha,' she said. 'You see? That's the problem. It *is* true. But it's also true that, should a woman who has been spousally abused later be murdered, the chances that her spouse is the murderer is way in excess of eighty per cent. Based simply on statistical patterns, there was enough evidence to investigate

Simpson, if not actually to convict him. But the jury lacked the insight to see through Dershowitz's creative use of statistical evidence. And so did the prosecution.'

'Blimey,' said Sam. 'You should've been a lawyer.'

'I know.'

'Why aren't you?'

'I don't have a degree.'

He said, 'Oh fuck. Excuse me. I assumed—'

'People do. But no. I started at the company as a trainee. I was sixteen, straight from O-levels. I worked my way up.'

'Then it's quite an achievement.'

'I worked hard.'

He looked at her with theatrical suspicion.

'So what do you actually do?'

'I told you,' she said. 'I'm in insurance.'

'In what way?'

'In a very boring way.'

'Why do I think that's not true?'

She put an elbow on the table and pointed the fork at him again.

'I don't know,' she said. 'Why do you think that's not true?'

He laughed and scratched an eyebrow and saw that he would get nowhere. He chased a mushroom round his plate, ate it, then laid down his fork with a bright clatter.

He said, 'Anyway, it's good to talk to another Robinwood escapee.'

'Isn't it?'

Anna raised her glass.

'Happy Birthday,' she said.

He clinked his glass against hers.

'It is,' he said, and she glanced away, perhaps pleased.

Later, the taxi stopped outside the house and he thanked her and kissed her chastely on the cheek. She squeezed his hand. He stood on the pavement, his tie loose at his throat, as the cab pulled away, watching to see if she turned in her seat. But she didn't.

He searched for his keys and quietly let himself in.

Mel and Jamie were waiting up. He flopped in an armchair and kicked off his shoes.

They said, '*Well*?'

Sam lit a cigarette.

'It was good,' he said. 'It was good.'

Something in his tone caused Mel and Jamie to exchange a glance. Jamie yawned and stretched and said he was going to bed. As he passed, he ruffled Sam's hair.

He said, 'Nice one, Loverboy.'

Sam swiped at his bony arse with the back of his hand.

'Bed,' he said.

Mel offered to make him a coffee, which was a coded instruction to tell her about the evening in forensic detail. He thanked her, and yawned into his fist. Waiting for the coffee, he closed his eyes for a second.

He was surprised, when he opened them again, to see Justine stood in the corner behind the television. Next to her was a gaunt old man he'd never seen before.

Ignoring the old man, he told Justine, 'It was only dinner. It was nothing.'

But her fixed expression, neither happy nor sad, didn't change.

Sam nodded at the old man.

'Who's this?' he said.

'He lives here,' said Justine.

Sam woke.

The house was dark. There was a cup of cold coffee on the floor next to him. At some point, Mel must have gone to bed, having decided that he was too deeply asleep to bother waking.

14

The maudlin, guilty happiness that followed Sam's first date for twenty years was a kind of contentment, and it saw him through to the weekend. He was on earlies. He got home late on Sunday afternoon to find Mel unsteady on her feet. He wondered if she'd been drinking all afternoon, alone.

He hoped not. A few minutes later, Janet rang the doorbell. Mel hugged her and planted a smacking kiss on each cheek.

Shortly before 9 p.m., the bell rang again. The ring had a peculiar, hesitant quality that immediately worried him. He glanced at his wristwatch, then he put down his drink and went to the door. He opened it to a stranger – a middle-aged man, tidy in slacks, shirt and windcheater. He wore bifocals that made the lower half of his eyes bulge and oscillate like poaching eggs.

'Mr Greene?'

'Yes,' said Sam.

The man didn't look like a policeman.

The man swallowed.

He said, 'It's Jamie.'

The world went liquid beneath Sam's feet.

'What about him? Is he all right?'

The man put out a soft, calming hand that hung uncertainly in the air.

'He's *fine*. Don't worry. He's fine. But he's in Casualty.'

Sam's voice broke.

'Jesus Christ,' he said. 'What happened? Why didn't someone call?'

'We tried. There was no answer.'

He was about to tell this idiot (whose name he still didn't know – he wondered if that was as odd as it felt) quite how ridiculous that was. They'd been home all evening. Then he remembered that his landline had been unplugged for days now and his mobile was likely to be turned off in his bag.

He said, 'Who are you?'

'Martin Ballard.'

He seemed puzzled by Sam's lack of response.

'Stuart's dad,' he said.

Sam thought he was going to vomit.

He said, 'My God.'

'Look,' said Martin Ballard. 'Really. He's all right. There was a dog.'

He read Sam's expression and saw that he was doing no good.

He said, 'Why don't you go and get your coat? I'll explain on the way.'

Numb, as if watching himself from some exterior vantage point, Sam stuck his head round the living-room door. He told Mel not to worry, but there'd been some trouble. Jamie was all right, but he was in hospital.

Two silent women looking at him in shock.

'Pardon?' said Mel.

Sam was already buttoning his coat. He realized he'd been garbling, and repeated himself, more slowly this time. His hands fumbled with the buttons, as Jamie's frightened hands had fumbled with his shoe-laces that fearful Saturday night.

Sam didn't want to cry.

He faced Mel with his unseasonal coat buttoned up incorrectly.

He said, 'He's all right. He's in Casualty.'

Mel stood.

'Do you want me to come?'

'No. Stay here. I don't want to . . .' he scowled, and looked for an excuse. 'I don't want to cause a fuss. It might frighten him. Do you know what I mean?'

Apparently she did, which was good because he wasn't sure that he did. He told her not to worry, they'd be home later that evening, he was sure, and he closed the door behind him.

Martin Ballard was waiting in the garden, examining the edge of the lawn with the heel of his shoe and twirling his car keys round his index finger.

Sam saw that Ballard's car, a Vauxhall Astra estate, was double-parked with its hazard lights blinking. This connotation of urgency made his legs go weaker still. But he made it to the passenger seat.

Ballard belted himself behind the wheel. For a moment there was a businesslike silence between them. Then Ballard turned the key in the ignition, looked over his shoulder to reverse, and told Sam not to worry. They were both all right.

'Both?' said Sam.

'Stuart,' said Martin Ballard.

'Oh, Jesus. I didn't even ask. I'm so sorry.'

'It's all come as a shock, probably,' said Ballard.

He was possibly the most careful, law-abiding driver with whom Sam had ever shared a car. At the junction with the main road, they pulled into the sparse traffic, accompanied only by the sound of the blinking indicator lights.

Ballard said, 'Stuart's fine.'

He nudged the brakes, adjusting the distance between him and the car in front.

'Or he will be. He's a bit upset and a bit frightened, but there's no real harm done.'

The journey was short and interminable. They had to circle the car park three or four times, and finally parked on the street, at a meter. They had no change between them. Sam jogged over the road and bought a pack of cigarettes from a corner shop. He handed over a twenty-pound note, asked for the change in one-pound coins and crossed the road with fourteen of them bulging in his pocket.

He overfed the meter, then followed Ballard into the hospital grounds and followed the signs for *Accident and Emergency*. Perhaps two dozen people were scattered over the waiting room, reclining variously in the fixed seating. There was a group of young men in muddy sports gear, a few solitary old people, funereal and silent, an Arabic family in the far corner by the Coke machine, and a newborn baby in its mother's arms. A happy toddler with white-blonde, blood-encrusted hair happily played call-and-response with a mad, dreadlocked tramp whose body was lost in infinite layers of greasy, grey-black clothing. A war-torn TV was bracketed in one high corner. Nurses came and went, unhurried. Never the same nurse twice.

Sam went to the desk and gave them Jamie's name. He was directed to a curtained cubicle some way down a faded green corridor. Sam thanked Ballard.

Ballard gave him a key-jangling thumbs-up and an encouraging smile, and shook his hand.

Once Sam was through the doors, he had to double-check with a nurse which was the correct cubicle. There were so many of them. They varied only in the quantity and ethnicity of attending, anxious relatives.

The young nurse diverted himself to show Sam where he should be going. Sam found the curtained-off cubicle and paused, as he might before entering the bathroom, knowing Jamie was in there.

He said, 'Knock, knock.'

He cringed.

'Come in,' said Jamie.

Sam pulled the curtain aside. He was reminded of camping, long ago, and the young child's fear of cattle.

Jamie lay propped on a number of pillows. His jeans had been cut away. His leg was dressed from knee to hip. The frayed end of the cut-off jeans was crusty with blood. Jamie's forearm and right hand were heavily bandaged. There was a bloody dressing on his forehead and a drip fed into his good arm.

Sam felt the world telescope away. He was balanced on a high building.

He wanted to say something, so he smiled encouragingly, but the smile wavered crazily at the corners.

Jamie was pale and there were violet half-moons beneath his eyes.

He wanted his father, but he was embarrassed by the presence of the helpful nurse.

He smiled.

'All right, Dad?'

Sam took the chair next to the bed. He thought of Jamie's baby skin, plump and butterscotch. The unquestioning singularity of his tiny devotion to his mother and father. The absolute knowledge that they would always protect him.

He took Jamie's hand and pressed it to his face, kissing the palm.

The nurse saw the moment and quietly excused himself.

Perhaps because Easter was in the air, Jamie and Stuart had decided to put their mountain bikes to the test. They cycled over the fields and through Robinwood, then on to the network of muddy tracks and gullies that ran between Farmer Hazel's land and the Robinwood Estate.

Later, Sam learnt that Martin Ballard was an amateur local historian. Ballard told him that the land which in the local imagination belonged to Farmer Hazel, now had several owners. But a Farmer Hazel had existed; in fact, generations of them had. The last of them, Jermyn Hazel, died in 1962, aged eighty-five, ten years after his long-delayed retirement. His widow promptly sold the land. So Farmer Hazel had been a spook even when Sam was a child.

The network of muddy tracks at the edge of Robinwood were a liminal territory. The miry lanes were littered with crushed lager tins and cider bottles and drug paraphernalia. There were used condoms and shit-smeared underwear. There were single shoes and rain-swollen pornographic magazines, distended to a semi-fungal state. There were the rusted-out remains of cars whose carcasses were filled with rotting leaves and stagnant water in which rippled teeming millions of mosquito larvae. These cars were never removed. They crumbled into red soil. Items of discarded clothing, rotted and beyond filthy, hung from low branches and flapped like defeated banners. There were bedframes and fridges and freezer cabinets. There was broken glass and the skeletal remains of motorcycles. Concealed by long grass and low hedgerows, snarling at the sky, were the corpses of foxes and badgers, unzipped from the throat and stuffed with maggots as if with rice.

Sam and his friends had played there as children, if played was the right word. In that ownerless borderzone, their behaviour had been temporarily and experimentally feral. They had done things they would otherwise never have dared.

Jamie and Stuart had apparently gone in search of Sam's stolen car, although Sam doubted that any serious effort had been made to locate it. The boys were thirsty for the kind of adventure to be had upon the wasteland between Farmer Hazel's fields and the Robinwood Estate, and they simply required a mission to justify it. It was possible that Jamie's stolen birthright (as it had become, for the purposes of the afternoon) might be discovered, wheelless but serviceable, and returned to his father in a symbolic act of manhood. But that wasn't likely. The object of the quest was the quest itself.

For several hours, the two boys explored the lanes. Once in a while, they stopped off to perform stunts from the knolls and hillocks, or raced down steep embankments into great, brown puddles. They had discovered much incidental treasure: Jamie had come across an ancient, sodden copy of *Moby Dick*, which he had stashed in his rucksack as a possible first edition. Stuart had found a watch they thought might be a Rolex. They had intended to take it down town on Saturday, to get it valued.

Finally, wearily, they cycled back towards Robinwood, taking the main track between a field of rape and a breeze-block wall. By way of a collapsed and sagging chainlink fence, the track led to a gap in the wall. The gap led to a cul-de-sac of garages of the kind that had been incorporated into the estate by forward-thinking, mistaken architects, a generation before.

Jamie hoisted the bike on to his shoulder and manoeuvred it through the gap. He saw a car propped up on oily blocks, the remains of an old Capri. It had no wheels and the arched cavities were black with grease. It made for an ugly spectacle and was therefore of some interest. Jamie propped his bike against a garage door and waited for Stuart, who was not so lithe and whose bike was heavier.

Beneath the car there protruded a pair of dirty blue jeans and oily Nikes. Tethered to its dented bumper was a muscular tan mongrel.

It swivelled its blunt snout in Jamie's direction and regarded him through tiny, idiot's eyes.

Nervously, Jamie remounted.

As he watched, the man freed himself from beneath the car. He was Craig Hooper. On Saturday night, he had tried to kick down Jamie's front door.

Jamie considered the wisdom of heading back the way they'd come. But Stuart had seen Craig Hooper too, and he was already astride his mud-splattered mountain bike.

With a flurry of hand movements, Stuart indicated to Jamie that it was best to keep silent and cycle past as fast as they could. The car was several metres away. It might be possible to gather enough speed to pass Craig Hooper without him even seeing Jamie, let alone recognizing him.

To Jamie, this sounded dishonourable. But he knew it was stupid to face Craig Hooper, who was at least eighteen and therefore a godlike and indestructible force. So he scanned the glass-sparkling concrete ground and gathered in his right hand a small, kidney-shaped pebble. He nodded that Stuart should go first, which he did with relief and without complaint, wobbling uncertainly at first on his oversized bicycle.

Craig Hooper was smearing his hands clean on his chest when Stuart passed him, a half-noticed blur. Craig Hooper was at an age when young boys are beneath contempt and all-but invisible.

Jamie settled his foot on the pedal and kicked off.

Stuart was right. By the time Jamie reached Craig Hooper, he had gathered some momentum.

Speeding past, he called out one word –

Wanker!

and threw the stone.

Hooper looked up. The stone hit him above the right eye. He fell back. His trousers caught on the Capri's loose bumper, which ripped free of its rusty housing.

This freed the dog. It set off in immediate, silent pursuit of Jamie.

All this Jamie knew because he glanced over his shoulder without reducing his speed. Because he was doing this, his front wheel hit the kerb and he was thrown, head-first, over the handlebars.

The impact smashed the wind from him. Before he could get up, the dog was upon him.

Jamie punched it.

It bit his hand.

That hurt so much, Jamie could *hear* it.

Jamie used his bodyweight to throw the dog from him. It scrabbled away, nails scratching on the concrete. Then it rounded to attack again. Craig Hooper was calling its name:

'Bronson! Bronson!'

But the dog had Jamie's blood on its tongue and in its hot throat.

As Jamie reached for his toppled bike, Craig Hooper ran towards them. One hand cupped his bleeding forehead. He was still calling the dog's name. There was panic in his voice.

Jamie's bike grew complex in his hands. He looked up, struggling with the handlebars, and saw that Stuart had turned and was cycling back towards him. In one hand, Stuart waved a wrist-thick branch. Stuart braked behind the dog. He steadied himself on one foot and brought the branch down, across the dog's spine. The dog yelped, perhaps in surprise. It turned, sinuously, and bit Stuart's leg.

Jamie was close enough to kick it. He aimed for its swollen testicles and instead punted it in the taut, pink stomach. The dog yelped, in pain this time. It took a moment to reorientate itself. In his haste, Jamie was unable to mount the bike. He swung one leg over the saddle and lost his footing. The bike slipped from under him. The dog bit into his thigh and worried the flesh like a rubber bone.

Jamie fell. The bike was beneath him. One leg was twisted beneath it. The dog was on top of him. He grabbed its collar to keep its jaws from his face. Its breath stank. Its snout flashed like a camera.

Finally, Craig Hooper's hand closed on the dog's collar. He lifted it, kicking and writhing, into the air. Craig Hooper was screaming at them to 'fuck off, fuck *off*' while the dog bent and curled and snapped its jaws and barked and snarled, three feet above the ground.

Jamie righted the bike and mounted it, successfully this time. He saw that Stuart was waiting on the nearest corner.

Jamie would never have believed it was possible to cycle so quickly. He seemed without weight and of infinite velocity, the bike skimming the surface of the earth like something devoid of friction.

They discarded the bikes in the Ballards' driveway. Stuart raced to the front door. Tears came with its familiar scent. He cried out: '*Mummy!*'

(Jamie had promised never to tell anyone, but he told Sam. They exchanged a look, and giggled.)

Mrs Ballard pressed a clean towel to Jamie's thigh, giving him a glimpse down her blouse and a head of her perfume. He thought she might detonate with repressed panic before the ambulance arrived.

The sound of its sirens brought some relief. Mrs Ballard and Stuart rode in the ambulance with Jamie. Stuart was given a dressing to press to his own wound, which seemed almost desultory compared to the great level of care and attention the paramedics paid to Jamie.

'There's like a big vein in the thigh?' Jamie told Sam. 'Apparently, if the dog had bitten the vein I might have bled to death.'

He marked a tiny measure between thumb and forefinger.

'It was this close,' he said.

Sam exhaled, whistling through his teeth.

'How many stitches?'

Jamie looked up at the female nurse who'd come in to change his drip.

'About sixty,' she said. 'In the thigh. After the wound was cleaned.'

'Sixty?'

'And twenty more in Jamie's arm and wrist. And a couple on his forehead, where he banged it.'

She tugged Jamie's earlobe and said, 'He's been in the wars.'

Jamie smiled up at her, subservient and proud.

Sam asked if he might have a word with her in private. He followed her from the cubicle. She told him that, yes, there would be some scarring. The bites were quite serious, and it was in the nature of such injuries that the flesh was ragged and torn at the edges, and difficult to stitch cleanly. But there'd been no real muscle damage and the scarring might not be as bad as Sam was expecting – modern colloid treatments had reduced the kind of permanent disfigurements that once had been common. Jamie was lucky to have suffered no concussion, despite giving himself a fair old whack on the head. She'd seen boys of his age killed by less serious tumbles. The worst of it was, he'd lost a lot of blood. He'd been fortunate to get to the Ballards' house without passing out, and more fortunate that Mrs Ballard had known how to fashion a tourniquet. It was she who'd done most to ensure that Jamie's injuries didn't have more serious consequences.

While she spoke, Sam cupped a hand over his mouth and nodded.

She asked if he'd like to speak to a doctor. He said no, and thanked her, then he put his head through the gap in the curtains round Jamie's cubicle and told him he was going to make a phone call. He went back through reception and into the car park, lit a cigarette, turned on his mobile and called Mel.

When he spoke the words '*savaged by a pit-bull fucking terrier*', the other smokers gave him impressed glances.

He put the phone in his pocket, ground the cigarette beneath his shoe and wandered back through to the ward. He already felt at home. Hospitals did that. They became too familiar, too quickly. He stopped off at the Coke machine and got a can for him and a can for Jamie.

He took them to the cubicle. Jamie couldn't move easily.

Sam popped the can for him, and sat back and watched his boy drinking.

They didn't really speak until Mel arrived. They heard her before they saw her, a rushing through the swinging doors, a low, theatrical whisper, asking where her nephew was. Jamie smiled at Sam's fond irritation, and called out to her. She must have been close because they could hear the catch in her throat and the accelerated clicking of her heels. She battered her way through the curtains and threw herself at Jamie. She smelt of wine and perfume.

Jamie was kept in overnight. Sam and Mel waited at his bedside long after he fell asleep. Finally, a nurse ushered them out.

Sam called a minicab from a vandalized free phone on the reception desk. The A & E department was beginning to fill with closing-time casualties.

The minicab, when it arrived, smelt of a hundred years of cigarettes. Sam and Mel were cold and grubby with tiredness. The streetlights slowly pulsed and strobed over their heads. The driver didn't attempt to engage them in conversation, perhaps judging them recently bereaved.

In the morning, Sam called at the Ballards'. Their front garden was orderly and groomed, with gardenias in concrete pots either side of the front door.

Martin Ballard was at work. His wife, Jane, came to the door. She was tall and as pink as a sugar mouse. She was very showered and perfumed and coiffed, as if permanently expecting company.

The house made Sam feel adolescent and scruffy, and when he explained who he was, he stumbled over his words. But Jane Ballard smiled and stepped aside to let him in.

She called Stuart downstairs. Barefoot in a Liverpool FC strip, he limped down. Sam thrust out his hand. After a nervous, confirming glance towards his mother, Stuart extended his hand and shook manfully.

'I wanted to thank you,' Sam told him. He was monitoring the tone of his voice, wary of the patronizing manner that crept in when people addressed the old or the young.

'It took some bottle,' he said. 'Doing what you did.'

Stuart looked proud. Sam guessed he had never been so praised in his mother's presence. He clapped him on the shoulder and broke the moment.

He said, 'Make sure you come and see him.'

'Is he home?'

'Later today. They kept him in overnight, just to keep an eye on him.'

'Is he off school?'

'For a bit, yeah.'

'He's all right, though?'

'Thanks to you, he is.'

That was perhaps a compliment too far. Stuart said, 'Nah,' in a strange tone and looked at his bare feet. Then he said he had to go (he didn't bother trying to explain where), and went back upstairs, greatly exaggerating his limp.

Sam watched him.

'Brave boy,' he said.

Jane Ballard was looking at the stairs where Stuart had been, as if noticing for the first time the space he had occupied.

'Yes,' she said.

There was a mystery behind that look which Sam had no desire to investigate.

He said, 'I wanted to thank you, too.'

She turned to face him. The odd look had gone and she had again adopted the self-conscious languor she'd worn to the door like a nightdress.

Sam was surprised to find himself responding to it. He shifted his weight.

He said, 'They told me at the hospital . . .'

He broke her bright, unblinking gaze.

'Well,' he said. 'You really helped.'

She smiled.

'It's very nice of you to say so.'

'Not at all. And please thank—'

'Martin?'

'Please thank Martin for me, too. I hope I wasn't rude.'

'Not at all.'

'It was a bit of a shock, that's all. I wasn't thinking straight. But I can't believe I didn't thank him.'

'Really,' she said, 'don't give it a thought.'

Sam looked down and smiled.

'I didn't know if I was coming or going.'

'Of course not. Your child was in pain.'

He couldn't predict from what angle this conversation would approach him next.

'Yes,' he said.

She touched his shoulder.

'They don't stop being precious,' she said, 'just because they're growing away from you.'

He brushed at his eyes.

'I'm sorry,' he said.

She squeezed his upper arm.

'Don't be silly.'

He smiled.

She said, 'Jamie's a lovely boy.'

'Yes,' said Sam.

'And he's always welcome here.'

Sam could feel the sun on his neck. He enjoyed standing there in the hallway being outmanoeuvred by Jane Ballard. But it was time to go. He jingled his car keys round his index finger, in unconscious and perhaps guilty mimicry of her husband.

On the way home, he stopped off to buy some things for Jamie: a pile of magazines, a couple of books, a new driving game for the PlayStation. He stopped off again at the local chemist to pick up some prescription painkillers and antibiotics, and while he was there he bought some Lucozade, a warm bottle of which had become such an integral component of British illness that it seemed to evoke another time, like a faded postcard of the Silver Jubilee.

He took the carrier bags to the boot of the car, and dumped them in. Then he went to the camping shop, to find something he could kill the dog with.

15

He'd known the camping shop by the railway station since he was a child. He was disappointed to discover that it was no longer the fusty, underlit store of his recall; its dustiness would have suited his furtive intent. But the camping shop had been rebranded as an Outdoor Adventure Centre, and it was vivid and halogen-lit. Somehow, extra floorspace had been acquired; there was now room near the back of the ground floor to erect a four-man tent on a square of Astroturf, around which browsed a number of young people in primary-coloured, sleeveless fleeces.

Sam wandered up and down before locked glass cabinets that contained racks of knives, multi-tools, binoculars, torches and compasses. He felt smug and wise. When the first rush of wisdom had passed, he became worried that a particular sales assistant was watching him too closely, so he went and examined with an expert eye the display of rucksacks and hiking socks.

When Sam was very young, he and his father had sometimes gone camping. He remembered little more than the pride he'd felt, the weight of the rucksack on his shoulders, the straps grating his skin and the sunburn on the back of his unprotected neck. Like Jamie, Sam had been scared of cows – except his fear had a precipitating event. His father had hurried them across a particular field, towards a stile that never seemed to get any closer. Too late, Sam's father realized that in the northeast corner of the field there stood a bull; solid and lumpy as an ingot of lead. The bull appeared to be uninterested in them. But it was built like a train, and it could charge like one if it chose. Sam recalled the repressed and fearful quiver in his father's voice.

This had been an acute, early moment of self-consciousness and separation. Although some years were to pass before he learnt the full extent of his father's weaknesses, and many more years yet before he began to understand them, Sam never again regarded him with uncritical awe.

He sometimes wondered if he'd passed that experience on to his own son. Perhaps at the sight of cows, Sam let off some pheromonal fear-signal, alerting Jamie at a pre-conscious level that his father, the divine protector, was himself frightened by these doe-eyed, slow-moving ruminants.

Approvingly, Sam fingered the nylon weave of an orange rucksack. He tested the padding of the shoulder strap. Then he wandered over to inspect the walking boots. His own pair had been brown leather, piously dubbined, and they had chewed his feet bloody for six months. His father had assured him it was worth it; the boots would last a lifetime. But Sam didn't want them to last a lifetime. He wanted rid of them. They ruined the camping weekends, and they ruined getting home, too – because his father insisted that newspaper be spread on the kitchen table and the boots be dubbined before Sam was permitted to slip into a cold, blissful bed.

He felt vindicated by history. During the intervening thirty years, the design and construction of hiking boots had been revolutionized. He felt old, and wiser still. The new boots were ranked on Pyrex shelves, mounted on the rear wall of the shop. His kind of boot still existed, but they were tucked away on the top left-hand shelf, where only the most determined customer could reach them. The new boots were constructed of strong, lightweight, waterproof, foot-friendly and colourful materials that required little or no maintenance.

Sam passed through wisdom to melancholy. It was sometimes disturbing, how quickly his memories of childhood had come to belong essentially as well as factually to another century. The colour was fading from his memory. He and his father slogged up rainy hills in their vicious boots and scratchy woollen socks, like characters in a Hovis advert.

He bought two Leatherman multi-tools, one for him and a miniature version as a gift for Jamie. He also bought two eight-inch fishing knives with serrated blades, a smaller version with a six-inch blade, a landing net, such as might be used for salmon, and a small spear-gun designed for deep sea fishing, the kind included in most boats' emergency ditch-kits. He bought a couple of compasses too, for no reason other than that he liked their weight and design. Finally, he bought a pair of gloves and some thick grey socks with a black heel and toe-piece.

He wanted to look like he was maintaining a permanent kit, but he needn't have bothered. The shopkeeper, a stringy man with grey, cropped hair, was as uninterested in Sam as his colleague was suspicious. He was poring through a colour catalogue, marking off items on a checklist with a chewed ballpoint pen.

Sam put the kit in his shoulder bag and hoped he wouldn't be mugged. It would be embarrassing to be rolled by two bored teenagers when he was carrying such a selection of weaponry.

It was a short drive to the builder's merchants, where he bought two broom handles and some duct tape. As an afterthought, he selected a couple of pick-axe handles, just to make sure.

Mel had gone to pick Jamie up from the hospital. There was no way to be sure they wouldn't be home early, but Sam couldn't wait. Without bothering to remove his coat, he made the first spear on the kitchen worktop, taping a fishing knife to the end of a broom handle. With it, he jabbed at the leg of lamb he'd left there to defrost. The blade penetrated the flesh, but the impact wrenched the handle from his grip, hurting his wrist, and the knife was torn free of its makeshift housing.

Next, he used an epoxy glue to bind the knife to the pick-axe handle and doubly secured it with duct tape. With this, he was able to hack and slash at the leg of lamb with some abandon. It was a happily remedial interval. When he was done, he stared at the ragged clod of flesh on the kitchen floor.

He cleaned off the knife blade and used a dustpan and brush

to sweep up the tatters of lamb from the floor tiles. Then he made a second spear to the same design. He carried the weapons to the car, wrapped in a blanket, and put them in the boot.

Mel and Jamie got home at teatime, three hours late. Sam ran to the door to welcome his son. He kissed Jamie's forehead and gripped him fiercely until Jamie said, 'All right, Dad,' and hobbled through to the front room and turned on the TV.

In the morning, Sam was brittle and withdrawn. When he refused breakfast, Mel assumed he was hungover.

Before leaving, he went upstairs and found his old beanie cap. He pulled the hat over his shaggy hair so it stuck out like the petals of an inverted flower. He removed his new watch and the old chain round his neck, and finally his wedding ring. He put them in a Ziploc plastic freezer bag, and the bag in his jacket pocket.

He looked for a long time at the pale blue band where the wedding ring had been. He flexed his fist. It looked unfamiliar, like a transplant.

He called goodbye from the hallway and hurried out before they saw him. He checked the stuff was still in the boot: salmon net, spear-gun, home-made spears.

It took some time to find the right garages. For a while he thought the written-off Capri had been moved and he would never find it. But it was there, still propped on piles of breeze-blocks.

Sam parked across the street and waited.

Craig Hooper appeared shortly after midday, his dog trotting primly alongside him. Craig Hooper wore his hair gelled in a Caesar crop, and a puffa jacket over stained blue overalls. His Nike trainers were split along the insoles.

The dog swaggered, its head held high and alert.

Sam's saliva evaporated. He sat there while Craig Hooper lightly hooked the dog's lead on the edge of a dented, loose chromium bumper and lifted the green garage door. The door was counterweighted by two concrete blocks. Craig Hooper emerged from the garage carrying a toolbox and a long torch. He wore a dressing above the ridge of his eyebrow.

Hate drew a swirling Mandelbrot set in Sam's gut. He grabbed the steering wheel and watched. He imagined he knew what a wolf felt, defending its cubs on some snowy tundra.

Something inside him that was not him decided when the time had come. Sam put the bag containing his jewellery into the glove compartment. He leant across the seats and opened the passenger door, leaving it slightly ajar. Then, having left the keys in the ignition, he stepped out on to the pavement. He walked round the car and opened the boot.

He paused. Craig Hooper was paying him no attention, but the dog had lifted its boxy muzzle and was tasting the air. Perhaps it could smell the cloud-burst of hatred blasting from Sam's skin. If so, Sam was glad. He wanted it to know what was about to be done to it.

The dog shuffled its feet. He thought it might be retreating, but it was simply repositioning itself. The muscles in its shoulders were bunched. The velvety skin was soft over massive mandibles, like a soldier ant's. Sam could see the black, fleshy ruffles inside its lips and its hot, red mouth. The yellow teeth and the stupid, hungry eyes.

Sam looked at the array of survival equipment. The speargun and the salmon net looked puny. He was embarrassed by them. He grabbed the two spears and slammed the boot. The dog yelped. It adjusted its footing again, to monitor Sam's progress.

As Sam approached, it gave out a short, warning bark. Craig Hooper reached out from under the car to tickle its belly, to comfort it.

Soon Sam had come within two or three metres of the animal. It didn't strain at the leash. It simply faced him, silently, and made cool eye-contact.

Sam looked into limitless malice. Beneath the car, Craig Hooper remained unaware of his presence.

Sam took the spear in both hands.

The dog exploded into gnashing rage. In a moment it had bucked and flexed free of its tether. Sam was startled by the speed of it. He took an automatic step backwards. The dog ran at him. Sam lost his footing and stumbled.

He lunged the spear at an acute, unmeasured angle. It entered the dog's pink belly, an inch or two above its swollen testicles. The sudden, unexpected weight wrenched the spear from his hands. He scrambled backwards like a crab.

The dog yelped and curled and thrashed.

While Craig Hooper freed himself from beneath the car, Sam stooped to retrieve the spear. He watched the dog find its feet. For a moment it tottered drunkenly. He saw a blue loop of intestine protruding from the gash in its belly. Alternately, it was snorting with pain and yelping with fury.

By now, Craig Hooper was standing beside the Capri. He had an oily yellow rag in his blackened left hand. Without comprehension, he watched his skittering, yelping dog.

Abruptly, the dog seemed to remember itself. It stopped yelping and lowered its head. Once again it ran at Sam.

Sam had been captivated by what he thought were its death throes. He had yet to get to his feet. He was still down on one knee.

The dog came thundering towards him on stumpy legs. This time Sam jabbed the spear deliberately, two-handed, and with force. The blade slipped into the dog just below the white diamond on its throat. This time it didn't squeal. It snarled and gnashed and kept coming, like a landed shark.

Sam fought to retain his grip. The dog's struggles worried him this way and that.

Craig Hooper approached. He was yelling something, but Sam didn't know what it was. The jaws of the enraged, impaled dog snapped at the air close to his testicles. He tried to push it away. But it was too heavy and too determined.

Sam levered himself to a half-standing crouch.

The dog continued to thrash. It had a surfeit of life. It was trying to free itself from the serrated blade. Sam wondered if he should let it. Perhaps it would simply retreat to a corner to lick its mortal wounds, but he doubted it. The dog was a knot of hate.

Sam gave the spear an exploratory prod. The dog screamed. It sounded like a baby. With greater urgency, it tried to scrabble backwards. He heard its claws skittering on the concrete.

The tip of the blade scraped bone. The dog was panicking now, kicking its legs uselessly in all directions. Another furious prod tipped it on to its back, like a beetle. It gave up. It grew calm. It rolled over, showing Sam its pink and wet, ruby-red belly.

Sam leant forward and put all his weight into a final downward thrust. The knife found a space between two vertebrae and sliced through the dog's spinal column. Its tip snapped on the concrete, causing Sam to stumble a few steps forward.

Sam stood straight.

He waited for Craig Hooper to turn on him. But no attack came.

Craig Hooper stood with collapsed shoulders, staring down at the dog. Sam saw that he was little more than a boy. He regretted the necessity of hurting him.

Craig Hooper got down on his knees. He took the dead animal, slippy and loose, into his arms. Its velvety fur was smeared black and spiked, as if with oil. The boy tugged at the spear. The dog's body bent to follow it, as if reluctant now to be parted. Then the dog flopped back on to the concrete. Its front paws twitched slightly, as if it dreamt.

Craig Hooper rocked the dog on his lap. He stroked its head with sweeps of his palm, as he had probably done when it was a puppy.

Sam picked up the spear. He supposed, vaguely, that he would have to get rid of it somewhere.

He said, 'Your dog hurt my son.'

Craig Hooper didn't look up.

He said, 'You didn't have to hurt him. You didn't have to fucking *hurt* him.'

He buried his face in the dog's neck.

It was an awkward moment.

'Get the next one trained,' said Sam, with a contempt he no longer quite felt.

As he walked back to the car, he half-expected Craig Hooper, feral with anguish, to come running after him. But Craig Hooper just stayed there, cuddling the corpse of his dog.

Sam took off the hat and gloves and jacket and threw them in the boot with the spear. He hadn't expected so much blood. His face and eyebrows were thick with it. His clothes smelt coppery, like a butcher's. He sat at the wheel, trying to clean his face and neck with a scrap of old tissue.

It took him three attempts to get the engine started. As he pulled away from the kerb, the passenger door, which he'd left ajar in case he needed to get in quickly, swung open. He stopped in the middle of the road to pull it closed. Somewhere past the Dolphin Centre, he drew in to the kerb. He was very hot and the black-pudding smell inside the car had nauseated him. He opened the door and puked into the road.

Then he put on his necklace. He left the wedding ring in the plastic bag. He wondered what he should do with it.

He'd planned to use the staff shower at work, then change into the clothes he'd mashed into his sports bag. But the unantici-pated gore made that impossible. Instead, he stopped off at home. He sprinted from the car, through the front door, up the stairs and into the bathroom so quickly that he was already in the shower when Mel banged on the bathroom door and demanded to know what the fuck he was *doing*.

The water ran pink over his feet. He threw the hair from his face.

'Nothing.'

'What do you mean, nothing? What are you doing here?'

'I had an accident.'

'What kind of accident? Why aren't you at work?'

'I'll explain later.'

'Why can't you explain now?'

He couldn't answer that.

'It's nothing,' he said.

He could sense that Mel was pausing, undecided, at the door. She said, 'Sam, are you all right? Has something happened?'

'I'm *fine*.'

She tested the handle. He'd locked the door.

He soaped himself hurriedly and rinsed the pink froth from his body and face. Then he jumped from the bath, wrapped a towel round his waist, wrapped the bloody clothes and shoes into a loose sausage, and opened the door. Mel was waiting there.

He hurried past her. Then he turned on the landing, as if exasperated, and said, 'Honestly, Mel. Nothing's wrong.'

In the bedroom, he stuffed the soiled clothing into a hold-all before dressing. He left for work with wet, tangled hair. As he passed Mel, who was still waiting on the landing, he saw her notice that he wore black leather shoes with his jeans, and no socks. He didn't bother trying to explain himself. He would be unable to tell a lie convincingly, even if he could think of a convincing lie to tell.

The first few working hours were difficult. He endured any number of comments about his timing, and not a few about the new trainers he'd stopped off to buy on the way. He was distracted enough to accept the derision as banter. He kept dropping things and bumping into furniture.

Many times he silently dared himself to go and open the car boot, to confirm to himself that the bloody weapons and soiled clothing were actually there. Each time, he dismissed the idea as ridiculous and tried to get on with his duties. He worked through his lunch- and tea-breaks to make up some lost time. But eventually his desire for confirmation won out. He jogged to the car. There was no need to open the boot. There were bloody fingerprints all over the bodywork. That was enough.

The call came an hour later. He was summoned from the ward and into reception. He thought it must be Mel. Or maybe Anna had misplaced his mobile number. He wandered off the ward, aware that he was in a state of some anxiety and would alarm himself if he allowed himself to hurry. He wormed his hands into his pockets and strolled. He practically whistled. He nodded a second, redundant hello to Molly, and picked up the phone.

He said, 'Hello.'

'You're fucking dead,' said Dave Hooper. 'You and your fucking son. And your fucking cunt sister. You're fucking dead.'

Sam's heart gave a single thump, like something dropped.

'Who is this?'

'You know who this is.'

'Look,' said Sam. 'Your dog hurt my son. All right? The problem is taken care of. Can we let it rest now?'

There was a silence.

'You didn't need to do what you did,' said Dave Hooper.

'Yes, I did.'

'It was evil.'

Sam glanced at Molly. He wondered if she could hear.

'We'd've got him put to sleep,' said Hooper. 'All you had to do was say.'

'I doubt that.'

'I don't think you heard me.'

'No, I heard you.'

'You're dead,' said Dave Hooper. 'End of story.'

He hung up.

Sam stared into the buzzing receiver. He looked at Molly. She stared back. Sam smiled with one side of his mouth and handed back the phone.

'Some people,' he said, and rolled his eyes. His hands were cold.

He could see she wanted more and smiled sadly, for not providing it. The matter, he suggested, was out of his hands. He returned to the ward, to all the mad people.

As soon as the opportunity arose, he took his coat from the rickety stand in the staffroom and hurried out. It was after 10 p.m. and the car park was lamplit and edged with darkness. Dave Hooper could be squatting, waiting, behind any of the Minis, Escorts, dented Puntos and rusty Polos. He paused, imagining the gentle, predatory slap of Dave Hooper's trainers on the tarmac. He wondered what kind of weapon Dave Hooper would use. A knife, possibly. Or a gun. He didn't doubt that Hooper was the kind of man who could easily get hold of one.

He hurried to the courtesy car. He grabbed the wheel and made himself calm down before turning the key in the ignition. He drove slowly through the car park, testing the brakes several times before turning on to the road.

He could feel the migraine gathering like bad weather at the base of his skull. The slight palsy in his right hand, the corned-beef complexion that greeted him in the rearview mirror. At home, Mel asked what was wrong. When he opened his mouth to speak, the migraine burst and he folded like a clothes-horse. Mel led him by the hand to the living room. Without needing to be asked, Jamie limped speedily to the kitchen and brought back the things that sometimes helped: Ibuprofen with codeine, a pint of room-temperature water, a can of cold Coca-Cola, a bag of granulated sugar with a tea-stained spoon stuck in it like a shovel. Sam thanked Jamie with a grunt but took only the Ibuprofen and the water.

Jamie helped him upstairs. He rested his hands on the boy's shoulders like a blind man. He fell on to the cool bed with great but temporary relief. Jamie closed the door softly behind him.

Sam lay perfectly still, sweating. The darkness and the stillness and the quiet controlled the migraine, until it began to recede to a distant, ominous drumbeat. His rigid musculature relaxed into the mattress. But every thought of Dave Hooper, every replay of what had happened that morning, was accompanied by a thump of pain. Bursts of colour glittered across his inner lid.

Later, Mel came in and sat on the edge of the bed. She stroked his hair. Her hand was cool. He thought for a sleepy moment it was Justine.

She said, 'What sparked this off?'

He pressed down on his right eye with the heel of his hand. Sometimes that afforded enough relief to let him speak.

But Mel didn't wait for an answer. She mashed her lips together and said, 'I suppose you've heard that he's been spreading rumours?'

'Who?'

'Who do you think? Dave Hooper.'

'What sort of rumours?'

'About us.'

'What about us?'

'About the nature of our relationship.'

Fireworks fizzed and whirled behind Sam's eyelids like a flock of luminous starlings. He sat up. The room plunged and dipped away from him.

He removed the hand from his eye and stared at her.

'What's he been saying?'

'You know,' she said. 'About you and me.'

'What *about* you and me?'

'Jesus, Sam. Do I have to spell it out?'

Gorge surged in his guts. He knew that soon he must vomit. He squeezed his bad eye shut again and tilted his head, to see her better.

'Who told you this?'

'Guess.'

He was in no condition.

'Janet,' said Mel.

'And how did it get to Janet?'

'It's a *rumour*. Rumours get to everybody. Especially really good ones.'

'And do people believe this?'

'Of course they don't.'

'You don't sound convinced.'

Mel sagged.

'Well,' she said, 'Janet asked me if there was any truth in it.'

Bilious confetti spread across his field of vision.

'Janet *what*?'

'She didn't believe it,' said Mel. 'But, you know. You hear something often enough and you start to wonder. She's only human.'

'She's a fucking shit-stirrer,' he said through his teeth. Then he said, 'Christ,' and lay back down. The ceiling seemed to expand and contract, as if breathing.

He said, 'I don't believe this.'

Mel said, 'I have to move out.'

'You can't do that. People will think it's true.'

More gently, she said, 'But what about Jamie?'

'What about him?'

'What if it gets to Social Services?'

He sat up again. He retched into his fist.

'What if it does?'

'You could lose him.'

'What do you mean, *lose him*?'

She told him to be quiet. He was shouting. She said, 'If Social Services think Jamie's living in an incestuous household, he'll go straight on the At Risk register. I don't know how long this rumour's been doing the rounds. All it needs is to reach one teacher who's inclined to listen – and that's it.'

Sam stood and rushed to the bathroom. He vomited into the sink. When the spasm had passed, he turned on the taps and pushed the scraps down the plughole. Then he rinsed his mouth and splashed his sweating face. He padded slowly back to the unlit bedroom.

He sat on the edge of the bed, next to Mel, a gloved fist inside his head.

He said, 'Don't leave us.'

'I have to.'

He put out his hand. Mel withdrew.

He let the hand flop heavily into his lap.

Mel stood as if to go. But she sagged again on the edge of the bed and put her head in her hands.

He said, 'Mel. We're a family.'

'Not that kind of family.'

'Don't even joke about it.'

'It'll blow over,' she said. 'He's just jealous – that's all.'

'Jealous how?'

'How do you think?'

He sat up.

He said, 'Did you and Dave Hooper—? With Dave *Hooper*?'

'A long time ago, yeah.'

'He's *married*.'

'Technically, yes. But that's beside the point. We had a fling, I don't know – three years ago? He got funny about it. He kept phoning. When he was drunk. You know what men are like.'

He sloughed the sweat from his brow.

'I can't believe you never told me this.'

'It didn't seem relevant.'

'Well, it seems pretty fucking relevant now.'

'Well,' she said. 'Yeah. Sam, he's had half the women in the Cat and Fiddle over the years.'

'And what? You didn't want to be left out?'

Their eyes met and locked and he was surprised by the ferocity of his emotion. But the pain was too great and he collapsed again, pressing the cool underside of the pillow to his eye.

Mel didn't slam the door, but she didn't close it quietly either.

Sam lay with the pillow pressed to his eyes. He imagined them together. Hooper was made of rage and tendon and sinew. The erotic charge of his murderer's hands. Mel's body, pawed and scratched and rammed. He thought of the bolt that pounded pig skulls, a thousand times a day. And Mel screaming and squealing and biting his back, until they were two pigs, biting and fucking, with wild, white-rolled eyes, in the back of a slurry-spilled, slat-sided lorry slowing to pull in to the white-lit slaughterhouse.

He lay and listened, hoping to hear Mel's footsteps on the stairs. Instead she paid a visit to the bathroom, then went to her room and began to pack. He heard noises that he interpreted as her struggling to lever her suitcase from the top of the wardrobe. He pictured her on tiptoes, straining.

He stood. The room oscillated and he reached out for the

wall, steadying himself. Like an inmate of a penal colony, shuffling as if in leg-irons, squinting against the fierce, unaccustomed light of the hallway, he shuffled to the bathroom. He ran the shower cold. He took a deep breath and, fully clothed, clambered under it. There was a bright, clear moment of shock. He yelled and stayed under. His scalp and the flesh of his face grew taut, his clothes sopping and heavy. He counted down from a minute, then gave it thirty seconds more. He gave up at twenty.

There were various ways to attack a migraine. There were those people who, at the first signs, went for a run, or played squash, or did as many press-ups as they were able. Some masturbated. For Sam, only the shock of cold water had ever proved even slightly beneficial.

He stepped out of the bath and shambled like a sea monster to Mel's room.

Her suitcase lay open on the bed. She was taking armfuls of clothes from the wardrobe, the floor and the bedside table and stuffing them in the suitcase. The bare soles of her feet were dirty and there were ancient chips of red varnish on her big toes.

She said, 'You're dripping all over the carpet.'

He shrugged. Cold, wet clothing touched his skin.

He said, 'Don't leave.'

'I've been here too long anyway.'

'But we like having you here.'

He heard Jamie on the stairs behind him and stepped aside to let him enter.

Jamie looked at Mel.

'What's going on?'

'I'm going home.'

'You can't do that.'

'Love, I have to. It's where I live.'

'But I'll get *bored*.'

'You'll be all right. I'll still be round here all the time.'

'But it won't be the same.'

'I know.'

'But it's a laugh, having you here.'

'I've had a laugh, too.'

Jamie glowered at Sam.

'Has Dad *said* something?'

Mel laughed. She stuffed a pair of tights, with a pair of knickers still visibly rolled into the gusset, into the suitcase.

'Of course not.'

'Then why are you going?'

She stopped and put her hands on her hips.

'Please don't,' said Jamie. 'Really.'

Mel hung her head and laughed again.

'Don't give me a hard time,' she said.

Sam watched them and understood that Dave Hooper's wrath was beyond his power to control. The police couldn't control him. The neighbourhood could exert no sanctions because it feared and liked him. Dave Hooper and his family could say what they chose and do as they pleased, and the only way to stop them was to be more terrible than them.

Sam looked at his son.

He saw a strange, frightened boy whose first battle had

proved to be unwinnable. Sam wondered what kind of lesson that would teach him. What kind of timorous adult would this turn him into? He marvelled at what the Hoopers – without doing much – had done to them, to the fragmented remains of his family. He wondered what the Hoopers, with the perfume of victory in their nostrils, might continue to do. He saw that killing the dog had been no victory. It was a small act of resistance, of terrorism. It hardly made up for the sour knowledge that Dave Hooper had fucked his sister.

He brushed the sopping wet fringe from his eyes. Then he went downstairs, to find Unka Frank's telephone number.

16

Dating in parts to the fifteenth century, the church of St Mary Whitcliff had finally fallen derelict sometime during the Cold War. Eaten away by time, its stone corpse was so old as to be almost invisible. But it occupied a great deal of valuable city-centre real estate and, two years earlier, the Town Council had sold the grounds to a property developer, who won the sealed bid with an audacious and committed plan to take the sacred ground into the furthest reaches of twenty-first century retail. The churchyard was to become part of a shopping mall and integrated leisure complex.

The church had been there since before the city was a city, while its boroughs and wards were a nexus of villages, beyond which their denizens seldom stepped. Not quite 3,000 people had been buried there. And they lay there still, interred in the graveyard and the vaulted crypt.

The presence of the dead was an inconvenience. Nobody cared much about what actually happened to the bodies, but nobody wanted to play squash or buy a handbag or a cappuccino on a shiny floor beneath which lipless skulls grinned upwards.

So the bodies had to be moved. To do this, the property developer had subcontracted one of its affiliates, Blueberry Hill Relocations Ltd, which specialized in this sort of thing. In turn, Blueberry Hill Relocations Ltd employed Unka Frank as foreman.

Sam made his way down there in the morning. He parked round the back of Castle Green, just the other side of the river, walked down Fairfax Street, then up towards Fulton-Mangle. The church stood at the tip of a broad peninsula that divided two one-way road systems. The site was surrounded by a lashed, heavily graffitied corrugated iron fence. Much of the spraypaint was faded and ancient, referring to bands long since split and teenagers long since become parents. Generations of posters had been ripped down by passing hands until only scraps and corners remained, thick as cardboard with months and years of overpasting.

He found a makeshift gate. He took its weight on his shoulder, lifted half the sagging, ropy construction clear of the ground and heaved it forward. The iron shrieked and he squeezed self-consciously through the gap he had created.

Despite the good weather, it was chilly within the iron walls, whose gloominess the spring sun barely penetrated. The ground had not dried since the last heavy rain. Thick, grey mud clung to the soles of his boots.

The church squatted in the middle of what resembled a building site. It was a low and stumpy building with a twisted spire like an ill-set finger. It could never have been beautiful. Its windows were boarded with plywood. Its studded doors had been removed from the great hinges, perhaps to be inspected by local historians. If so, they had been rejected as of little interest and now stood propped against a mossy wall, close to a generator that vibrated and leapt from side to side like an excited child. A thick snake of cable ran inside the church, into the darkness.

Men in workclothes, steel-capped boots and hard-hats came and went, smoking roll-up cigarettes. They didn't look like typical builders. There was something variant and diverse about them. They had the air of stragglers at a motorcycle rally.

Long neglected, the graveyard was now a ploughed mess of oozing clay and ancient, leaning headstones, worn smooth and discoloured like dentures. Among them, earthmoving machines, wheelbarrows and men were parked indiscriminately. Although there was a great deal of miscellaneous activity, Sam could see little actual work being perpetrated.

Two men in suits and hard-hats appeared to be inspecting the site. Sam assumed they were Frank's employers, come to ensure the dead were being disposed of in the quickest, most cost-efficient manner permitted under European legislation.

In all the random activity, it was difficult to single out an individual. Sam seized on a prematurely wizened little man with a dried-apricot face and asked if he knew where Frank was. The small man responded in a language Sam didn't understand and pointed. Sam's gaze followed his index finger to the south end of the grounds, where a clutch of antiquated caravans were propped up on oily breeze-blocks. The caravans had gone yellow like old Sellotape and they rocked visibly when a large vehicle passed by on the other side of the fence. Sam watched the caravans for a while, but they seemed to be empty.

Instead, he walked into the shadow of the church and through its doorless portal. Inside, the cold dampness settled on him. The familiar smell of church was undercut by fragrant ribbons of cigarettes and wet soil. The interior was illuminated by a rickety lighting rig, which took its energy from the fat main cable that snaked across the floor. Shovels, spades and pick-axes were arranged haphazardly in the available empty space, from which the pews had long since been removed. There was old graffiti on the inside walls – white, dripping anarchy signs and more long-dead bands: Sam gazed sadly at an aerosoled marker that read THE SPECIALS 2 TONE RULES. There was a great variety of other equipment: boxes in wood and metal, wheelbarrows full of unidentifiable junk, corners of skirting board, bits of plaster, wiring, crushed Coke cans. And against the far wall, where the altar had once stood, were stacked a large number of rotten old coffins wrapped in plastic sheeting.

A broken stream of clay-caked, long-haired men in hard-hats emerged from the crypt, three or four to a team, carrying coffins as if they were delivering sofas.

Sam stopped one of the teams and, attempting to ignore their freight, asked where Frank was. A bearded man with a small pentagram tattooed between his eyebrows told him that

Frank was 'downstairs'. He smiled with such satisfaction that Sam felt challenged and he stomped off in the direction the coffins were coming from.

It was like entering a shallow-cast mine. The crypt was lit with arc lamps that cast quick, extravagant shadows. It was cold and damp. Sam clutched the neck of his jacket and wished he'd brought his scarf.

He couldn't guess at the size of the crypt: its far edges bled into the shadows. The walls, as far as he could see them, were lined with shallow recesses, in many of which a coffin was still placed. Few of the coffins were complete. Some had rotted enough to offer a glimpse of their contents. He averted his gaze, and he averted it again. There was nowhere safe to look.

More systematically than he might have guessed, the coffins were being removed from their recesses and organized on the ground. As he watched, one of the five or six men clearly assigned to the task prised open a lid and knelt to assess the contents. After applying what criteria Sam could not guess (the men pried around like car mechanics, probing the interiors with powerful torches whose beams he could see from this distance, like luminous glass rods), the coffins were wrapped in plastic, awaiting transport to the surface.

Finally, he spotted Frank. He wore blue overalls, muddy at the knees and arse, and work boots whose leather toes had worn away to reveal dull grey steel toecaps. He'd grown a full beard and his waist-length hair was tied in a ponytail. He was deep in conversation with a similarly dressed man.

Unka Frank's authority appeared to be designated by the clipboard he held in his right hand. Now and again he'd glance at it, occasionally lifting the soiled top sheet to read what lay beneath. From where Sam stood, he could see the white paper was a patchwork of grubby fingerprints. He thought of the boot of the courtesy car.

He approached Unka Frank and held out his hand.

Unka Frank turned and regarded him with alarm.

'Jesus,' he said, 'you can't come down here without a hard-hat.'

Immediately and quite uselessly, Sam ducked. He looked up into the darkness, within which was concealed the ancient ceiling.

'Why?'

'Because you're on site, dickhead, and because we've got the fucking *inspectors* in.'

Sam knitted his hands above his head.

'OK,' he said, stooping. 'I'll see you up top.'

'Don't you fucking *move*,' Unka Frank told him. He put two fingers in his mouth and whistled. A member of a coffin team looked up.

Unka Frank called out, 'Ted. Do us a favour! Chuck us your hat.'

Ted, who was neither clean nor delighted, removed his hat and chucked it like a Frisbee in Unka Frank's direction. Then he scooted quickly to the surface.

Unka Frank retrieved the hat and handed it to Sam.

'Jesus,' he said. 'You'll get me shot.'

'Sorry,' said Sam. He made an apologetic face. Then he inspected the greasy interior of the hard-hat. Inside, two strips of white plastic intersected, forming a cross designed to save his skull from the impact of heavy stone objects accelerating at 30 feet per second squared. He settled the hat on his head. His scalp crawled.

He looked up again.

'Is the roof unstable?'

Frank joined him. They stood there, looking up.

'I doubt it,' said Frank. 'This place has stood for seven hundred years. I'm sure it'll last another five minutes.'

He reached up and rapped on Sam's helmet.

'Besides,' he said, 'there's not much a hard-hat can do for you, if this place collapses.'

Sam had thought so too.

'So why all the fuss?'

'Rules are rules,' said Unka Frank. Then he clapped his hands and said, 'Time for tea.'

Sam followed him, ducking all the way.

Outside the church, Unka Frank broke away to have a brief conversation with the inspectors. Sam hung round awkwardly, then followed Frank towards the antediluvian caravans. Frank's was the smallest of them. An upended milk-crate functioned as doorstep and welcome mat.

Inside, the tiny space smelled strongly of Frank, and unwashed clothing and Calor gas. The kitchenette was in browns and mustards. Its stained and torn work-surfaces were dotted with squeezed, dried tea-bags, yolky forks, empty bean tins and handle-less mugs in which pooled stagnant tea. Frank emptied two of them into the sink and put a beaten aluminium kettle on to boil. He gestured for Sam to sit.

Sam found an orange, foam rubber bench and sat facing a
black and white portable television with a wire coat-hanger
for an aerial.

'It's not much,' said Frank. 'But it's home.'

Sam peeked behind an orange paisley curtain at the activity
outside.

'You're *living* here?'

Frank poured boiling water into two cups. He made a face:
his skin concertinaed into deep crevasses and valleys. Sam saw
that he really was not a young man any more.

'I'm not living here,' said Frank, 'not exactly. But I'm sleeping on site, yeah.'

Sam went cold.

'Christ, with all these *dead* people?'

Frank shrugged.

'The dead can't hurt you. It's the living who'll do that, every
time.'

'Well,' Sam said. 'Yeah. But – Jesus. Doesn't it get creepy?'

Frank handed him a mug. Sam found a few square inches of
floorspace and put it down there.

'Does your place?' said Frank.

'What do you mean?'

'Well, how old is it? A hundred years? Hundred and
twenty?'

'I don't know,' said Sam. 'Eighty, maybe?'

'OK, say eighty years. During that time, how many people
have died there? Do you ever think about that?'

Sam shrugged, uncomfortable.

'That's different.'

'How is it different? Put it this way: you die, right? And then you're a ghost. Where do you haunt? The place you know and love, or some grimy shit-hole of a church, just because that's where they've stashed your bones. It's home, innit? Stands to reason.'

'I'm not talking about haunting,' said Sam. 'Not as such.'

'Then what are you talking about – as such?'

'I don't know. Atmosphere.'

'Listen,' said Unka Frank. 'The reason we're sleeping on site is, this is hard work. It's hard work, and we're doing it against a tight deadline, with about sixty per cent of the man-power we need to do it. We work from dawn, sometimes until midnight, seven days a week. And it's bloody back-breaking, believe me. I'll tell you, mate: you work that hard, you don't have the luxury of seeing spooks or listening for rattling windowpanes when you get your head down on that pillow.'

Sam was vaguely ashamed.

'No,' he said. 'I suppose not.'

A silence fell between them.

'Still . . .' said Frank, and slurped his milky tea.

Sam looked up sharply.

'Still what?'

'There was one night,' said Frank. 'About a week ago . . .'

Sam leant forward.

'Yes?' he said.

Unka Frank had grown reflective. He looked into his tea.

He said, 'I'd just packed it in for the night. It must've been half ten, quarter to eleven. Jesus Christ, I was knackered. I could hardly put one foot in front of the other. So anyway. I kick off my boots, take off my trousers, have a fag and that's it: I lie down and pull the blanket over my head and in a second I'm gone. Out like a light.' Frank put down his mug and twiddled at a muddy bristle of beard. 'Next thing I know,' he said, 'I wake up and it's pitch black. And I mean pitch black. There's no electric light, no ambient streetlight, nothing. I can't see an effing thing. I try to look at my watch. Can't even see that. Then something pokes me in the back.'

Frank demonstrated by jabbing himself in the kidney with a rigid index finger.

'It couldn't have been more clear,' he said. 'First thing I think, I think it's a muscle spasm. Like I say, it's been a hard day, and the place I always feel it first is my lower back. You know how it is. So I take a deep breath and think, Thank God for *that*, and I punch the pillow and prepare to settle down. And then it happens again.'

Slowly, Sam's hand had crept to his mouth.

Frank tapped himself in the ribs.

'Except this time it's higher up,' he said. 'Right up here. It feels like someone's poking me in the back. So, by now I'm a bit freaked out, right?'

Sam blinked at him.

'So I sit up,' said Frank, 'and I reach for the light and I turn it on, and there in bed with me, plain as day, is the biggest fucking sewer rat you ever saw.'

Sam recoiled and flexed his fists in helpless disgust.

Unka Frank's gold tooth gleamed malevolently in the caravan's soupy half-light.

'Now,' he said, 'I've seen a few rats in my time, but this thing, it's big as a bastard. I mean, it's the size of a cat, easy, with a tail as long as my leg. And all night it's been curled up in bed with me, having a kip.'

Sam scratched at his upper arms.

'Oh,' he said. He glanced over his shoulder. 'Jesus. What did you do?'

'This thing's teeth,' said Frank, 'are like vegetable knives. And they're about four inches away from my bollocks. What do you think I did?'

'I don't know,' said Sam, with a sense of rising panic. 'That's why I'm asking.'

'Very slowly,' said Frank, 'I inch my hand over, bit by bit, until I'm cupping my balls. By now, the rat knows something's wrong. It's coiled there, watching me. I can see myself, little tiny Franks upside down in its eyes. Then I kick it.'

Involuntarily, Sam stood. He banged his head on the metal roof.

He said, 'Oh fuck, where did it *go*?'

'Over there,' said Frank, and pointed at the kitchenette.

'Where did it go after that?'

'Nowhere. It came back at me.'

'It *what*? Do they *do* that?'

'This one did.'

'Fuck this,' said Sam. 'I don't want to hear any more.'

'Fair enough,' said Frank, and picked up his tea.

'No,' said Sam. 'Go on. What happened?'

'It fucking jumped at me. Right at my throat, the little bastard. I caught it in both hands and held it out like this—'

Frank extended his arms to their fullest '—and do you know what? I can feel the tip of its tail, tickling the hair on my belly.'

Sam massaged the back of his head.

'Oh Jesus,' he said.

'Anyway,' said Frank. 'Long story short. I got it out the door and it goes scampering away.'

'Scampering away where?'

Unka Frank shrugged.

'Dunno. Wherever it came from.'

'Why didn't you *kill* it?'

'I don't think it wanted me to.'

Sam was indignant.

He said, 'That's a *terrible* story.'

Frank's phlegmy chuckle.

He reached into his waxed jacket and took out a pack of red Marlboro. He lit a cigarette with his brass Zippo.

'Anyway,' he said. 'You wanted to talk about Jamie.'

'Look,' said Sam. He stared around at the debris. 'Can we go to a café or something?'

Unka Frank blew smoke along his nose and through his slitted nostrils. He said, 'If I understood what you told me, I think we'd be better off keeping our chat within these four friendly walls. Don't you?'

Had the caravan belonged to a stranger, Sam would have been too disgusted to draw breath. But it was Unka Frank and Unka Frank's rubbish. It was even Unka Frank's rat. Sam moved the greasy suede cowboy hat from the corner of the bench and stretched out. He balanced his cup of tea on his sternum and, with the occasional nervous glance into the corner where the rat might lurk, he told Frank all about it.

Later that afternoon, Frank gave him a proper tour of the relocation works. He introduced Sam to his colleagues. Sam had already met some of them – at least one of them while visiting Unka Frank in prison. They greeted Sam like a distant relative. Their unquestioning approbation made him feel strong and included. For the rest of the afternoon, he wished he worked here with them, a misfit among misfits, an ersatz family, kept from the real world by self-erected fencing. He thought how good it would be to work so closely alongside people that you developed a language of slang and private, dry-mocking reference.

Frank showed him the full extent of the catacomb. Intact coffins were wrapped in cellophane and parcel tape, later to be reburied on designated land in an out-of-town graveyard. Incomplete skeletons were shovelled into green rubble sacks that were later sealed with tape.

Frank told him that the majority of the coffins had been found open. Sam's first thought was of rats. In the darkness, hemmed in by those damp stone walls, mortal despair seeped into his bones. But Unka Frank corrected him. It wasn't the rats. The rats got in later. You couldn't blame them, they were just following their instinct.

'It's the kids,' said Frank.

Sam didn't believe him.

Frank shrugged. 'What do you want me to say? They're after thrills. And jewellery. A lot of these people were buried wearing necklaces and wedding rings and what have you. Not many are wearing them now, I'll tell you that.'

Sam was weighed down by a terrible sadness.

He said, 'I didn't need to hear that.'

'What can you do?' said Frank.

He stepped aside to allow a cellophane-wrapped coffin to be borne into the church, and from there to a second Christian burial in some anonymous field.

'It's in their nature,' he said.

17

That Sunday, Frank came back to the house on Balaarat Street.

Jamie was excited to see him. He hugged Unka Frank's beanpole frame and told him at great speed and with much tangential detail how he had come to be savaged by the mad dog. Frank leant in the front doorframe like Gary Cooper while Jamie enumerated the wounds beneath his bandages, then lifted a leg to demonstrate to Frank how close to the artery the dog's incisor had come.

During all this, Sam sat on the stairs passing his necklace through his fingers, watching. When Jamie was done – or at least when he drew breath for long enough to allow it – Frank reached out a leathery hand and ruffled the boy's hair.

He said, 'You put up a pretty good scrap.'

Nothing more was required. Jamie was silenced by his pleasure. Frank entered the house, bringing the smell of sweat and patchouli oil and earth with him. His leathers creaked as he sauntered to the kitchen, Jamie at his heel. Sam waited on the stairs, watching the sunlight stream on to the welcome mat and the stripped boards in the hallway, the pistachio green paint. It was a good moment. The young summer entered into him.

Through the open door, he saw one of his neighbours, an elderly man, heading towards the fields. Alongside him waddled a fat, wheezing bulldog.

Sam wondered if he should just forget everything: have a pint with Unka Frank and put the last few months behind them. Perhaps he'd send Jamie to a fee-paying school. There was a good one, only a bus-ride away. He'd only have to leave the house ten minutes earlier in the morning. Fifteen, maybe. But he'd soon get used to it. And fuck it: a year might seem like an eternity when you're thirteen. But a year was nothing.

Sam had made mistakes. But here, in the summery day, it all seemed so ridiculous. How could he allow someone like Dave Hooper to ruin his life?

He stood and stretched, content as a big, fat cat. He smacked his lips and walked slowly to the door, pushed it closed against the summer. In the sitting room, the white linen blinds clattered against the windowsills.

All that was missing was Mel. He wished she'd let herself in and embrace Unka Frank, kissing his crevassed, bearded face. Frank would slap her arse. But Mel had left the house in a taxi and she and Sam had not spoken since.

Frank said, 'Come on, sunshine. Time to hit the road.'

'Where are you going?' said Jamie.

'Hunting,' said Unka Frank.

Jamie was thrilled. 'What for? Foxes?'

Sam urged Frank down the hallway.

'We're going fishing,' he emphasized, over his shoulder.

'Same thing,' said Jamie, siding with Frank as always.

Frank had brought his car. It was a long, low and cancerously rusted American Cadillac convertible. Its white roof was scabrous and torn: the cabin furniture was cracked and stiff with age. The car's name was Linda Blair. Three of its tyres were white-walled. The fourth was fully black and under-inflated. The front seat was a naugahyde bench.

'Perfect for heavy petting,' Unka Frank said. His eyes were lost behind Raybans and his gold tooth shone devilishly in the sunshine. He put on his Stetson.

Sam said, 'Aren't you a little old for heavy petting?'

Beneath a flap of mouldy carpeting, he could see tarmac.

Frank pulled over into the local Esso station, to inflate the slow puncture.

Sam wandered into the forecourt shop. He glanced at the soft porn magazines in silver-grey wrapping that revealed only a title and glint of forced smile. He thought about Anna. He looked at the aisle-end shelving, whose space was devoted to toothbrushes, soap, toothpaste and small bottles of mouthwash. He walked up and down the crisp aisle, then went to the fridge and bought two cans of Dr Pepper.

The doors hissed open and Frank's cowboy heels clattered on the floor. He'd filled the capacious tank and paid in cash, counting notes from a greasy wad retrieved from his back pocket.

The forecourt attendant commented on Frank's car. Frank was pleased. He leant his pointy elbow on the counter. Both men looked through the reinforced window at the remains of the Cadillac while Frank rattled off her specifications. The attendant crossed his arms and nodded.

'English bikes and American cars, mate,' said Unka Frank. 'Accept no substitute.'

The shopkeeper seemed wholeheartedly to agree.

Sam followed in Frank's loping, creaking wake.

Back in the car, Unka Frank turned on the stereo. Whatever Linda Blair's other faults, her stereo worked perfectly. They left town with a blue plume of exhaust expanding behind them, and Mott the Hoople making noise about the kind of young dudes they no longer were.

Frank believed that motorways were psychic power lines that distanced people from the land. One result of this was that he knew the scenic route between any two points on the map of England. His knowledge of Scotland was good but not encyclopaedic. His knowledge of Wales was scanty and neurotic. Something about Wales unnerved him. It was the last bastion of the Celts, and Unka Frank considered himself to be an Anglo-Saxon. Unka Frank preferred the French to the Welsh, which was saying something.

His xenophobia was cordial, almost affected, and did not extend to the peoples of any nation beyond the British Isles, except France. Unka Frank was an enthusiastic European Federalist, but would never voluntarily set foot in Liverpool.

After driving for an hour or so, they hit the coast road. Sam could smell the sea. Unka Frank put on some Hawkwind, and turned on to a minor road. A few miles further and he turned again. By now they'd seen no traffic for perhaps half an hour. They passed through a long canopy of trees, a verdant tunnel that surrounded the empty country lane. Lozenges of pale green shimmered and danced on the tarmac and the long bonnet of the car.

They arrived at a gate, half-hidden by ivy and other climbing plants. Next to the gate hung a sign that read STRICTLY NO ENTRY. Unka Frank pulled the car to long grass at the roadside and approached an intercom that hung lopsided from the wall. He pressed the buzzer and waited. He turned and gave Sam the thumbs-up. Then he turned again and leant in to the intercom. He listened, then said,

'It's Frank. He's expecting me.'

There was another pause, while Frank listened, his ear pressed close to the intercom. He scowled, then said,

'He's my brother-in-law. Yeah. *Sam*. He's expecting him, too.'

Frank waited, stooped. Then he announced, 'Thank you,' in a manner that made it sound like *fuck you*. He wandered back to the car, wearing a big grin that split his greying, auburn-streaked beard.

He took his place behind the wheel. The metal gates opened.

'We're on,' said Unka Frank.

Something inside Sam lurched.

He said, 'Tell me again how you know this bloke.'

Behind the lenses, Unka Frank's eyes slipped sideways.

He said, 'We share a tattooist.'

It seemed like a private joke. Sam let Frank enjoy it as he eased the basking shark of a car through the gates and on to a narrow, gravel path that curled deeper into the trees. The forest absorbed much of the sunlight. Sam glanced back and saw the black metal gates swing closed behind them.

He said, 'So. How long have you known him?'

Frank was concentrating on the road. He took one hand from the wheel to remove his sunglasses and laid them, upside down, on the dash. The murky green semi-darkness seemed to oppress him, perhaps because it was like driving through shallow coastal waters.

'I don't know,' he said. 'Twenty years?'

'How did you meet?'

'I did him a favour.'

'What sort of favour?'

Frank gazed rigidly ahead.

'The kind of favour you do,' he said, 'when a man like him asks you to do it.'

Sam laughed.

'Blimey,' he said.

Unka Frank put his foot on the brake. Sam was pitched forward. He turned to face Frank.

He said, 'What the fuck was *that* for?'

'Listen,' said Frank. 'I know you're nervous, but trust me. Don't joke about this. And don't joke around him. Just – you know – act like I told you.' He glowered at Sam down the length of his hawkish nose. 'Be polite.'

Sam wanted to go home.

'OK,' he said.

They drove on. Presently, they entered a clearing. The sunlight was instant and dazzling. Unka Frank hit the brake again and fished blindly for his Raybans.

Three cars were parked in the clearing: an Aston Martin, a Jaguar and a Range Rover. They gleamed in the sunlight, like showroom models aligned for a photo shoot. Against the Aston Martin leant a man. He wore a dark suit and tie, shined shoes and sunglasses. He was reading the *Daily Star*. His curly hair blew like a hedgerow in the summer breeze.

'Is that him?' said Sam.

'No,' said Frank. 'It is not. That's his driver.'

'His chauffeur?'

'His driver.'

'OK. Whatever.'

'There's a difference,' said Frank.

He looked at Sam accusingly, as if he regretted bringing him. Sam looked apologetic. Before either could speak again, the man leaning on the Aston Martin closed the paper, tucked it under his arm and waved. He wore leather driving gloves.

Frank's hands tightened on the steering wheel, then released it. He killed the engine and unfolded into the sunlight, settling the beaten-up hat on his head.

'Frank,' said the man, and extended his hand. He looked at the car. 'What's this piece of shit, then?'

Frank patted the bonnet.

'There's more going on under here than meets the eye,' he said, and shook the man's hand.

By now Sam was standing in the clearing, the breeze cooling his brow and the diamond of sweat between his shoulders.

'Phil,' said Frank, 'this is Sam, my brother-in-law. Sam, this is Phil.'

Phil extended his hand.

'Nice to meet you.'

'And you.'

Phil smiled.

'I didn't know Frank was married.'

'Well,' said Frank. 'You know how it is.'

'I do,' said Phil. 'I really do.'

He threw the *Daily Star* on to the front seat of the Aston Martin.

'So,' he said, and made a sweeping gesture. 'If you'd like to follow me.'

He pointed to a track that led yet further into the woods. They had taken only a few steps towards it when they heard a loud crack, like the clapping of a giant hand. It was followed by a second of utter stillness. Then birds erupted from the trees. There was the sound of slow, gentle applause and mutters of approval, like the sound of a village green cricket match.

'Oh,' said Phil. He looked at them over his shoulder. 'You're lucky. He'll be in a good mood. I think he got one.'

The trail was narrow and steep, muddy at the edges. They ascended in single file, Sam bringing up the rear. After a few minutes of this, Phil paused, leaning against a tree.

'Fuck me,' he said. 'I hate the country.'

Frank clapped him on the shoulder.

'Too much time at the wheel, mate,' he said. 'You need to get out more.'

Phil said, 'I've had enough of this. I'm too old. I've worked too hard. Look at my shoes.'

Frank looked down.

'They'll scrub up nice,' he said. 'With a bit of effort.'

Phil looked him up and down.

'Yeah,' he said. 'Like you'd know.'

Frank flicked his ponytail from his shoulder.

He said, 'Shall we press on?'

Presently, the track reached a plateau. Shafts of light penetrated the leafy canopy, lighting thousands of tiny, flying bugs. They heard another loud crack, and more amiable laughter.

They stepped into a clearing. Two large picnic baskets had been arranged on a gingham sheet. There were three empty bottles of champagne, and three half-empty flûtes. Close to the picnic, a wooden frame had been erected. It creaked like a boat. Four large mammals hung from it, twisting slowly in the breeze. Their fur was spiked with blood and their lips pulled back in rigor. At first, Sam thought they might be badgers. They were big enough, but they were the wrong colour. And they looked feline.

Three men were on the brow of the low hill. One seemed to be an attendant. Dressed like Phil, he was lugging a fifth animal corpse towards the picnic. The other two men were dressed for shooting. They carried shotguns across their forearms. One was very tall, with long, white-blond hair. The other man was smaller, cropped, with a stance like a boxer.

Phil stopped and held up a warning hand, like a Cherokee scout. Frank and Sam halted at his shoulder.

Phil coughed into his fist. The cropped man turned to face

them. The barrel of his gun was smoking. The edges of Sam's nose were tickled by cordite. Even from a distance, the man looked physically powerful, with a much-broken pugilist's nose. But he moved with a cultivated, assured grace.

He saw Phil and smiled. He had tiny teeth, like little ivory pegs.

He cracked the gun over his forearm and strolled towards them. He might have been sixty, lean and strong and weathered like hardwood.

The man with white hair wandered over the brow of the hill, followed by the attendant, leaving the dead prey to attract flies in the grass.

The cropped man stood before Frank. His eyes were periwinkle blue.

'Carnie Frank,' he said. His voice was deep, edged with accent and irony. 'You look like a whatsit. A Village Person.'

Frank laughed and scratched the back of his head. He glanced at the ground.

'Where did you get that hat?'

Frank removed the greasy Stetson and passed it through his hands like a steering wheel.

'I like it,' he said.

The man made a face.

'I didn't say I didn't like it,' he said. 'It suits you. A man should have a hat.'

The man handed the shotgun to Phil, who took it without a word. He appeared to have no idea what to do with it. In the end, he propped the weapon against the frame from which swung the feline, badger-sized mammals.

The man glanced at Sam. His briefest scrutiny seemed jocular and inclusive. He was letting Sam in on the joke.

He looked at Frank and said, 'So?'

'Christ,' said Unka Frank. 'I'm sorry. I'm forgetting myself. Bill, this is Sam.'

Bill smiled. His eyes sparkled pleasantly. Sam found his grip, strong and restrained, oddly reassuring.

Sam said, 'I hear you share a tattooist.'

Bill stepped back and put his head at an angle.

'Oh,' he said. 'You hear that, do you?'

Bill looked at Frank.

There was a long, still moment.

'It was a joke,' said Frank.

'I'll bet it was,' said Bill. 'You cheeky monkey.'

His eyes were dead in his face.

The moment passed. Bill smiled again, and it was like the sun coming out. He turned that inclusive, intimate grin on Sam and said, 'I was sorry to hear about your trouble.'

Phil came strolling back, his hands buried in his pockets.

'Thank you,' said Sam.

'And Carnie Frank here tells me you'd like something done about it.'

Sam hesitated.

'Listen,' said Bill, pleasantly. 'You've come here today because you've already made a decision.'

Sam lowered his eyes.

'I'm sorry if I cut to the chase,' said Bill. 'But this is my day off.'

Sam looked around.

'Oh,' he said. 'Right. I'm sorry. I thought you *lived* here.'

Bill examined the vast horizon, the unbroken forests stretching away in all directions.

'Good God no,' he said. 'I'm not one for the country. I just pay the occasional visit. For the constitution.'

Sam nodded, as though he understood. He had the peculiar impression that Bill was far, far older than he appeared.

Bill came closer. Sam could feel his force field.

'I never had children,' said Bill. 'Never needed them. But I understand a father's love.'

Sam said nothing.

Bill looked at him.

He said, 'And you love your boy? Jamie, is it?'

'Yes,' said Sam.

Alongside him, Unka Frank shuffled, uncomfortable.

Bill smiled, fascinated.

'And is it a fierce thing, that love?'

Sam blinked.

'Yes,' he said.

Nobody spoke. Sam watched a murder of crows describe a loose spiral in the air.

Bill said, 'All right then.'

Sam hesitated, fearing that he didn't understand. But the meeting was over. Bill turned his back and wandered towards the frame, to get his gun. He paused on the way, to sip champagne.

Phil took Sam by the elbow and guided him back towards the canopy of trees. Without speaking, the three of them made their way back down to the clearing where the cars were parked. Halfway down, Phil lost his footing. They watched him toboggan on his arse, smearing his trousers with a broad, muddy stripe. He stood up and, disgusted, dusted himself down.

He said, 'Fucking typical.'

Sam and Unka Frank waited, without looking at each other, while Phil collected himself.

When they reached the cars, Phil opened the boot of the Aston Martin and took out a suit-holder. He laid it on the low roof of the car and unzipped it. Inside was a clean, pressed suit identical to the one he wore.

Loosening his belt, he said, 'I told you he'd be in a good mood.'

Unka Frank touched an index finger to the brim of his Stetson.

He said, 'Nice one, Phil.'

Phil looked distracted. He was pulling his belt free of its loops.

'No problem,' he said. He placed the belt in a coil on the roof of the car and began to remove his trousers. Then he stood in jacket, shirt, tie, socks and shoes and held the muddy trousers up to the sun. His legs were white and hairy.

'Look at that,' he said.

Frank tutted and nodded his head.

'Bad news,' he said.

'Do you know how much this *cost*?'

'No,' said Frank.

'Well,' said Phil, 'I didn't buy it at M&S, if you know what I mean. We can't all be New Age travellers, mate.'

Frank chuckled.

He said, 'I'll see you in a bit, then.'

'Yeah,' said Phil. 'See you, then.'

Frank beckoned Sam to get in the car. He remained silent until they reached the gates, which swung slowly open on creaky hinges, allowing them access to the public, if empty, highway.

Then Sam said, 'What the fuck was *that* all about?'

Frank shrugged. He was chewing the beard that sprouted beneath his lower lip.

He said, 'I think he wanted to see if he liked you.'

'If he *liked* me? What does that have to do with it?'

Frank shrugged.

'He's that kind of bloke.'

'What kind of bloke,' said Sam, 'exactly?'

'The kind of bloke,' said Frank, 'whose tattoos you don't mention.'

'I'm sorry,' said Sam. 'I was just being friendly. I didn't even see any tattoos.'

'That's not the bloody point,' said Frank. 'Jesus Christ. Didn't I ask you to be careful what you said?'

Sam watched the blue sky flickering through the leaves overhead.

Quietly, he said, 'You're really scared of this man, aren't you?'

'Too bloody right I'm scared of him,' said Frank. 'And so should you be.'

They arrived at a junction. There was no traffic, but Frank paused there anyway. He took a series of slow, deep breaths.

'Anyway,' he said, turning right. 'No harm done. He liked you. Let that be an end to it.'

Sam lit a cigarette. His hands were shaking.

He said, 'So, what happens now?'

'They'll call you,' said Frank.

He put on another tape. They didn't speak again until they were back at Balaarat Street.

18

On Monday, Sam took delivery of the Chrysler.

Jamie saw the shining globular form hunkered down behind the hedge. He ran from the house. He was in the passenger seat, pushing buttons, before Sam had signed the delivery chit. Then he joined Jamie in the front seat. They looked at the empty road, hooking away from them.

Jamie said, 'Can I drive it?'

'No.'

'Go on. Let me.'

'You can't.'

'Yes, I can.'

'How?'

'I've watched you do it.'

'It's not as easy as it looks.'

Jamie sighed.

'There's the brake,' he said, 'and there's the clutch. And there's the accelerator.'

'There's more to it than that.'

'Like what?'

Sam looked inside the glove compartment. Then he adjusted the driver's seating position. He toyed with the steering wheel.

He said, 'Do you fancy going somewhere?'

'Where?'

'I don't know. Let's go for a drive.'

'Where to?'

'Surprise. Go and pack.'

'Don't you need to?'

'Need to what?'

'Pack.'

'Look behind the sofa.'

Sam had already booked them a room in a seaside hotel, and he'd packed an overnight bag the day before. It was hidden behind the sofa. While Jamie went in to pack, Sam flicked through the driver's manual. His eyes slid down the words without purchase. He put the manual back in the glove compartment and searched for the indicators, the windscreen wipers, the horn. He looked up to see Jamie lugging both their bags down the garden path.

They drove with the windows open and the radio on, hardly bothering to speak. Sometimes, Jamie passed comment on the car's performance and Sam's occasional slips – several times he forgot where the indicators were, and twice he stalled at a junction. They both cheered when they saw the first distant sliver of ocean, glinting like a knife on the horizon.

Sam had booked them into a white-washed bed and breakfast hotel. It stood on a hill that dipped steeply into the cobbled centre of town. The day was at its highest and they were lazy with the baked heat of the car's interior. Sam parked up and registered them at the desk. They ascended the musty stairs and dumped their bags at the foot of two monastically taut single beds, and went straight out. They lingered in the narrow streets, window shopping at rather baroque tourist shops. Sam bought them each a pair of sunglasses, cheap Rayban copies, and a Cornetto. They sat on the sea wall and watched fishing boats bob on the receding tide.

'So,' said Sam. 'How are you feeling?'

Jamie shrugged and took a bite from the last quarter of his ice cream.

'Are you feeling any better?'

Another shrug.

Sam put his hands down behind him, taking his weight. He kicked his heels against the wall.

'You're going to have to think about going back, pretty soon.'

They watched a flock of gulls gathering in the sky. Individual birds broke away and dived, white and silver flashes. Others crowded and cawed at a faded boat chugging in against the tide. Sunlight reflected on broken water. A low bank of cloud lay on the horizon, coloured like the gulls.

'How do you feel about that?'

'About what? Going back?'

'Yeah.'

Jamie dropped the ice cream's wrapper. It went helicptering

down, landing in the shallow, oily water that lapped at the slick harbour wall.

'Don't know.'

They watched the birds.

'You don't have to.'

'Don't have to what?'

'Go back.'

Jamie brushed the hair from his eyes. The wind ballooned his jacket.

'I've got to go somewhere,' he said.

'Somewhere, yes. But not back there. Not if you don't want to.'

Jamie hugged his knees.

'Everywhere's the same,' he said. 'It doesn't matter.'

Sam wanted to answer him, but no answer presented itself. He laid a hand on Jamie's back, between his shoulders. He felt the delicate, bony knobs of his spine.

He said, 'Do you like the car?'

Still hugging his knees, Jamie grabbed the scuffed suede toes of his trainers and rocked on the fulcrum of his coccyx.

'It's great,' he said, without looking up from the water.

Two days later, Sam went back to work. He was about to leave for home after finishing his Thursday shift when his mobile rang in his briefcase. He dug for it urgently, fearing an emergency.

'Hello?' he said.

'Sam?'

'Yes?'

'Phil.'

'Phil?'

'Phil. We met.'

There was a pause.

'In the *country*,' said Phil.

'Oh,' said Sam.

He turned away and cupped the phone close to his mouth, like a soldier lighting a cigarette.

'I'll see you tomorrow,' said Phil. 'Six-thirty a.m.'

'Look,' said Sam. 'I'm not too sure about this. You know.'

'No,' said Phil. 'I don't know.'

Sam pinched the bridge of his nose.

He said, 'Where do I meet you?'

When Phil had finished issuing instructions, Sam gathered his things and walked to the car, the Batmobile shape in the gathering darkness. He didn't imagine that Dave Hooper was squatting like a troll behind the cars and in the corners. Instead, he imagined Dave Hooper at home, in front of the TV with a beer in his hand.

Without making a conscious decision, he consulted the *A-Z* that he kept, new and unused, in the glove compartment. He kept it there for much the same reason that one might bake bread in a new house. On the way home, he took a detour and parked outside Dave Hooper's house. The street was quiet and narrow. Cars were parked half on the pavement. Sam had to double-park. He crossed his forearms on the steering wheel and stared at Dave Hooper's house. It was much the same as the houses either side of it. Much the same as Mel's, and Janet's.

Much the same as the house Sam had grown up in. There was a scrap of front garden, bordered by a low hedge. The lights were on in every room.

He sat there for perhaps an hour, without knowing what he was waiting for. The Hoopers didn't reward him with as much as a shadow passing across a window. Possibly nobody was home.

Eventually, he turned the key in the ignition and pulled away. There was no movement in the Hooper household. The combination of illumination and stillness was eerie. He glanced in the rearview mirror, as if looking for a passenger on the back seat.

He took a second detour, this time past Mel's house. Again, all the lights were on. He thought about calling her – *Where are you? Outside. In the car.* – she would laugh and invite him in. Or perhaps she would be afraid the neighbours would see, and draw the wrong conclusion. For the same reason, he didn't want to be seen staring at his sister's house, disconsolate as a lover, so he stayed for only a moment. But he had the strong impression that Mel's house too was empty. Then it seemed to him that all the houses on the estate were empty, and all the houses in the city beyond it. The city spread, a patchwork of hills and roads and rivers and estates, to every horizon. It was empty of all life, except the foxes and the rats and the pigeons. Houses stared at him as he passed. Only he and Jamie remained, and their memory of Justine. And he knew that even that connection was insubstantial and fading fast. It wasn't enough to keep them together. Whatever joined them was dissolving. Soon it would rupture and they would fall separately into different worlds. Perhaps it had already happened and only Jamie knew it. Perhaps that accounted for the pitying looks Sam sometimes caught coming from his son's direction. The mildness of that pity was terrible and debilitating. Jamie looking at him as if something were over.

Sam thought he was vanishing.

He walked to the door, trying not to panic. The key turned in the lock without noise. He rolled into the living room as if on castors. Jamie was watching TV and eating a tub of Cherry Garcia. He barely looked up.

'You're late,' he said.

'Yeah,' said Sam. 'Sorry. Stuff to do.'

The explanation could hardly have been less necessary. Jamie's eyes flicked back to the television.

Sam lay all night with a portable radio close to his ear, an indistinct, ghostly murmur that lulled him into a state that was not sleep but was not quite consciousness either. He rose, exhausted, while it was still dark. He stood before his wardrobe and wondered what he should wear.

The absurdity of the thought made him catch his breath, and stifle a giggle. He selected clothes that would not draw attention, but which could be easily discarded without their absence being noted: an old pair of jeans, through at the knee, a cashmere sweater gone raggedy at the cuffs. (The sweater was a gift from Diane, his mother-in-law. But it was an unflattering beige and clung too tight to his belly and the rolls beneath his armpits. Like all big men, he showed the fat easily.)

He splashed cold water on his face and made a pretence of

cleaning his teeth. Then he vomited up a yolky green bile. He sat on the lavatory, shuddering, while the nausea passed. The feeling was familiar. He had vomited similarly on the morning of every exam he'd ever taken, and on the morning of his marriage too.

He marvelled that things could change so utterly and yet remain so much the same.

He cleaned his teeth again.

He moved through the house as he did in dreams. He fought the urge to look in on Jamie. He didn't want to contaminate him with the deeds of the morning.

He slipped on his jacket and closed the door quietly. In the garden it was cold and still. His breath condensed in clouds. In the sky a number of winking aircraft described an intricate mandala. Speeded up, they would have knitted a golden filigree, a hemispherical net that enclosed the city like a sugar cage. At the gate, he stopped to dry-heave.

There was very little traffic on the roads. He passed a few nightworkers on their way home and a few people pulling an early shift. After so many years as a shiftworker, he could easily tell who was going and who was returning. He saw himself reflected in the puffy, tired faces that sped by in their little bubbles of light.

He drove through Robinwood, past the Dolphin Centre, past Farmer Hazel's fields. In the shallows of the country, he followed the road that led eventually to the slaughterhouse. Soon the last, trailing edge of the city was behind him. He drove at a reduced speed, until he located the lay-by Phil had told him about. It was a gravelly scoop taken from the side of the road. As instructed, he parked the car and killed the engine. It was cold and he wished he'd worn better clothing. He juddered his legs for warmth, and hugged himself. He muttered songs through inert lips.

The hiss of an engine and the sweep of headlights caused him to start and sit upright. But whoever was at the wheel of the vehicle that passed, it wasn't Phil.

He glanced into the back seat, as if somebody might be there. Since the previous evening, he had found it difficult to shake the feeling that somebody was with him. Here in the darkness, he was giving himself the creeps.

He convinced himself that nobody was on the back seat. Then he saw movement in the bushes. It was too abrupt to be the wind. He supposed it was a bird, hopping from spindly branch to spindly branch, awaiting the dawn. Or perhaps it was some ground-dwelling mammal, some hangover of an agrarian past: a badger, a hedgehog. Perhaps it was a fox or even a feral dog, attracted here by the permanent spoor of carrion that issued from the slaughterhouse. Sam wondered if the undeviating smell was like pornography to a carnivore.

There was a hiss on the gravel. He glanced up, sharply. In the mirror he saw that a pearly black Renault Espace people-carrier had cruised to a halt behind him. It was the size of a small bus. Already a man he recognized as Phil was jumping down from behind the driver's seat. Phil wore a donkey jacket and a beanie cap pulled low on his forehead. He buried his hands in his pockets and, breath steaming, he crouched at the driver's side window of Sam's car.

Sam engaged the engine to lower the window.

'All right?' said Phil.

Sam swallowed and said he was.

Phil nodded. He seemed quite cheerful.

He patted the bodywork and said, 'Couldn't you have brought something more conspicuous?'

Sam shrugged, embarrassed.

'It's new,' he said.

'You don't say,' said Phil. He stood, dug his fists into his kidneys, and bent backwards. Then he looked round himself: a slow, broken spiral of vapour followed his mouth. He rested his splayed hands on the roof of the Chrysler.

'How is it?'

'How's what?'

'The car. Does it handle like a bus?'

Sam recalled Mel and Jamie's excitement when he agreed to buy the car. He felt protective of that moment.

'It's surprising,' he said. 'It handles all right.'

Phil was smiling.

'I'm still getting used to it, though,' Sam said.

Phil nodded.

'It reminds me of a taxi,' he said. 'A proper one, a black cab. It's surprising. Those things can swivel on a sixpence.'

He clapped his gloved hands.

'So,' he said. 'Are we ready, then?'

Sam looked up at him.

'What do I have to do?'

'First thing,' said Phil, 'I'd nudge your car along a few feet. Just so it's a bit more hidden from the road. Nudge it behind those bushes up there.'

'What about my tyre tracks?' said Sam. 'Should I rub them out with a branch or something?'

Phil laughed obligingly, then he saw that Sam wasn't joking. He smiled.

'I shouldn't worry about that,' he said. Then he rapped on the roof three times, a signal that Sam should get under way.

Sam nosed the Chrysler six or seven feet forward. Getting out of the car, he had to fight past a tangle of bushes. From the tip of one there hung a short length of used-looking toilet tissue. Sam edged past it with extreme care.

'Look at that,' said Phil. 'That's disgusting.'

He dug his hands deeper into his pockets and scuffed his feet on the muddy gravel.

'I hate the fucking country.'

He offered Sam his hand. The shake was friendly enough.

'You can sit in the front,' he said. 'With me. Since you're the guest of honour.'

Sam did as he was told. In the doorway, he paused to nod hello at the two men who sat silently in the back seat. The Espace smelt new.

Phil made himself comfortable behind the wheel. This took a good deal of squirming and seat adjustment.

He said, 'I see you've met Hinge and Bracket here.'

One of the men told Phil to fuck off. Phil smiled all the more broadly for it.

'Boys,' he said. 'This is Sam. Sam, this is the boys.'

Sam turned in his seat. He nodded a second hello, still more awkward than the first. The two men in the back didn't look like thugs picked up for a few quid in some terrifying inner-city pub. They had the businesslike air of soldiers or policemen. One of them was perhaps a gaunt forty, with cropped curly hair and a bitter rash of ancient acne scars. The second was younger, with a chubby face and short, fine hair that looked blond in the half-light.

The younger, blond man leant forward.

He said, 'I'm Damien. And this is Terry.'

'Hello,' said Sam, for the third time.

He faced the front. Damien sat back. Phil had turned on the radio and was fiddling with the tuning.

He said, 'No fucking pre-sets,' and turned his head. 'Any preferences?'

Nobody answered.

'What, nothing? You don't care?'

He waited. Still no answer. He turned off the radio and crossed his arms, as if sulking. Then his mobile telephone rang. Sam had noticed it when he got in – an outdated model, perhaps five years old, that lay on the dashboard. Phil answered it. He said 'yes' a number of times, then terminated the call. Immediately, he engaged the engine.

'Gentlemen,' he said. 'We have lift-off.'

He suggested that Sam put on his seat belt. Then he struggled with the steering until the Espace faced the road at 90 degrees.

A car passed.

'Second one after this,' said Phil. 'It's a whatsit . . .'

He clicked his fingers.

A sense of unreality closed in on Sam. He wondered what he was doing here.

Phil stopped clicking his fingers.

'. . . a Golf,' he said. 'A flash one.'

'GTI?' said Damien.

'Probably,' said Phil. 'Something like that. A prickmobile of some kind.'

A second car passed them. A Nissan Micra.

Inside the Espace, it had grown tense and silent. In the back, both Damien and Terry had engaged their seat belts.

Briefly, the brow of the low hill was illuminated by an oncoming car. As yet unidentifiable behind the glare of headlamps, it came accelerating towards them.

'Blimey,' said Phil. 'He's going some.'

Surprise made him fumble with the unfamiliar controls. The Espace lurched forward. Then it stalled. It stood laterally across the tarmac, blocking the road.

The oncoming car was travelling greatly in excess of the speed limit. Sam heard its brakes. He noticed that Phil was struggling to restart the Espace's engine. Then the car hit them, side on.

The Espace was slammed sideways. It hung in the air on two wheels for a long, uncertain moment, then righted itself with a juddering crash.

For several seconds they sat, staring straight ahead. Then Phil slapped the steering wheel.

'Fuck,' he said.

He turned in the seat and yelled at Damien and Terry.

'What are you waiting for – a confirmatory fucking email?'

Sam stared ahead while Damien and Terry got out of the van. He pretended not to watch them as they hesitated on the road, checking themselves for injuries. It seemed to Sam that things were not going according to plan, but it didn't seem appropriate to ask.

Phil gritted his teeth and slammed his foot down on the accelerator. The Espace screamed and pitched a few feet forward. Its rear wheels seemed to lose purchase.

Sam looked out the far window. He saw that a Golf GTI convertible with a crumpled front end and a shattered windscreen had attached itself to the Espace like a pilot fish. When Phil gunned the engine, the Espace dragged the nose of the Golf with it, giving off a migrainous shower of blue sparks.

Damien was dragging a bloodied man from behind the wheel of the Golf. The bloodied man was Dave Hooper. Once he was free of the car, Damien took Dave Hooper by the armpits and hauled him towards the Espace. Meanwhile, the older man – Terry – was using his weight to bounce the front end of the Golf free of the people-carrier. Terry gave up. He got behind the wheel of the Golf and threw it into hard reverse. The Golf parted from the Espace with a metal shriek. Terry reversed again. The Golf curved backwards, into the lay-by. Terry parked its remains as deep in the roadside bushes as time would allow. A few bits of it – a hubcap, the front bumper, tyre-shreds – were scattered over the road. Terry considered this shrapnel, decided to ignore it. Instead, he ran to assist Damien, who was still heaving Dave Hooper towards the Espace. They hoisted him and threw him inside like a side of beef.

Sam looked at Phil for reassurance.

Phil saw the look.

'Don't worry,' he said. 'The situation's a bit fluid, but we'll be back on course in a minute or two.'

Phil pulled away before Damien had fully closed the sliding door. The Espace travelled faster than Sam might have believed possible, and Phil didn't seem especially perturbed. The slaughterhouse flashed by on their right. They followed the road deeper into the countryside.

Sam swivelled. Dave Hooper lay on the floor behind him. His eyes were open. He was breathing noisily through his mouth. Small nuggets of windscreen were embedded in his forehead and scalp. His nose appeared to be broken.

Without reducing his speed, Phil twisted in the driver's chair.

'You,' he said.

Dave Hooper looked at him.

'Yes,' said Phil. 'You. Do you know what? You drive like a cunt, mate.'

Dave Hooper tried to say something.

'Yeah,' said Phil, and mimicked the wordless, fish-like opening and closing of Hooper's mouth. 'I hope you're fucking brain-damaged. That'll teach you to use a seat belt.'

Damien produced a roll of duct tape and proceeded to wrap it around Dave Hooper's mouth. Sam didn't look, but he heard the ripping sound of unspooling tape. There were noises in the back, a confused banging and thrashing and muffled grunts, some frustrated swearing from Damien and Terry.

Phil glanced sideways, examined Sam's fixed expression. He turned on the radio. Terry Wogan's breakfast show was just beginning.

Phil shifted gear.

'Don't worry,' he said.

Sam swallowed.

'I'm all right.'

Phil grinned at him, not unkindly.

'I knew a bloke once,' he said, 'who would've done this all by himself. He'd be finished by now. One word by the side of the road and Mr Cooper there would've spent the rest of his life treating you like the Queen of Sheba.'

Phil's grin turned into a broad, private smile.

Sam said, 'Where's this bloke now?'

'Oh,' said Phil. 'He's not around. You know how it is.'

Sam was beginning to.

'Shame,' he said.

'Not for Mr Cooper.'

'Hooper,' said Sam.

'Whatever.'

Phil swore and braked. He'd missed a turning. He reversed, then nosed the Espace into a road that was little more than a country lane, bordered on either side by thick hedgerows. Sam saw that the sky was beginning to lighten.

He risked a look in the back. Dave Hooper's mouth was bandaged in silver-grey tape. He was breathing with difficulty through his broken nose. Behind his back, his hands had been taped at the wrists. Terry and Damien were resting their feet on him, crossed at the ankles.

Hooper's eyes met Sam's and widened. He whinnied and bucked.

Sam looked away.

They drove for perhaps fifteen minutes. They passed no

other vehicle. Finally, Phil turned the Espace on to a narrow track barely wide enough to accommodate it. Twigs and low bushes brushed its bodywork. By now there was a definite strawberry-milkshake smear across the base of the sky.

Eventually, the track opened up into a scruffy glade. Three wooden picnic benches were arranged close to a small river. Sam could see the road by which the picnic area was more commonly approached: it ran off to a motorway access road. About half a mile downriver was a bridge over which ran some early-morning traffic.

He said to Phil, 'You've been here before, haven't you?'

Phil brought the van to a stop.

'Once or twice,' he said. He opened the door and got out. On the damp grass, he yawned and stretched and knuckled the small of his back. He walked round the van, examining it, kicking its tyres.

Then he said, 'Come on, lads. Let's get on with it.'

Terry opened the door and leapt out. The ground was soggier than he'd expected. He corrected his balance and looked with distaste at his mud-splattered trousers.

Phil leant against the bonnet and lit a cigarette. Smoking, he stared at the river.

Damien and Terry pulled at Dave Hooper's ankles. He fought hard to stay in the van, kicking at them. They slapped his flailing feet from their faces and laughed, then hauled him down into the mud.

Hooper struggled to his knees. Damien kicked him in the stomach. Hooper curled in the mud. He made urgent choking noises.

Sam looked away. He got out of the car. The air was colder

than he'd expected. He saw that the side of the Espace was punched in, as if by a fist. Then he walked to the edge of the picnic area. He crossed his arms and watched.

Dave Hooper lay on the ground. Damien lined himself up and took a penalty kick at Dave Hooper's head. It made a lonely, hollow noise in the stillness.

Sam reached out for the cool solidity of the Espace. But without being aware of it, he had continued to approach the scene. The van was some way behind him.

Terry hoisted Dave Hooper to his knees. A flap of the tape had come loose and hung like a bandage. Thick, intermittent streams of vomit were expressing themselves through Dave Hooper's nostrils. Between them, he struggled to breathe. Damien and Terry laughed at his bulging eyes.

Terry caught Sam's eye and winked. Then he kicked Dave Hooper in the throat. Hooper was chopped to the ground. He began to fit. His legs kicked like a baby's. His fingers, taped at his back, formed straining claws.

Terry and Damien bundled Hooper face-down and began to unwind the tape around his mouth. Hanks of hair adhered to it. Hooper opened his mouth and released a wad of vomit. He lay in the mud, trying to breathe.

After a long time, he laboured to his knees, then his feet. His head hung low. He coughed up more vomit, blew it from his nostrils. Then he just stood there, swaying, hands tied at his back, dripping blood and mucus and vomitus. Terry kicked him in the testicles.

When he had finished screaming, Dave Hooper lay at Terry's feet.

Phil chucked away the stub of his cigarette and, pointedly, looked at his wristwatch.

Damien held up an acknowledging hand and pressed a foot down on Dave Hooper's mouth. Hooper flexed and strained beneath him while Damien reached into his inner pocket and removed a telescopic baton, such as might be used by any European police force.

Damien removed his foot, stepped back, and prodded Hooper in the jaw with his toe. He kicked and nudged and prodded Hooper into a better position. Then he and Damien spent a minute or two beating Hooper about the head and body. Sam could hear the crack of unprotected bone.

Having worked up a sweat, they stepped back. They watched Hooper try to crawl away, wriggling through the mud like a lungfish. From his pocket, Terry produced a small lock-knife. With it, he cut Hooper's hands free, then hoisted him to his feet by the collar. It took several attempts. Hooper's feet kept collapsing from under him. Eventually he found his balance. Then he tried to run. They let him stumble a few metres before setting off in laughing pursuit. Terry swung the baton at the base of Hooper's skull. There was a sound like a single, muffled handclap. Hooper ran on for a few steps before his legs gave way.

Close to the picnic tables, he lay on his back, looking at the sky.

Terry sat on the edge of the picnic table and lit a cigarette while Damien circled Hooper, prodding him now and again with the end of the baton.

Sam approached Phil.

Phil turned away and looked at the river.

The sky was much lighter now. Sam could clearly see the picnic table. On its surface he could read many years of knife-carved graffiti, decades of Carolines for Tonys and Ians for Lisas. And he could see the Coke and Stella Artois cans that littered the surrounding mud and patches of grass.

Damien was squatting next to Dave Hooper, the baton resting on his knees. He was speaking to him as he might to a bedridden relative.

The wet grass had soaked Sam's socks and trousers. He stood several feet away from the picnic area and crossed his arms.

Terry glanced at him.

He didn't know what to say. He looked at the ground. His jeans were black with mud almost to the knees.

Dave Hooper's tongue was swollen and his teeth were gone and his lips were split, and his voice was hardly a voice at all.

He said, 'Jesus Christ, Sam, make them stop.'

Sam was shocked. He had almost forgotten that Dave Hooper was a person. His teeth lay scattered like a broken necklace. His eyes were swollen labia.

It would be so much easier, and so much better, Sam thought, simply to roll him down the riverbank and into the water, to let the current take care of him.

Damien and Terry were watching him. He saw his own disgust mirrored on their faces.

Dave Hooper reached out. He grabbed the hem of Sam's jeans and tugged, once. He tried to force words past his ripped and bloated tongue. He spoke quietly and it was difficult to understand him.

He said, 'Jesus. Please.'

Sam felt nothing but abhorrence. He wanted the remaining light wiped from Dave Hooper's eyes.

He looked at Terry.

'What would happen if we just left him here?'

The tugging at the hem of his trousers grew more urgent. Sam shook it off, irritated.

Terry flicked away his cigarette. It went careening like a firefly towards the dewy, wet bushes. Sam could see the detritus collected at their roots: toilet tissue, cans, a rolled-up magazine, a collapsed KFC box, several used condoms.

'He's bleeding inside,' said Terry.

Damien grunted confirmation.

'He'll be dead by lunchtime, latest.'

Hooper tugged at Sam's ankle.

'Stop it,' said Sam, irritably, and kicked the importunate hand away.

Hooper lay flat and stared with one swollen eye into the gathering dawn.

'Please,' he said. 'Sam.'

Sam ignored him, as one might a persistent child.

'What do we do now?'

Terry prodded Hooper with the blood-spattered toe of his shoe. Then he produced the small lock-knife.

'We've got rope in the van. Let's string him up and cut him open.'

'That'll learn him,' said Damien.

Dave Hooper tried to scream.

Sam looked at Damien for help, but Damien didn't seem interested. He lit a cigarette and perched on the edge of the picnic table, next to Terry.

Hooper was chanting something. One word: a single, throttled syllable.

Sam was distracted by it. He couldn't think straight.

He said, 'What's he saying?'

Terry shrugged, indifferent. Sam looked to Damien. But Damien still wasn't listening.

Sam became aware by a small displacement of energy that Phil had joined them. He stood at Sam's shoulder and looked down.

'He's asking for his mother,' said Phil. He put his hands in his pockets. 'They do that. Even the big boys.'

'Jesus,' said Sam. He ran his fingers through his hair.

He stooped, heel to haunch. He listened hard.

Abruptly, he straightened.

'Right,' he said. 'That's it.'

Damien, Terry and Phil looked at him.

'That's what?' said Phil.

'That's enough.'

Sam stood with his legs slightly apart, anticipating a challenge.

Phil shrugged.

'Fair enough.'

Terry put away the knife.

'What?' said Sam. 'That's it?'

'You're the boss,' said Phil.

Sam wished he hadn't said that.

Phil hitched his trousers and squatted.

He said, 'Did you hear that, Mr Hooper?'

Dave Hooper nodded. His hand slapped at the wet ground.

'Mr Greene has told us to stop,' said Phil. 'So we're stopping. Believe me when I say, the boys don't want to. They'd like to cut your cock off and stuff it down your throat.'

Dave Hooper made an urgent, animal noise.

'And personally,' said Phil, 'I'm inclined to let them, after what you did to my fucking van. But orders are orders.' He glanced at Sam, as if seeking approval. Sam half-nodded and Phil continued: 'But listen to this,' he said. 'If you or your family so much as look at Mr Greene or any member of his family, I'll hear about it. And I'll be back. Do you hear me? Not because I have to. Because I want to.'

He prodded Hooper's sternum with a rigid index finger, the first and last time he ever touched him.

'And next time,' he said, 'I'll kill you. And I'll kill your sons and I'll kill your mother and father and I'll kill your wife. I'll kill your fucking dog and your fucking goldfish and I'll burn your house down and when it's stopped burning I'll come and shit on the rubble. Do you understand that?'

Phil took the mobile phone from his pocket and held it between finger and thumb, like a sheet of shit-smeared paper. He dropped it on the ground close to Hooper's head.

He said, 'Here's your phone. Wait five minutes, then call yourself an ambulance. If you're lucky, it'll get here in time.'

Phil watched Hooper's hand scuttle slowly to the phone like a spider. Then he said, 'I don't care what you tell the police, because I'm assuming you won't mention me, or Damien or Terry. But most of all, you don't mention Mr Greene. He's taking a big risk, leaving you alive. He's acting against every piece of advice I've ever given him. Do you understand that?' He waited. 'Do you understand the gravity of the commitment Mr Greene is making to you? If you reject that gift, then may God damn your eyes, Mr Hooper, because that's all that'll be left of you when we've finished. Do you understand that?'

Dave Hooper pronounced the word 'yes' with an exaggerated lisp that made Damien and Terry exchange a smile and dangle limp wrists in the air before them.

'Good,' said Phil.

He straightened up.

'Gentlemen,' he said. 'Shall we?'

They walked back to the damaged Renault Espace. Sam didn't look over his shoulder. He could hear the wet rattle of Dave Hooper's breathing.

He belted himself in the passenger seat. In the back, Damien and Terry lit cigarettes.

Phil started the engine and pulled away from the picnic area, down a dark lane the morning had yet to touch.

After they'd been driving for a while, Terry said, 'That was some spiel you gave him there, Phil.'

Phil glanced in the rearview mirror. His dead face split into a sudden grin.

He said, 'It's good, innit?'

'Where'd you get it from?'

'I nicked it,' said Phil, 'off another bloke, a bloke I used to

work with. I heard him saying it and I thought, I'll have some
of that. So I wrote it down and memorized it.'

'It's good,' said Damien.

'It comes in handy,' said Phil. 'You know how it is. You can
never think of the right thing to say.'

They paused at the junction; turned back on to the main
road into town.

'Who was it, then?' said Terry. 'This bloke you got it from.'

'You wouldn't know him,' said Phil, in a friendly manner
that put an unambiguous end to the conversation.

The traffic was growing heavier. They passed the gates of
the slaughterhouse. A few minutes later, Phil pulled up in the
lay-by.

Sam sat as if hypnotized.

'Right you are, then,' said Phil.

Sam detached himself from the seat belt and opened the door.
He said, 'Well?'

'Well,' said Phil. 'That's it. Go home and forget all about it.'

Sam laughed, like a man admiring a car he can't afford.

He said, 'I'm not sure I'll be able to do that.'

Phil shrugged. 'Don't worry about it,' he said. 'You've heard
the last of Mr Cooper.'

He looked at Sam as if expecting him to say something.

Then he said, 'Right. We'd better be off.'

Sam climbed out of the MPV. The gravel crunched beneath
his feet.

He said, 'I'm sorry about your car.'

'Oh,' said Phil. 'Don't worry about it. It's no skin off my
nose.'

'Right.'

Sam scuffed at gravel with the toe of his shoe. He saw it was flecked here and there as if with dark paint.

'See you, then,' said Phil.

Terry and Damien raised their hands in a casual goodbye. Sam was still trying to think of what to say when, with a final wheelspin, the MPV pulled away from the lay-by. He waved lamely as it passed over the low brow of the hill.

Dazed, he stared at Dave Hooper's car, its snub nose cracked and concertinaed by impact, Hooper's blood on the crazed windscreen. It waited there like a sculpture to the missing.

Sam felt in his pocket until he found his car keys. They felt strange, powerful, a talisman of home.

He got behind the wheel of the Chrysler and reversed into the gathering traffic.

On the way home, he stopped off at the garage and put the Chrysler through the car-wash. The brushes hammered vengefully at the windscreen and windows. He waited patiently, without expression. Then he drove to the McDonald's drive-thru and ordered a Big Breakfast each for him and Jamie. When he got home, the coffee in its paper cups was still hot. Jamie was asleep in bed.

Only then did Sam look at his watch. It was not yet nine o'clock in the morning.

19

The Easter holidays ended that week. On Monday, Jamie went back to school.

When the morning arrived, they might have been preparing for a funeral. Jamie produced his uniform with military ceremony, holding it to his father's eye as if for inspection. He put on the blazer and draped the tie round his neck like a scarf, then stood facing the mirror and practised making the knot. Before he had finished, he ran to the bathroom.

Sam heard him vomiting. He pretended not to have heard. Instead, he offered Jamie a cup of tea and a bacon sandwich. Jamie told him no, he wasn't hungry.

Ten minutes later, Stuart knocked on the door. He greeted Sam with a big, pleased smile. Sam reciprocated, with some effort. Jamie squeezed past him.

'All right, Jay?' said Stuart.

'All right, Stu?' said Jamie.

Sam smiled. He watched them saunter down the garden path. He could sense the emptiness in Jamie's guts, just by looking at the angle at which he held his head.

Jamie got home at four o'clock. His shirt was open to the third button and his tie loosened almost to the navel. His hair stuck up and out at all angles. A few sweaty spikes of fringe dangled over his brow and into his eyes. He dragged his bag on the floor behind him, as if exhausted. Sam had seen other kids walking exactly like that, dragging their bags behind them. He guessed it to be one of those mini-fads that can possess a school for a few months. Jamie's shoes were scuffed and dusty and he kicked them off in the hallway. He dumped his bag and his blazer on the floor. His sweaty socks left damp patches on the wooden floor that evaporated in his wake.

Sam poured orange juice into a pint glass. He topped this up with a handful of ice cubes. Jamie took the sweating glass and drank off half of it. He wiped dilute orange beads from his downy moustache and set the glass down on the worktop, next to the sink.

Then he said, 'What did you do?'

'What do you mean?'

'Everyone's *scared* of me.'

'Scared of you? That can't be right.'

Jamie pushed hair from his eyes.

'Liam was waiting for me at the gates this morning. He told me he didn't want any trouble.'

'I expect he's just grown out of it.'

'Dad, he *cried*.'

Sam turned away. He opened the fridge and took out a low fat blackcurrant yoghurt.

'Liam's dad's in hospital,' said Jamie.

Sam raised his eyebrows and took a spoonful of yoghurt.

'I'm sorry to hear that.'

'He's in intensive care.'

Sam examined the spoon. It was stained dark with years of stirring strong tea. His inverted reflection was dark; like a fading photograph in an antique shop.

He said, 'I'm sure that's an exaggeration.'

Jamie drained the orange juice. He didn't take his eyes from Sam.

'It's not an exaggeration.'

'What makes you say that?'

'Because it was Liam who told me about it.'

Sam dug the spoon into the yoghurt pot's base and muttered something noncommittal.

'He might die,' said Jamie.

'Anyway,' said Sam. 'How was your day?'

'Dad – what did you *do*?'

'Nothing.'

'I don't believe you.'

'Do you want more orange?'

There was a long moment.

Jamie said, 'I'm going to my room.'

Sam asked him to put his dirty clothes in the washing basket, and to move his bag and his blazer and his shoes from the hallway.

But he didn't.

Earlier that day, Mel had left a message on his answer machine. She seemed hysterical about something and the long message veered several times between incoherent fury and quieter moments of disbelief when she simply repeated the words *I can't believe it*.

Sam could imagine her, running a hand through her frizzy, curly hair. He didn't need to see her to know what her expression was, her stance. He could even judge those moments when she wielded the cigarette as a jabbing, rhetorical tool. He smiled sadly and erased the message.

First there was the school term to get through. He imagined it would be easier now. Then the long summer lay ahead. The thought filled him with a sense of peace and the serenity of accomplishment.

He saw Mel once, in the street. But she turned her head and pretended not to see him. He learnt from Jamie that she was spending a lot of time with Dave Hooper. Apparently she was helping him through his physiotherapy. Stuart had seen her in the streets by the Dolphin Centre, pushing Dave Hooper in a wheelchair.

During the summer term Jamie fell in love with a girl called Michelle. But this trauma was something Sam could do little about. When summer term ended and the weeks stretched out, Michelle-less before him, Sam could only seek to reassure Jamie that there was no pain worse than the pain he was currently enduring. And there was no time worse than the first time.

Jamie seemed to accept the wisdom of this. It added an heroic undercurrent to his sense of romantic martyrdom.

Sam indulged him. He encouraged him to enjoy every moment of his final summer as a boy, because next year, he would be something else.

Jamie looked at him strangely, but said nothing.

At the end of June, Sam got fired. He accepted it with equanimity and felt sorry for Barbara, who was clearly so nervous when she summoned him to her office. He didn't mind. He was done with nursing. He had some money in the bank. He was sure he could do some labouring for Unka Frank, which would tide him over until he made up his mind about the future. He was still a young man. He would requalify – perhaps even as a teacher.

He was single, with one child. He thought they could live on a teacher's salary, since there was no mortgage to pay. He considered phoning Ashford to discuss it. In the end he decided not to. He was sure there were better people to talk to.

He saw Ashford once, one afternoon near the end of the summer term. Sam had gone to pick Jamie up from swimming.

Clutching his briefcase, Ashford was struggling to open the door of his Citroën. He saw Sam but didn't look away. He looked at Sam the way some visitors looked at certain patients on the ward.

Jamie and Stuart and a third boy Sam didn't recognize bundled into the back of the car. Their hair was wet and spiked and they smelt of chlorine. Distracted, Sam didn't acknowledge them.

Stuart said, 'Why are you staring at Mr Ash Bandit?'

Stuart was seldom less than respectful. Sam suspected he was showing off for the benefit of the third boy.

'Sorry,' said Sam. 'I was miles away.'

Ashford dumped his paperwork on the passenger seat and perched behind the wheel. The Citroën pulled out of the Exit gates.

Sam left it a few seconds before following. He glanced at Churchill School in the rearview mirror. It looked dilapidated and diminished, smaller than he remembered.

He and Jamie joined the Ballards for a fortnight's holiday in a Spanish villa. The Ballards were dull but easy company. They began drinking at breakfast and didn't stop until midnight. Sam let their conversation wander over and around him, just as he did the endless shouting and splashing of the boys, who spent all day in the swimming pool.

When they got back, he tried to call Anna. She wasn't home. She wasn't home when he tried again the next day, and she wasn't at work either. He wondered if Mel had said something. He decided that, if she had, there was no point bothering.

In September, they went shopping for a new, bigger school uniform. Jamie got his hair cut. He seemed happy. He returned to Churchill Comprehensive, Year Eight. He started going to parties on Saturday nights.

On the evening of December 12th, Jamie killed himself. He slashed his wrists with a vegetable knife and bled to death in the bath while Sam slept in the room next door.

Jamie didn't leave a note. All he did was tidy his room and hang his clothes and shoes and schoolbag neatly in the wardrobe.

Sam never learnt why he did it.

20

Drunk, he phoned Mel and told her she would not be welcome at the funeral. She screamed and called him a bastard and he called her a bitch and they were like children.

But she respected his wish. Or perhaps she was thinking about Jamie's dignity. For the dreamy length of the funeral Sam couldn't concentrate. He couldn't listen to what the man who didn't know Jamie was saying about him. He kept expecting Mel to walk in. Many times, he glanced over his shoulder to see if she was standing quietly at the back of the room. But she never was.

When it was over, he endured a revolted hug from his mother-in-law. This time, there was no invitation to spend a recuperative few weeks at her house in Bath. Sam stank of death and loss. Diane was in a taxi shortly after Jamie was in the ground, and he never saw her again.

Few had come to mark Jamie's life. The Ballards were there. There were some cousins, few of whom Jamie had given a second thought to while he was alive.

Unka Frank was there. He'd shaved his face and washed his hair and plaited it neatly down his spine. He wore a neat grey suit and a white shirt and a dark tie and he looked like an old man, he moved on stiff joints. Jamie's death had sucked the life from him as surely as a tumour. He was desiccated and weak and the naughty crow's feet at the corner of his eyes were deep wrinkles now.

Unka Frank held Sam's hand like Sam was a child and he was grateful for that. He felt like a child. He felt lost in the woods. He felt as if somebody had punched his heart.

Later, Unka Frank came back to the empty, echoing house on Balaarat Street and sat with his haggard, narrow head hung while Sam worked his way through a bottle of whisky and buried his head in his hands and wept so hard he thought something inside him had torn.

Frank tucked him up in bed, as he had done once before.

Sam woke in the night, having dreamt of Jamie and Justine. But instead, he saw the moonlit profile of Unka Frank, laid out flat on his back. Sam's heart shivered in his chest and he thought the morning would never come. But morning came, like morning always did, and he woke and stared at the ceiling and wondered how he was going to continue.

It wasn't even grief yet.

Unka Frank had to leave that morning. He promised to be back soon. Sam thanked him. Then he turned and walked back into emptiness. When he closed the door, the universe outside popped like a soap bubble. He was alone with his imaginary friends. In the silence, he thought he could hear them upstairs, moving around. He imagined they were hiding from each other in corners and behind wardrobes, exchanging secret smiles. Perhaps they would sneak up behind him and tap him on the shoulder and giggle and disappear.

Even that would be enough.

At some point during the unending day, somebody rang the doorbell.

Sam consulted his watch. It was the watch Jamie had bought him. He'd given a great deal of thought about which of his two watches would be the most appropriate to wear to his son's funeral. The thought rushed through him like a drug.

He saw it was getting late. He wondered where the time had gone, and concluded that it had not. It was simply that the universe outside this haunted house moved at a different rate. Time in here was slowing down. Soon it would come to a halt altogether. Outside, walls would rise and fall, empires would crumble, wars would be fought and lost, there would be plague and pestilence and flood and fire. The stars would align in apocalyptic configuration. And nothing in this house would change. Sam would shuffle from room to room in bare feet, listening out for the giggling of his ghosts.

He went to the door, and opened it. There stood Dave Hooper.

Sam's first reaction was to laugh, as if somebody was playing a joke.

Dave Hooper seemed greatly diminished. One shoulder

drooped and he held his head low. Sam could see a curlicue of purple scar tissue around his eye.

Sam leant on the door for support.

'I'm sorry to bother you,' said Dave Hooper. He slurred his words. His powers of speech had not fully recovered.

'That's all right,' said Sam.

Dave Hooper said, 'I really need to speak to you.'

'Not now,' said Sam.

'Please,' said Dave Hooper.

Sam shook his head. They stood there, on the doorstep, two men with their heads hung as if over a grave. Sam heard a noise and when he looked up he saw that Dave Hooper was crying.

Dave Hooper said, 'It wasn't my boy.'

Sam had to bite back laughter.

He said, 'What?'

'It wasn't Liam. He left Jamie alone.'

Sam couldn't speak. He tried, but nothing came out. He stared at Dave Hooper.

He said, 'You don't have to do this.'

Dave Hooper tugged down the hem of his jacket.

He said, 'I'm sorry. About your boy.'

'Thank you,' said Sam.

There was nothing to say.

Dave Hooper said, 'How are you?'

'I'm fine,' said Sam.

'Do you need anything?'

It was the cruellest possible question.

He said, 'Really. I'm fine.'

'Okay,' said Dave Hooper. He made as if to leave, hands in the pockets of his windcheater. But he stopped.

'Did you hear?' he said. 'About me and Mel?'

'Yes,' said Sam.

Hooper put his weight on one leg.

He said, 'You're welcome to come. If you'd like to.'

Sam laughed and nodded and blinked.

'Thanks,' he said.

'Really,' said Dave Hooper.

'I'll think about it,' said Sam. Then he said, 'How is Mel?'

'She's good. She misses you. It would be good if you called her.'

'OK,' said Sam, and smiled, knowing he never would.

They looked at each other. Two fathers.

He watched Dave Hooper limp down the garden path, and into the car that waited, idling, at the kerb. He didn't see the driver.

He waited until the car had gone. Then he went back inside the house on Balaarat Street and closed the curtains on the daylight, on the time-rotten world outside. He wondered what he would do with the time he had, with all the time until the end of the world.

POCKET
BOOKS

Neil Cross

Holloway Falls

Meet William Holloway: Family man. Gentle man. Wanted man.

Holloway has secrets. Years ago, he witnessed his wife's betrayal and his life fell apart. Now someone's toying with his mind and the life of a missing woman, the prostitute Holloway pays to imitate his ex-wife. When she is murdered, his ex-wife's name scrawled on her abdomen, Holloway is trapped by the consequences of love and sex, of infidelity and violence, in a world of his own terrible making.

Hunted as a rogue policeman and a killer, he's on the run.
And planning retribution . . .

'A compulsive tale of abduction, coincidence,
psychotic jealousy and imaginative daring'
Chris Petit, *Guardian*

'Powerfully atmospheric and hypnotically rendered . . .
a hell of a ride'
Literary Review

ISBN: 978-1-84739-463-7
PRICE £7.99

POCKET
BOOKS

Neil Cross

Natural History

Patrick's son Charlie has left home in disgrace. His zoologist wife Jane is on a field trip in Zaire and his daughter Jo is engrossed in her studies. So Patrick is left alone to look after the ailing Devonshire monkey sanctuary that he and Jane took on in a bid to save their marriage. Alone, that is, but for the big, panther-like cat that preys around the park, evading capture, lurking in the shadows and in the back of Patrick's mind as he tries to uncover the truth behind the murder of their oldest female primate.

Patrick's fears begin to fade. But then one night something happens that is so shocking, so deplorable, that it rips apart everything he ever held to be true – and unleashes a horror he could never have imagined . . .

'A masterpiece . . . seductively readable . . . dangerous'
Daily Telegraph

'Fierce and poignant'
Sunday Times

ISBN: 978-1-41652-279-9
PRICE £7.99

POCKET
BOOKS

Neil Cross

Burial

Nathan has never been able to forget the worst night of his life: the party that led to the sudden, shocking death of a young woman. Only he and Bob, an old acquaintance, know what really happened and they have resolved to keep it that way. But one rainy night, years later, Bob appears at Nathan's door with terrifying news, and old wounds are suddenly reopened, threatening to tear Nathan's whole world apart.

Because Nathan has his own secrets now. Secrets that could destroy everything he has fought to build. And maybe Bob doesn't realise just how far Nathan will go to protect them . . .

'Stunning . . . It has been a long time since I've read
a novel so compelling, chilling and satisfying'
Peter James

'A terrifically scary and all too believable tale . . . brilliantly written . . .
exceptionally well observed and paced'
Daily Mirror

ISBN: 978-1-41652-616-2
PRICE £7.99